"Beautiful Risk"

R.I.S.C. Series

Book 3

Anna Blakely

"Beautiful Risk"
R.I.S.C. Series
Book 3

First Edition

Publisher: Anna Blakely
Cover by Lori Jackson Design
Content Editing by Trenda London
Copy Editing by Tracy Roelle

Other Books by Anna Blakely

R.I.S.C. SERIES

Taking A Risk, Part One
Taking A Risk, Part Two

Because He's Perfect Anthology

Unexpected Risk (A R.I.S.C. Novella)

Dedication

This book is dedicated to my grandfather, or as we affectionately called him, Ol' Pa. He was 97 years old, and sadly, he passed away during the writing of this book.

My grandfather was the kind of man we all love to read about. He was a WWII Army Veteran. He and my grandmother were married for over 50 years, and he was one of the most loving, caring, and protective husbands I've ever seen.

Before my grandmother passed away due to complications from Alzheimer's, he would drive the thirty-mile round trip to her nursing home twice a day to be with her. Every morning, he would sit and help her with her breakfast, and then sit in her room with her for a few hours after. He'd go back home, rest or do what needed to be done around the house, and go back to the nursing home to sit and help her with her dinner. He'd then stay with her in her room until it was time for bed. (To this day, I can't make it all the way through watching The Notebook without breaking down like a blubbering fool, because those two characters remind me so much of my grandparents.)

Ol' Pa was an amazing husband, father, grandfather, great-grandfather, and great-great grandfather. He will be dearly missed by so many, but I find peace and solace in knowing he and Ol' Ma are back together after seventeen years apart and have finally gotten their very own Happily Ever After.

Prologue

"It's empty. Did you know that?"

From behind his dark glasses, Trevor Matthews stared down at the shiny new casket. Its silver hue shimmered in the summer sun.

Jake McQueen—his Delta Force team leader and best friend—stood silently beside him. They were the only two who had yet to leave the gravesite.

Beads of sweat formed on Trevor's forehead, his wool beret doing nothing to fight off the warm, sultry air. He was so hot he thought he'd suffocate if he didn't get out of his dress uniform soon.

Would be a hell of a lot better than the way Lisa died.

"Why the casket?" he wondered aloud.

Not the most appropriate question, given they were standing less than two feet from her grave. For some reason, Trevor couldn't let it go.

"There wasn't even enough left for her parents to bury."

"Don't do that, man," Jake tried to deter that line of thinking.

"I'm serious. Why spend the money? Why go through all this?" He waved his arm toward the numerous floral arrangements and now-empty seats. "It's not like she's here to…"

He shifted gears mid-thought. "I shouldn't have let her go in there. I should've listened to my gut, but I"—his voice broke, and he cleared his throat—"I shouldn't have let any of them go."

Jake turned to face him. "I'm there; I make the same call, all day long." Trevor shook his head in denial, but Jake kept going. "Listen to me, Trev. You can't do this to yourself, you hear me?"

Trevor turned to his friend, grateful the sunglasses hid his red-rimmed eyes. "I knew it was off, Jake. In my gut, I knew *something* wasn't right with that guy, but I still gave the go-ahead."

"And if it hadn't been for the fucking flu knocking me on my ass, *I* would have been the one giving those guys and Lisa the green light to enter that building."

"You don't know that. You may have seen something. Noticed something I missed, or—"

"Bullshit. I've read the reports. We got bad intel. Period. You didn't miss a fucking thing." When Trevor remained silent, Jake said, "And let's not forget, Lisa's the one who brought Hadim in to begin with."

Trevor's gloved hands fisted at his sides as he spoke through clenched teeth. "Don't do that. You do *not* get to blame her."

"Why? Because you want to shoulder all the blame yourself? Lisa was CIA, Trev. She knew the risks. You shared your suspicions about Hadim, but she chose to ignore them and moved forward as planned. That's on *her*. Not you."

"It wasn't her fault," Trevor growled, defending the woman he'd grown to care for. One he'd been sleeping with for two months, despite regulations against it. A woman he'd just said his final goodbyes to. "Hadim was a long-time asset. She trusted him."

"And that trust got her killed."

Except Lisa hadn't just been killed. She'd been held captive for nearly a week. Tortured that entire time. With each day that passed, a new wave of pain and terror had been brought down on her until finally…mercifully…she took her final breath.

Using his shoulder, Trevor wiped away the single tear that had escaped beneath his glasses. Turning, he glanced at the casket one last time and made a silent vow.

Never again, would he allow himself to feel this way. Dealing with the loss of those he'd served with was bad enough. Knowing someone he'd been intimate with had died because he'd failed to protect her…that was a brand of pain all its own.

One he never wanted to experience again.

Chapter 1

"Just grow a pair and ask her, already."

"Shh! Keep your voice down, dipshit," Trevor warned his teammate and friend from across the table. "She'll hear you."

Derek gave him an unapologetic smile. "Good. At least then she'd know you've got a thing for her."

Derek West was R.I.S.C.'s technical analyst and all-around smartass. R.I.S.C.— Rescue, Intel, Security, and Capture—was an elite, private security firm based out of Dallas.

R.I.S.C.'s Alpha Team—the team both he and Derek were on—was comprised of five men and one woman. All former military, they provided several different services, ranging anywhere from installing and testing out high-end security systems to trudging through the swamp looking for Homeland Security's latest target. And pretty much everything in between.

Jake McQueen, Trevor's best friend and former Delta Force teammate, owned the company and was Alpha Team's team leader. Trevor was his SIC, or second in command, but for the past two weeks, he'd been the one in charge.

While Jake was away with his new wife, Olivia, Trevor had been left to man the fort. He'd learned quickly how this side of the job could be a pain in the ass, but he'd gladly deal with the headache so his friend could take his long-awaited honeymoon with the love of his life.

The guy had wasted years pining away for his childhood friend's little sister, but after Olivia was kidnapped and nearly killed by a sadistic drug lord, Jake had finally come to his senses and married the woman of his dreams.

Seeing those two together and happy had made Trevor think about his life. His future. He didn't, however, want to discuss it with Derek or any other member of Alpha Team.

"I don't have a…*thing* for her." It was the first lie Trevor had ever told his friend.

"Right. That's why we've been coming here, to this outta-the-fucking-way diner to eat, instead of going somewhere in the same time zone as the office."

Trevor rolled his eyes. Derek could be so dramatic. Joe's was less than a twenty-minute drive from R.I.S.C.'s downtown office. "I like the food here."

D laughed so loudly, several customers turned their direction. "One, the food here is greasy as shit. And two, with the exception of your lady, the service has been mediocre, at best. Just admit it, Trev. You've had a hard-on for that tiny little thing ever since we first stumbled across this place."

Trevor's gaze slid over to the petite blond. Wearing a pair of perfectly fitted jeans and a black T-shirt, she began to take an elderly couple's order.

Like every other time he'd come here, she had her long, blond hair pulled up in a messy bun. A few wavy tendrils had escaped, framing her face and brushing the back of her neck.

She smiled at something the older man said, deepening the matching set of dimples on her cheeks. Trevor suddenly found it hard to breathe.

"I don't get it, man. You're single. Haven't had a girl—

serious or otherwise—the entire time I've known you. What's the deal?"

Trevor looked back across the booth at his friend. Not in the mood to go all Dr. Phil with the guy, he remained quiet. It turned out to be the wrong choice to make.

"This isn't about that one woman, is it? What was her name…Lisa?"

Hearing the name was a shock to his system. Several seconds passed before Trevor could even speak. "How do you know about her?"

Derek looked at him incredulously. "You're kidding, right? Hell, the first thing I did when Jake hired me was look all you assholes up."

Of course he had. "No," he finally answered D's original question. "Lisa has nothing to do with this." *Liar.*

Even though his friend nodded, Trevor knew he hadn't sounded as convincing as he'd have liked.

"Glad to hear it. 'Cause that was a long damn time ago, Trev. You've got to move on from shit like that."

"I already told you that isn't it, so drop it."

After giving him an assessing gaze, Derek said, "All right. If what happened in Syria isn't the problem, what the hell is?" Then, as if he'd just realized something big, Derek's eyes widened, and he began tripping all over his own words. "Ah, shit, man, I'm sorry. I-I didn't know. It's cool, though. Really."

Thoroughly confused, Trevor asked, "Didn't know what?"

"Seriously, man. I don't judge anyone for shit like that. Your lifestyle's your business. Even if we are battin' for different teams, that don't change the way I look at you, or–"

"Batting for…what in the hell are you talking about, D?" Trevor lifted his glass of his sweet tea to his lips, wondering if his friend had lost his mind.

"I'm just sayin', bein' gay ain't nothin' to be ashamed of."

A small geyser of tea shot out of Trevor's mouth, covering the front of Derek's shirt.

"Jesus Christ," Trevor grumbled as he reached for the metal napkin dispenser.

"Whoa!"

Scooting back in his seat as far as he could go, Derek pulled out several napkins of his own and started patting the front of his shirt.

"You know, for a genius"—Trevor wiped his mouth and chin—"you can be a real dumbass."

Now Derek was the one who looked confused. "What?" he asked, wiping down the table. "What did I say?"

"What did you—"Trevor cut himself off and ran a frustrated hand over his jaw. "Just because I don't go to bed with every woman who has a pulse doesn't make me gay."

"Well, good. I mean, if you were, that would be cool, too. I just meant that..."

"Hey, guys! Sorry it's taken me so long to get back here. We're short-staffed today, so it's been kind of crazy."

Trevor glared at Derek before turning and giving the five-foot-nothing angel standing next to their booth a smile. D had better pray she hadn't overheard their conversation.

"Hey, Alexis. I'd ask how you've been, but I'm thinking this may not be the time," Trevor joked.

Grinning, she said, "Well, you know me...just livin' the dream."

Her sarcasm made him smile even more. *Man, she's pretty.*

Looking at Derek's chest, Alexis shook her head in amusement and chuckled. "Nice shirt, Derek. I think I like it better than the last one."

Trevor glanced down at D's shirt. He was so used to the computer geek's oddball T's he hardly paid them any attention anymore.

Today's was a picture of a computer power symbol with the words 'Turn Me On' below it. Trevor fought an eye roll.

"So, what are you guys going to have? Your usual?"

They'd eaten here a handful of times, and each time, he'd ordered the same thing. Trevor ignored the silly beat of emotion he felt because she'd remembered. Hell, she probably knew what everyone who came in regularly ordered.

"Actually…" Derek directed his response to Trevor. "I think we should branch out tonight, Trev. You know, go for somethin' new. Somethin' you've *really* wanted but have been too afraid to try. We should all do that once in a while, ain't that right, Lex?"

Trevor had never wanted to punch Derek…until now. And if the guy kept this shit up, that was exactly what was going to happen.

Giving Derek a cute as hell giggle, she answered, "Sure. I guess so."

"See, Trev? Even Lex agrees with me."

Clearly amused by the jackass, Alexis was still smiling when she asked, "Well, then…what are you going to try, Derek?"

"I think I'll go for the fish tacos. Haven't tried yours yet, and I'm curious to see if it's any good." Derek glanced across the table at Trevor, a giant shit-eating grin spreading across his face. "Don't you think it sounds good, Trevor?"

Schooling the murderous expression trying to make its way to the surface, Trevor fought against the desire to reach across the table and beat the hell out of the other man. Lucky for D, Alexis didn't catch his double entendre.

"Fish tacos. Got it." That sweet voice had his head turning back around. A set of crystal blue eyes found his. "What about you, Trevor? Have you decided what you want yet?"

Derek let out a few loud, exaggerated coughs. Trevor barely squelched the urge to kick the asshole's shins beneath the booth.

"Oh, my gosh. Are you okay?" Alexis asked, sounding genuinely concerned. She looked down at Derek's empty glass. "Hold on, I'll go get you some more water."

Before Trevor could stop her, the sweet woman was heading back to the other side of the counter and reaching for a pitcher and a glass.

Leaning on his elbows, Trevor spoke low and through his teeth. "What the hell's the matter with you?"

"What?" Derek cleared his throat and shrugged innocently, his coughing fit suddenly over. "I had a frog in my throat,"

"Yeah? Well, you're gonna have my fist down your throat if you don't knock your shit off. What are you, twelve?"

With humor in his eyes, Derek coughed loudly a couple more times right as Alexis came back with the full pitcher.

"Here"—she quickly poured the ice water into his glass—"this should help."

"Thanks, darlin'."

Derek took the glass from her hand. While he sipped the water, Alexis turned back to Trevor.

"Sorry. What did you decide? Did you see anything new that caught your eye?"

No, not new. Trevor wanted the same thing, every time he came in here. Too bad he hadn't worked up the nerve to ask for it yet.

"Trevor?"

Shit. He hadn't answered her. "I-I'll just stick with my usual."

For some reason, this made the corner of Alexis's lips turn up, her dimples becoming more prominent with the movement.

"One patty melt and fries, coming up." Then, staring a little deeper into his eyes, she added softly, "Let me know if you think of anything else you need."

Jesus. The temperature in the small diner seemed to instantly rise. "I will. Thanks, Alexis."

She smiled even more. "I've told you before. Call me Lexi. All my friends do." With a little wink, she turned and walked away. Trevor's eyes couldn't help but follow.

Alexis—no, *Lexi*—might be small, but the woman was still packed with curves in all the right places. He'd spent many a recent night imagining how those hips would feel beneath his as he held on to them while he—"

"Just here for the food, huh?"

Trevor blinked and looked across the table at Derek. He had that, *I know you're full of shit* smirk on his face.

Resigned, Trevor sighed. "Fine. I think she's cute. Whatever."

"She *is* cute. And she likes you."

Shaking his head, Trevor started to argue, "She doesn't—"

"Dude. She was practically eye-fuckin' you while you were givin' her your order. And then there was the whole"—Derek made his voice all low and husky—"let me know if you think of anything else you need."

Despite his irritation, one corner of Trevor's mouth rose slightly. "She was talking about what I wanted to eat, you idiot."

"Oh, I *know* what you want to eat. Not that I can blame

you. Lex is a hot little number. She's got that whole girl-next-door-thing goin' for her. Personally, I usually like my women to have a little more to hold on to, but if you really don't plan on makin' a move there, I think I might just have to—"

Trevor did kick Derek then. Hard.

"Ow!" Derek leaned down, rubbing his leg beneath the table. "What the hell?"

Leaning forward, Trevor made sure Lexi wasn't within earshot and growled, "Don't."

"What's your problem?"

"My *problem* is Alexis isn't like all those other women you screw around with. She's not a one-and-done kind of girl. She's a…a take on dates and buy flowers kind of girl. Hell, she practically screams white-picket-fence, and kids, and a dog, and…"

Derek's brows rose. "You got all of that just from her taking your order a few times?"

Shit. Okay, so maybe he'd observed her a little more closely than he had any other women in a while. Or…ever. So what?

"I'm just saying she seems genuinely nice, and I don't want to see her get hurt by some jackass like you, who's just looking for his next piece of ass."

The corners of Derek's mouth turned up slowly, stretching into a wide smile. The booth's cheap, imitation leather creaked as he settled back into his seat.

"I'll be damned."

Trevor knew better than to ask, but he did it anyway. "What?"

"You like her. I mean, you *really* like her."

Trevor opened his mouth, the lie ready to fall off his tongue when a man's loud voice coming from behind them caught their attention.

"Well, there's my Lexi-Loo. I was wondering when you were gonna come over here and give *me* some attention."

Trevor turned around to see Alexis standing next to a booth closer to the door. The man who'd spoken was alone, and sitting on the side that put his back to Trevor. From this angle, all Trevor could tell was that the guy had blond hair.

"Hi, Rob. What can I get you?"

Trevor could tell from the change in her voice that Lexi wasn't nearly as excited to see this Rob guy as she had been him and Derek. He ignored the jolt of happiness that gave him.

"You know I don't like to share you, Lexi-Loo."

Lexi's smile seemed forced as she bypassed the obvious line the man had thrown her way and simply asked for his order.

"I'll have my usual. And put a boost in that sweet ass of yours. I'm really hungry today."

Clearly biting her tongue, Lexi told the douchebag she'd have his order out as soon as possible. Trevor turned back in his seat.

"What a dick," Derek bit out. "I can't believe she let him get away with that 'sweet ass' comment."

Trevor would be happy to let the asshole know what he thought about it, but it wasn't his place. He had no claim over Lexi. *Not yet.*

Whoa. Where the hell had that come from?

"She seemed to handle herself all right," Derek pointed out, his eyes still watching the other guy. "Working here, she probably gets hit on all the time."

Jealousy and anger began to boil as Trevor thought of Lexi having to deal with jerks like that.

"Here she comes," Derek whispered, then glanced back at Trevor. "Jesus, man. You'd better get that look off your face before she sees you, or you'll scare the shit out of her."

"Here ya go, guys. Careful, the plates just came out of the dishwasher, so they're pretty hot."

She glanced to Trevor as she sat both meals on the table. "Hey, you okay? You look upset."

His unexplained need to protect this woman prevented him from keeping quiet. "Who's the blond?" he asked a little too harshly.

Derek cleared his throat loudly, and Trevor knew his friend was telling him to calm down. He was right. *Cool your shit, Matthews.*

Lexi looked a little surprised at the intensity in his voice. "Who, Rob? He's just a customer. Why?'

Those beautiful, blue eyes drew him in. "I'm sorry. I know it's not my place, and we weren't trying to eavesdrop, but—"

Understanding filled her eyes, and she interrupted him. "You heard that, huh?"

"I think everyone in a two-block radius probably heard that jackass," Derek told her.

"Yeah," she agreed. "He can be pretty loud sometimes."

"Again, not really my business, but you seemed pretty uncomfortable around him." Trevor hated the man for that alone.

Lexi's gaze slid to where Rob was sitting then back to Trevor. "It's fine. He's a shameless flirt, but he's harmless."

Trevor couldn't help but ask. "How often does he come in here? Is he always alone, or does he ever bring anyone else with him?"

Those gorgeous eyes lit up with her smile. "You know, when you two first started coming here, I pegged you as military. Now, you've got me wondering if you're cops."

That made Trevor grin a little. "Pretty and perceptive. We're not cops, but we are both former military."

Pretty and perceptive? What the hell was that? He looked for any signs *he'd* made her uncomfortable, but the only change was a slight, pinkish hue beginning to tint her pale cheeks. And God, if that wasn't a turn-on.

"Well," she said, still smiling, "I'm not worried about Rob. He's loud and obnoxious, for sure, but…other than asking me out every time he comes in here, he's never done anything but annoy me."

A concoction of jealousy and concern began to swirl around in his gut. "You sure? Because I"—he glanced at Derek, then back to Lexi—"we could say something to him, if you'd like."

She laughed a little harder. "What are you going to do, warn him away from me, like a big brother or something?"

Before he knew it, Trevor heard himself say, "Or something."

His tone and choice of words were telling, but suddenly, Trevor realized he didn't care. They barely knew each other, but he wanted that to change. Soon.

Derek was right. He liked her. For reasons he'd rather not think about, Trevor had gone far too long even without having any kind of romantic relationship with a woman. In that moment, he knew he was ready to try again. With Lexi.

"Oh." She moved some of that loose hair behind her ear. "Um…thank you, but that's not necessary."

Her crimson blush deepened, and Trevor suddenly found himself wondering if she got flushed like that just after she came. *Damn.* The thought had him shifting in his seat to get more comfortable.

"Hey, Lexi-Loo!" Rob called out. "If you're done flirting with your boyfriend, I need a refill." This time, the guy sounded annoyed.

Lexi stiffened. Trevor watched as she took a deep breath and plastered that fake smile on her face again. "Be right there," she hollered over her shoulder. Clearly embarrassed, she quickly handed Trevor and Derek their checks and whispered, "Sorry," before turning and walking away.

"What an entitled prick," Derek said none-too-quietly.

"Yeah," Trevor ground his teeth together.

After finishing their meal, Trevor pulled his wallet from his back jean's pocket and tossed two twenties on the table. It was nearly double the amount of their checks, but he knew waitresses didn't make shit. Especially working in a place like this.

Whistling between his teeth, Derek glanced at the cash. "That's quite a tip."

"She's worth it," Trevor mumbled as he scooted out of the booth.

Standing with him, Derek's face lit up like the goofball that he was. "That's the spirit!"

Chapter 2

Trevor's own smile vanished instantly when he turned and saw the expression on Lexi's face. Rob had called her back to his table.

The guy was actually keeping his voice level low for a change, so Trevor couldn't make out his words. Whatever he'd just said had clearly upset Lexi.

After unceremoniously setting the man's check on the table, she told him, "Let me know when you're ready, and I'll get your change."

She'd just turned to leave when Rob's hand snaked out to grab her wrist.

Sonofabitch.

"The fuck?" Derek growled from behind him.

Clearly startled, Lexi tried to pull free from his grip, but the man refused to let her go. "I wasn't done talking to you."

Trevor saw red. His protective instincts flared to life, and in just a few long strides, he was standing next to Lexi.

Not bothering to hide his anger, his voice turned lethal when he said, "Get your hands off her."

Trevor and Derek both stood with their legs shoulder-width apart, hands hanging loosely at their side. Free to make their move, if necessary.

"This doesn't concern you," Rob spoke as he swung his gaze up to Trevor's.

Before he could hide it, Rob's eyes widened slightly. Oh, yeah. He was intimidated. *You should be.*

"I'll say it one more time, asshole. Let. Her. Go."

The diner went completely silent. Not even the clinking of a fork on a plate.

Giving them both an arrogant smirk, the preppy blond asked, "And if I don't?"

Rather than answer the jerk, Trevor slid his eyes to Lexi's. The pain reflected there only added fuel to his already-raging fire. Sensing he was about to lose his shit, Derek spoke up.

"Oh, you're gonna let her go. The only question is, do you plan to do it by yourself, or do you need our help?"

The man's eyes moved from Trevor's to Derek's and back again. After weighing his options, he made his first smart move since he'd walked into the place.

"Fine," he released his hold on Lexi's wrist with enough force, she stumbled back a couple steps.

Don't kill him. Don't kill him. Don't kill him.

Straightening his shoulders, the dick actually had the nerve to say, "You know, Lex. I don't think Joe will be able to keep this place open very long if word got out about the poor customer service." He looked at Trevor and Derek, then back to her. "Not to mention, the riffraff you've been letting in here."

Trevor opened his mouth to tell the guy to go to hell, but Lexi beat him to it.

With a surprisingly strong and steady voice, she said, "Joe can hold his own just fine. As for the riffraff, *you're* the only one I see who fits that description. So why don't you grab your coat and get the hell out before I call the police."

"The police?" The jackass laughed nervously, but Trevor saw the fear flashing behind his eyes. Turning his voice buttery-smooth, he said, "Oh, come on, Lexi-Loo. You can't really blame a guy for trying, can you? I mean, who wouldn't be disappointed, getting turned down by a gorgeous, intelligent woman like yourself?"

"Layin' it on a little thick aren't ya, buddy?" Derek asked from beside him.

Rob glared at Derek before making a show of checking his watch. Then, he smiled at Lexi as if nothing had happened.

"As much as I'd love to continue this little chat, I have an appointment I can't miss." He pulled out his wallet and laid out just enough money to cover his drink.

"Oh, I think this gorgeous, intelligent woman has earned a nice tip today, don't you, Rob?" Trevor sounded casual, but the look he gave the other man was anything but.

Rob's control slipped just a little, and he shot daggers back at Trevor. "Right."

He laid down two singles, adding a ten when Derek crossed his large arms and cleared his throat loudly.

Trevor stepped back just enough to let the jerk move out of the booth. If looks could kill, he and Lexi would have dropped where they stood as Rob walked past them and out the door.

Without a word, Derek followed, standing at the door to make sure the dickhead actually left. Trevor turned to check on Lexi.

"Are you okay, angel?"

Holding her wrist, Lexi gave him a shaky nod. "I'm good." She blew out a breath. "Thanks."

Towering over her with his six-four frame, Trevor

couldn't keep from reaching for her.

"May I?"

Lexi nodded, and Trevor had to force himself to ignore the spark shooting through his fingertips as he took her small hand in his. He must have made some sort of noise when he saw the red marks on her wrist, because Lexi quickly tried to reassure him.

"It's nothing, Trevor. I-I bruise really easily."

A familiar sense of guilt and regret bubbled to the surface as long-buried emotions began to awaken. He'd only been a few feet away, and she'd still gotten hurt.

"This shouldn't have happened," he offered softly, his thumb barely caressing the tender skin. "I'm sorry."

Lexi scoffed at him. "Why? You didn't do anything except try to help me. You *did* help me." She turned to Derek who was walking back toward them. "You both did. Thank you."

"He's gone. For his sake, he better stay that way."

Trevor looked down at her hand still in his. He needed to let her go before he did something stupid like pull her into his arms in front of all these people. After one final sweep of his thumb, he eased her arm back down to her side, immediately missing the contact.

"I-I should get back to work."

Turning, she offered the customers and the young man working back in the kitchen an extra-big smile. "Everything's fine now." To those eating, she added, "Let me know when you're ready for dessert. It's on me."

Looking back up at Trevor, she spoke more quietly. "I'm really sorry about all this."

"Nope"—he shook his head curtly—"you don't apologize for something like this, Lex. Not ever."

The intensity in Trevor's voice had her big, blue eyes

peering deep into his. For a moment, they just stood there, staring at each other. *I wish we were alone.*

"Do you have a boyfriend, Lex?" Derek asked out of nowhere, reminding Trevor they most definitely were not alone.

Lexi's head swung toward him, the question clearly throwing her for a loop. She wasn't the only one.

"What the hell, D?" Trevor growled.

Derek threw his hands up defensively. "Take it easy, man." To Lexi he said, "I only asked because I know Trevor and I would both feel better if we knew you had someone who could be here with you when you lock up. Somebody to walk you to your car, that sort of thing." He glanced back toward the kitchen where the young cook was watching them. "Someone over twelve."

Damn. I should have thought to ask that. Trevor relaxed his shoulders, feeling more anxious than he should, while waiting to hear Lexi's response.

"Oh, um…no. There's no boyfriend," she answered, sounding almost embarrassed by that fact. "And Caleb is nineteen, not twelve." She grinned.

Trevor slowly let out a breath he hadn't known he'd been holding and prayed she couldn't see how relieved he was.

"But," Lexi continued, "Joe almost always comes in to help with the dinner rush and stays until closing. He helps me clean up and then walks me out."

Doing his best to sound indifferent, Trevor cleared his throat. "Joe…I'm assuming he's the owner?"

"Yeah," she nodded. Her eyes softened when she added, "He's great."

"Oh," Derek said with recognition. "Is that the older, African-American man who helped in the kitchen the last time we were here?"

Lexi's eyes shone with genuine affection. "That's him. Joe's a sweetheart. He's also a former Marine. The man might be pushing sixty, but I'd still put my money on him over a guy like Rob, any day."

"Marines are tough sons of bi—uh, I mean, they're really tough guys." Derek censored himself at the last minute. "Is Joe planning on coming in tonight?"

"I'm assuming so. He usually calls if he can't make it, and I haven't heard from him today."

Trevor pulled his wallet out, removing his business card. "Care if I use that?" he asked, pointing to the pen clipped to the pocket of her canvas waist apron.

She lifted her arms out of his way. "Be my guest."

Trevor released the pen from the apron and clicked its top with his thumb. After scribbling down his personal cell on the back, he handed her both the card and the pen.

"Here."

"What's this?"

"My business and personal cell numbers."

Her brows turned inward as she studied the overly simple card. It was white with the company's name and number typed in a simple, black font.

"R-I-S-C?" she asked, spelling out each letter in the acronym. "What's that?

"It's pronounced, 'Risk'. And it's where we work." He tilted his head to include Derek.

"Okay," she drew the word out.

Trevor took a step closer, his low words only for her. "Lexi, Derek and I work for a private security company. Protection is one of the things we specialize in."

"Oh," she said as if she understood completely, even

though she clearly didn't. Then, as if his words had just made sense, she blinked, and her eyes widened. "*Oh*," she repeated with a little more emphasis. "I appreciate your concern, Trevor. I really do, but I don't need a…bodyguard or whatever." She looked to Derek, then back to him. "I'm pretty sure you two scared the daylights out of Rob already. I don't see him coming back anytime soon. If ever."

Trevor smiled down at her. "I'm sure you're right. And I'm not trying to get you to hire us. I just wanted you to have my numbers on the off chance you don't feel safe or need an escort to your car or…something."

"Something," she repeated his word. Lexi looked back down at the card, then back up at him. He could practically see the wheels turning, as if she wanted to say something but wasn't quite sure if she should.

"I, uh…I think I'll go wait in the car," Derek offered in a not-so-subtle way. "Lexi." He tipped his head to her. "Always a pleasure."

Looking both amused and a bit embarrassed, Lexi said, "Bye, Derek. Come back soon. Hopefully, it won't get quite so intense next time."

"Are you kiddin'? That shi…stuff is what we live for." Then, with a wink and a smile, D was gone, leaving Trevor and Lexi still standing there.

"So." Trevor's deep voice rumbled awkwardly as he shoved his hands into his pockets. *Christ, you'd think I'd never talked to a woman before.*

"Thanks, again, Trevor."

He shrugged it off. "No need to thank us. Like I said, it's kind of what we do."

"Right." She smiled before nervously skittering her gaze away from his.

Several seconds of silence stretched between them. Derek's words from earlier began to ring between his ears.

Just grow a pair and ask her out already.

D was right. Trevor had faced down the worst the world had to offer. Surely, he could ask this woman on a date.

"Lexi, I was wondering if you'd—"

He'd just started to ask her out to dinner, when a loud crash from the kitchen echoed loudly through the diner.

Their heads both spun in that direction.

"Crap. I'd better go see what I can do to help." She looked up at him, regret swimming in her eyes. "Sorry."

"Never apologize for doing your job, angel. You have my number. Don't hesitate to call if you need anything."

She grinned and held up his card. "Got it."

"Good. Now, go. We can talk another time."

"Okay." Lexi started to walk away, but turned and asked, "Will I see you again, soon?"

Loving the hopeful tone in her voice, Trevor answered with, "Count on it."

With another big smile, she turned and walked through the kitchen's swinging doors, sliding his card into her back pocket as she went.

****

"That's it." Joe Walker, the diner's owner, slapped the palm of his hand down onto the counter. "Effective immediately, that man is no longer welcome here."

"He comes in pretty regularly. You'll be losing money."

Lexi tested the running water's temperature. Sure, she was still pissed as hell about what Rob had done, but she'd had a few hours to calm down.

She pushed the faucet handle down, cutting off its steady stream of hot water. Sliding on a pair of bright yellow dishwashing gloves, she grabbed the nearest pan and scouring pad, and began to scrub.

"Your safety comes before money," he said angrily. "You should know that. He had no right to put his hands on you. Period."

Caleb took the pan from Lexi's hand and rinsed the suds off before setting it into the drying rack. The tall, lanky kid was cute…or, at least he would be when he got a little older and filled out some.

Using the back of his hand, he swiped at a sprig of dark hair from his forehead. "Don't worry, Joe. I don't think we'll see Rob again. Not after the way those two guys went at him, anyway."

Lexi's insides danced at the memory, but she ignored it. "They didn't go *at* Rob."

A snorting sound came from the back of the younger man's throat before he gave her a sarcastic, "Okay."

"They didn't," she insisted, grabbing another pan to wash.

He stopped what he was doing and faced her. "What would you call it, then?"

Focusing on the food stuck to the bottom of the pan, Lexi replayed the incident in her mind. It had all started with Rob telling her she shouldn't be flirting with Trevor and Derek. He'd said it was going to make people think she would do anything for a good tip. God, just thinking about it still riled her up again.

Her heart beat a little harder in her chest when she remembered how strong his grip had been and how scared she'd felt when she couldn't break free.

Then, *he* was there.

Though, she'd still been caught in Rob's grasp, Lexi had immediately felt safe. Protected. Thanks to Trevor.

Not that she didn't appreciate Derek's help and support, too, because she did. There was just something about Trevor that made her feel…different.

Lexi looked up and realized Caleb was still waiting for an answer.

"They just talked to him."

Clearly not agreeing, Caleb shook his head and went back to rinsing the dishes. Afraid Joe would think the guys had tried to start a brawl in his place of business, Lexi turned to Joe to reassure him.

"Trevor and Derek both calmly and respectfully talked to Rob. They made him understand he'd made a mistake. Rob chose to leave. End of story."

The older, bald man wiped his hands on his dirty apron and rested his hands on his hips. Joe was lean, and the tattoos on both biceps were old and faded, but the muscles in his arms were still clearly defined. It was easy for Lexi to imagine him as a young, fit Marine.

"Trevor and Derek. Those the two men I've seen you talking to a lot lately? Started coming in here a few weeks ago?"

"Yes. But, they're not trouble-makers, Joe," she was quick to say. "In fact, they're both former military, like you."

Joe's salt and pepper brows rose at that. "Marines?"

"I'm not sure what branch they were in. Just that they used to be in the military. Oh, and they work for a private security company here in the city. Trevor said they offer protection to people." Then, because she felt the need to stand up for them as they had her, she added, "I really think they're good guys, Joe."

"You don't have to sell me on those boys, Lex. They stepped up and took care of you when you needed it. The fact that they both served is just icing on the cake." He gave her a wide, toothy grin, the gold cap on one of his top teeth shining beneath the kitchen lights.

Lexi smiled at the way Joe called them 'boys'. They weren't anything like Caleb. Especially Trevor, who was a strong, confident man.

"Uh, oh. I know that look."

Lexi swiveled her head back to Caleb. She turned her brows inward. "What look?"

Putting his fists beneath his chin, Caleb rapidly blinked both eyes and raised his voice to falsetto heights. *"Trevor's so dreamy. I hope he asks me out."*

Lexi grabbed the nearest washrag and threw it at him. "I did not have that look."

"Oh, you *so* had that look. You get it every time the guy walks in."

"Trevor, huh?" Joe asked as he hung the newly cleaned and dried pots from the ceiling rack above the metal counter.

"Ughhhh," Lexi growled. "Not you, too."

"Sorry, Lex." Joe shrugged. "I'm afraid I'm with Caleb on this one. Even with eyes as old as mine, I can see it."

Don't ask him. Don't ask him.

"See what?"

"The way you look at him when he's not paying attention."

Damn it. *You asked.*

"I also see the way he looks at you when you're busy taking orders or behind the counter filling drinks and what not. He likes you, too, Lex. The only question is when are the two of you going to do something about it?"

Caleb laughed loudly. Lexi narrowed her eyes at him, but he simply shrugged and said, "Told ya."

Reaching behind her, Lexi untied her apron. "First of all, I don't give him a look. Second, and most importantly, my love life isn't any of your business." She eyed both men. "So, I'd appreciate it if you stayed out of it."

Caleb actually looked a little chagrined, but not Joe. The man who'd come to be more of a father figure than just her boss just stood there, smiling.

After locking the place up for the night, Caleb said his goodbyes and headed for his small, beat-up car while Joe and Lexi continued walking to theirs. They were parked next to the wooded area that butted up against the diner's parking lot, where all employees were supposed to park.

"You know," Joe said, as they stood behind his car's bumper. "There's nothing wrong with liking a man, Lex. Trevor? He sounds like one of the good ones."

"Joe," Lexi warned. Of course, the stubborn old fool didn't listen.

"You're too young and much too pretty to waste all your days stuck in this place"—he jutted his chin toward the diner—"and your nights alone in your mama's house."

Lexi swallowed at the mention of her mom. "I-I'm good, Joe. Really."

"I may be old, Alexis, but I ain't stupid."

Joe used her full name. He only did that when he was being serious. Shit.

"I know you're not stupid."

"Well, good. At least we agree on that." Joe's expression softened, and he put a comforting hand on her shoulder. "Look, Lex. I know losing your mama was hard. And, I know her illness and dying put you in a tight spot, but you still have a life to live. Your mama and I didn't know each other long, but one thing's for certain…she wanted you to be happy."

A stinging sensation began in her nose, and Lexi blinked away the tears that always came when she thought about her mom. "I know that."

"Do you? Because all I see is you working yourself to the bone, with nothing to show for it. Don't get me wrong, honey. You're the best employee I've had in all my years of owning this place, and I'd hate to lose you. But I'd manage, especially if I knew you were moving forward with your life. A life you *deserve*."

"I'm not unhappy, Joe."

"But you're not exactly happy, either."

That comment took her by surprise. Mainly, because he was right.

"Told you"—Joe pointed to the corner of his right eye—"these old eyes see more than anyone ever thinks."

Lexi leaned in and gave her friend a hug. "I'll see you tomorrow. Drive careful."

Hugging her back, "See you tomorrow, baby girl."

An hour later, Lexi had showered the day away and was sitting up in bed, trying to read. Normally, she could get lost in a good romance novel for hours. Tonight, however, she was having trouble concentrating on the words.

When she realized she needed to scroll back three pages because she had no idea what she'd just read, Lexi gave up and set her tablet on the nightstand to the right of her bed. She glanced at her phone and the business card lying beside it.

Checking the time, she wondered if he would even be awake. Thinking of what Joe had said, Lexi decided to throw caution to the wind and send Trevor a text. Just to thank him.

You already thanked him.

Ignoring the little voice in her head that was saying she was making excuses, Lexi snatched her phone from the nightstand, along with the card. With her pillow propped up between her back and the headboard, she flipped the card over.

Running her thumb across the handwritten numbers, she remembered the way his strong fingers had held her pen. Of its own accord, her mind brought forth the image of him holding her wrist and the gentleness with which he'd caressed the skin there.

He'd seemed so upset at the idea that she'd been bruised. Even apologized, as if it had been his fault. She looked at the number again. Surely, someone who stood up for others the way he did today had to be a good guy. Right?

Decision made, Lexi typed the number into her phone and then her message.

Hi, Trevor. This is Lexi. Sorry to bother you so late, but I wanted to let you know I made it home safe and sound. I also wanted to thank you again for today. Have a good rest of your night.

Before she could talk herself out of it, she hit send, then set the phone and card back down next to her tablet. She'd just repositioned her pillow and started to lie down when her phone dinged, notifying her she had a new text.

Oh, shit. Had he just responded? Holding her breath, she sat back up and quickly grabbed her phone. Sure enough, there was a new text from the same number.

Hey, angel. No bother. And I already told you…there's no need to thank me. That guy was a jerk and needed to learn he shouldn't treat a lady like that. Hope the rest of your day went smoother?

Her heart did a little flip at his use of the word 'angel', the way it had when he'd called her that at the diner today. She wrote back.

It did. What about yours? Did you have a good day?

She hit send and waited. Seconds later, her phone dinged again.

I did. Spent the afternoon at the office, went to the gym, then came home. Nothing too exciting.

Then, almost immediately after receiving that text, she got another.

Can I call you?

Lexi's heart gave a hard thump. Having a conversation while in the middle of a crowded diner was one thing. Talking to him over the phone, however, seemed…different. More intimate. *Because it is.*

Lexi shook her head at herself. This was silly. Trevor was just being nice. Nothing he'd said so far indicated he wanted to be anything more than friends. And friends talked to each other on the phone all the time, so this was no big deal.

Except, in the diner, she could have sworn he'd been on the verge of asking her out. Something about the way he'd been looking at her…just before Caleb dropped a tray and broke two dishes, essentially ruining the moment.

Her phone dinged again.

You still there, angel?

Crap. She hadn't answered his question.

Yeah, I'm still here. And yes, you can call.

Butterflies danced in her stomach, and she nervously tapped her thumb against the edge of her phone as she waited. Four seconds later, it rang. Swallowing her nerves, Lexi slid the same thumb across her screen and answered the call.

"Hi."

"Hey, angel." His deep voice rumbled. "I hope this is

okay. I needed to ask you something, and I felt lame doing it through text."

Lexi could've sworn he sounded almost as nervous as she was. That didn't seem right, though. A guy like him wouldn't get nervous simply over talking to her.

"You're fine," she assured him. "You can call me anytime."

She regretted the words as soon as the invitation was out of her mouth. Not because she hadn't meant them, but because she was afraid they made her sound desperate.

She could almost hear his smile when he said, "Good to know."

After a few seconds of awkward silence, Lexi bit the bullet. "You said you wanted to ask me something?"

"I do." She heard him inhale, and then, "I was wondering if you'd like to have dinner with me."

Her inner teenager wanted to squeal. Luckily, she kept it on a tight leash. "Yeah. Sure. I'd love to go out with you."

"You would? Great." Trevor sounded relieved, which put her more at ease.

"When would you like to go?"

"When are you free?" he shot back.

"Um…" She thought for a moment. "I close the next three nights, so I won't be able to go for a few days. Unless you like to eat late, that is."

"Late works for me."

"Oh," Lexi laughed. "I was just kidding about that."

"I wasn't." He actually sounded serious.

"Really, Trevor. It's okay. The diner closes at eight on weeknights, which isn't horribly late, but I'd have to come home and shower and change. It would be nine o'clock before we could even go anywhere. Everything will probably be closed by then."

Without any hesitation, he asked, "Do you like Mexican?"

"Uh…sure. Who doesn't?"

"Good. There's a great little place over on Jefferson. Not too fancy, but the food is excellent. I know the owner and his wife pretty well, so, I'm sure it'll be fine if we're a little late getting there."

"Seriously, Trevor. You don't have to—"

"Are you reneging on our deal?" he asked, sounding hurt.

"What? N-no. Not at all. I just don't want you to feel rushed during dinner, that's all."

"Relax, Lexi. I was just kidding. How about I pick you up tomorrow night at nine? Or we can meet at the restaurant, if that makes you feel more comfortable."

God, he was sweet. "No. You can pick me up here. I'll text you the address."

"Then, it's a date."

"It's a date," Lexi said, unable to contain her smile.

"Well, then…I'd better get off here and let you get some rest."

"Okay."

"Don't forget to text me your address."

"I won't."

"Goodnight, angel. Sleep tight."

"Goodnight, Trevor." With that, she ended the call. She laid her phone on top of her radio-slash-alarm clock-slash wireless charger and turned off her bedside lamp.

Lexi fell asleep with a smile on her face, completely unaware that someone had followed her home from the diner.

A man had stood on the ground below her bedroom window as she'd talked with Trevor. The same man who was currently watching her house as she slept.

Chapter 3

Trevor looked at the clock. It was already seven thirty, and he was running late.

The day started off great. He'd met the rest of Alpha Team at Jake's private shooting range on his ranch outside the city. They shot up a few targets, got cleaned up, and went into the office. The next three hours, Trevor sat through two very long meetings with some potential clients.

With the others busy with their own tasks, Trevor then spent the remainder of the day in Jake's office, ready to attack the rest of his to-do list. His intentions of getting it all done early were shot to hell within the first two hours of sitting down.

After nearly forty-five minutes on the phone with the bank, he'd finally managed to straighten up a payroll issue. Trevor then spent the next hour returning half a dozen emails and twice as many phone calls.

The last one took the longest. It was with Jason Ryker, R.I.S.C.'s Homeland handler. He'd called to talk to Trevor about an upcoming job that was going to require Alpha Team's assistance.

He had no idea how Jake did this part of the job on a

regular basis. The guy seriously needed to hire an office manager.

When it was all said and done, he barely had enough time to rush home, take a quick shower, and head to Lexi's house to pick her up for dinner.

Grabbing his jacket from the back of the chair, Trevor stood and pulled his phone from his pocket. He needed to text Lexi to let her know he may be a couple minutes late. With his head down and his thumbs flying across his phone screen, Trevor exited Jake's office at the same time one of his teammates was passing by.

"Whoa." Sean "Coop" Cooper quickly stepped to the side to avoid the near hallway collision. His brown eyebrows rose in surprise. "Easy, man. Where's the fire?"

"Sorry," Trevor offered as he stopped just in time. "I didn't see you."

"Clearly." Coop smirked sarcastically. "What's the deal? You got a hot date, or something?"

No sense in lying. If things went as well as he hoped, these guys would be getting to know Lexi soon enough, anyway.

"As a matter of fact, yes. I do."

"Well, hot damn. It's about fuckin' time."

Both men turned to see Derek coming out of his office at the end of the hallway. Ignoring him, Trevor rolled his eyes and headed toward the office's reception area.

"Wait up." Coop took a couple extra steps to catch up to him. "So, who's the lucky girl?"

"The blonde I told you about." Trevor heard D answer for him.

Looking to Trevor, Coop asked, "The one from that diner?"

Trevor quickened his pace, bringing himself a few steps

ahead of Coop. He hollered over his shoulder as he reached the office door. "Glad to see you two have nothing better to do than talk about my love life. Be sure to lock everything up before you leave."

From behind him, he heard Derek say, "Yeah? Well, you'd better name your first kid after me, since I'm the reason you two are finally getting together."

Without looking back, Trevor gave D a one-finger salute and left. He texted Lexi as he rode the elevator down to the building's main floor.

****

Lexi locked the door to the diner and quickly headed for her car. She'd gotten a text from Trevor a little under an hour ago saying he might be a few minutes late, which actually worked out well for her, since she was running about twenty minutes behind herself.

The dinner rush had been crazier than usual, which meant clean-up took longer than it normally did. Glancing at her watch, Lexi grimaced when she saw it was already eight-thirty. Crap. She still had a ten minute drive to her mom's house before she could even start to get ready.

No, not mom's house. It's my house, now.

Shaking off those thoughts, Lexi ran through her plan as she high-tailed it to her car. With minimal traffic, she'd be home by eight-forty. Her simple sense of style would allow her a five-minute shower and five more minutes to get dressed and put on a little makeup.

With the rest of the time, she'd blow dry her hair as best she could. Worst case, she'd just throw back up in a bun.

Thinking her plan was very much doable, Lexi approached

the driver's side of her car and stopped cold.

"Damn it." Of *course*, she would have a flat tire. Tonight of all nights.

She wanted to scream, or cry, or…scream. Instead, she took her insurance card from her wallet and called the roadside service number on the back of the card. After that was taken care of, she texted Trevor.

Hey, Trevor. Sorry for the short notice, but I'm at work, and my tire's flat. My insurance company called a tow service, and the guy said he'd be able to give me a ride home before taking it into the shop. They said he's on his way to another job right now and wasn't sure how long it's going to take. I'm really sorry. Hopefully we can reschedule soon.

Ending it with a fingers crossed emoji, Lexi sighed loudly and hit send. Within seconds, her phone was ringing.

"Hello?"

"I'm on my way." It was the only greeting Trevor gave.

"What? No." She grimaced at how harsh she'd sounded. "I mean, I appreciate the offer, Trevor, but that really isn't necessary. I told you, the insurance company already called someone."

"Go back inside the diner and lock the doors behind you. Then, call and cancel the tow. I'll be there in fifteen."

The concern in his tone took her off guard.

"Lex?"

"I-I'm here, but I gotta say, you're starting to scare me a little bit."

A muttered curse reached her ear. She then heard Trevor take in a deep breath before exhaling loudly. "Sorry. I don't mean to scare you or bark orders. Occupational habit, I guess."

Not quite sure how she should respond, Lexi simply replied with, "That's okay."

"Is Joe with you?"

She had a feeling he wasn't going to like her answer. "Joe's sick, Gina, the other waitress who works the dinner shift didn't show, and Caleb has a big algebra test tomorrow, so I sent him home as soon as we closed. He needed the extra time to study."

"So, you're *alone*?" he asked, clearly alarmed.

"This isn't the first time I've closed the place down by myself. I'm a big girl, Trevor," Lexi assured him. "I'll be okay."

He cleared his throat before apologizing again. "I'm sorry. I didn't mean to imply otherwise, but I don't like the idea of you waiting in the parking lot alone. Especially not at night. I just want to make sure you're safe, that's all."

"Oh. That's, um…really sweet, actually."

"Well, I've definitely been called worse."

She could practically hear his smile through the phone. "Okay, you win. I'm walking back to the diner now."

"Thanks, angel. I'll see you soon."

Twenty minutes later, Lexi was standing by her car, waiting as Trevor rolled up the sleeves of his light-blue button up. She could have sworn her mouth had watered when he'd first stepped out of his truck.

The man was like a GQ G.I. Joe in that shirt, a pair of dark, slightly worn jeans, and brown cowboy boots that clearly weren't just for show. She watched as he pulled a small flashlight from his back pocket and squatted down next to her flat tire. Thumbing the light on with his left hand, he began to slowly inspect the tire with his right.

"What are you doing?"

"Looking for anything obvious that could have caused the leak. I'm not seeing anything, though. Could be on the part of the tire that's trapped under the wheel." He turned off the light and stood to face her. "You probably just ran over a nail or something."

"Lucky me," Lexi said sarcastically.

"Where's your spare?"

With a chagrined expression, she said, "The flat tire *is* my spare."

She'd known for a while that she needed new tires, but had been putting it off for as long as she could. The money she made waitressing either went to pay her bills or buy groceries. Anything left at the end of the month—which was never very much—went into a jar she had hidden in her bedroom closet. Her version of a savings account.

Trevor shoved the flashlight back into his pocket and used that same hand to pull out his phone and shoot a text.

"One-handed, that's pretty impressive."

Grinning, Trevor said, "I'm a man of many talents."

I bet you are. The words nearly fell from her lips. Damn, she really needed to watch herself around him.

After receiving a response from whomever he'd texted and sending another message back, Trevor shoved his phone into his pocket and looked at his other hand. "You mind if I go in and wash up?"

"Of course."

They walked back to the diner. Lexi unlocked the door and led him to the sink behind the counter. Standing beside him with her back against the Formica top, she bit her lip and watched his corded muscles as they moved with the motion of his hands. Holy hell, even his *forearms* were sexy.

Trevor turned off the faucet and reached for the paper towel dispenser on the wall. He quickly dried his hands and tossed the used towels into the small trashcan below it. "You ready?"

"Ready? For what?"

"Dinner." Then, he gave her a lopsided grin, and…holy hell, the guy was seriously hot.

Ignoring the tingling in her lower belly, Lexi looked at her watch. "There's no way we'll make it to the restaurant in time."

He shrugged a shoulder. "No, but I'm sure we can find something close."

She thought about the food places in the nearby area. They were all fast-food. This was their first date, damn it. She didn't want drive-through. She wanted a nice dinner.

Something memorable. Something like—

"I know just the place," she offered.

His brows rose slightly. "Is it close by?"

"Very." Excited about the idea that had just formed, she held out her hand and smiled. "Come on. I'll show you."

Trevor placed his hand in hers, and Lexi had to force herself not to react. The feeling she got when they touched was nothing short of an electrical charge. It was unlike anything she'd ever experienced before.

Maybe it was wishful thinking, but Lexi could have sworn he felt it, too. It was there, in his eyes he looked down at their joined hands and then back up to her.

Swallowing hard, Lexi quietly whispered, "Follow me."

Without another word, she turned and led him out from behind the counter and to the left…through the kitchen's dual-swinging doors. Though, she hated to, Lexi let go of his hand and turned to face him.

"We're here."

Confusion filled his face. "Uh, Lex. This is the kitchen."

"I know," she grinned. "Here," she went to the sink and grabbed the metal stool Joe sometimes used to help his back when he was washing dishes. Setting next to where Trevor was standing, she patted its seat. "You sit here, and I'll take care of everything."

Turning his brows inward, Trevor grinned suspiciously as he sat down. "What are you up to, angel?"

Lexi couldn't help but laugh at the befuddled expression. "You'll see. Oh! I almost forgot. Do you like wine?"

Still looking suspicious, Trevor grinned. "I do."

"Red okay?"

He gave her a slight nod. "Red's fine. But, Lexi, what are you—"

"Don't worry about a thing. I've got this under control."

Walking over to the commercial-size refrigerator, she grabbed the large handles with both hands and pulled the doors open. The rush of air that hit her heated flesh was a shock to her system, but she welcomed it.

She used the stolen moment to draw in a deep, calming breath. Feeling this nervous was silly, but it had been a very long time since she'd cooked for anyone but herself and didn't want to screw the night up any worse than she already had.

After moving a few things around, Lexi pulled the chilled bottle of merlot from the fridge and went over to one of the many utensil drawers. After some digging, she found what she was looking for.

"I didn't know Joe's served wine."

Lexi smiled as she screwed the opener into the top of the bottle's cork. "We don't. I keep a bottle in the back of the fridge, just in case."

"In case of what? A wine emergency?"

She chuckled, twisting the opener. Looking as though she meant business, she said, "Hey, you joke, but that's actually a thing."

When she glanced over her shoulder, she was rewarded with a heart-stopping smile. *God, just look at him.*

With one boot on the floor and his other heel propped on the stool's bottom ring, Trevor's legs were set casually apart. Lexi couldn't help but notice how the denim stretched perfectly over a pair of toned thighs. It took everything she had not to look directly at the bulge between them.

"Um…" She licked her lips nervously and continued opening the bottle. "Gina and I will sometimes have a glass before heading home after a long day."

Pouring some for each of them, Lexi walked a glass over to Trevor. "Here ya go."

"Thank you." His low voice rumbled.

Their fingertips met, and damn, if she didn't feel that same spark again. Sitting this way brought him closer to eye-level, and when Lexi's gaze found his, she knew he'd felt their connection, too.

"You're welcome." She swallowed hard before returning her focus back on the task at hand. If she didn't, it would be midnight before they ever ate.

After taking a sip of her own, Lexi put her glass down and began gathering everything she needed for what she had planned.

"I already know you like red meat," she stated, pulling out two steaks wrapped in butcher paper. Do you like rice?"

"Rice is fine."

She bent down and opened one of the vegetable drawers. "What about salads?" She looked back over her shoulder, and Trevor's eyes shot to hers. Lexi schooled her expression, but inside she was grinning from ear to ear. *He was checking me out.*

Clearing his throat, Trevor said, "I've been known to eat a salad or two." With his wine glass in his hand, he stood from the stool and walked over to where she was setting the food out on the counter. "But, I don't want you going to any trouble for me, angel. Honestly, I'm good with hitting a drive-thru or something."

"Well, I'm not." She began chopping the lettuce. "Not tonight."

"You've been working here all day, Lex."

She shrugged it off. "This is different."

"How?"

She stopped chopping and faced him with a smile. "For me, cooking like this is…cathartic."

"Cathartic?"

"Yeah. I don't know; I guess it gives me time to think. It's relaxing."

Lexi scooped the lettuce up from the wooden chopping board and placed it in a large bowl. She then wiped the board down and reached for the steak. She expertly trimmed the fat from its edges, then began slicing the meat into thin, bite-size pieces.

"So, what do you think about when you cook?"

She smiled. "My mom, mostly."

"How long has she been gone?"

Her head whipped up in surprise. "How did you know?"

The corner of his mouth rose slightly. "The tone of your voice. That and the way your eyes looked when you said the word 'mom'."

Lexi stared at him for a moment, and then, "You see a lot, don't you?"

He grinned. "Another occupational hazard."

Firing up two gas burners, Lexi set a pot of water to boil for the rice on one, and a large, cast-iron skillet on another. After quickly seasoning the meat, she placed it in the pan with some olive oil.

"My mom died almost two years ago. Breast cancer."

"Damn, Lex. I'm sorry."

Lexi focused on stirring the sizzling meat. "Thanks. I won't lie; it was the hardest thing I've ever had to go through, but I'm okay, now."

"Still, losing a parent has to be rough. What about your dad?"

"You mean the sperm donor?" When Trevor's brows rose in reaction, Lexi quickly tried to recover. "Sorry. Filter malfunction."

Trevor's shoulders shook with a laugh. "No need to filter yourself around me. I like a woman who says what she's thinking."

"Really?"

"Yeah. I never understood why some people feel the need to talk or act a certain way just to impress someone."

"Right? That's exactly how I feel. I guess I'm a 'what you see is what you get' kinda gal. Take it or leave it, I always say."

Heat flared behind his dark brown eyes when he said, "I'll take it."

Staring up at him, Lexi nervously bit her lip. When Trevor's eyes found her mouth, he started to lean inward.

Holy, crap! He's going to kiss me.

More than ready to feel his lips against hers, Lexi was about to throw caution to the wind take charge when a loud pop came from the stove right before she felt the burn on her arm.

"Ouch." She quickly rubbed the spot where the hot oil had landed.

"You okay?"

"Yeah, the oil just got too hot." Turning the burner down a bit, Lexi used a wooden spatula to stir the meat. With a smirk, she looked at him and said, "Occupational hazard."

Trevor's entire face lit up when he laughed. "Touché."

****

Thirty minutes later, they were both nearly finished eating. Not wanting passersby to think the diner was still open, Lexi had told Trevor they were going to eat in the kitchen.

He'd offered Lexi the bar stool, but she chose instead to sit up on the stainless steel countertop and hold her bowl as she ate. God, she was adorable.

In typical, first-date fashion, they'd gotten to know each other a little more over dinner. He'd learned Lexi and her mom moved from Missouri to Texas when she was a little girl. Her mom had been a teacher and had gotten a job in one of the smaller schools here.

Lexi's dad—aka the 'sperm donor'—had left her mom when he found out she was pregnant. Her mom never married and had no other children, so it had always just been the two of them, which made it even harder when Lexi lost her.

Imagining Lexi as a little girl growing up without a father pissed him off. Knowing she had no one to turn to during that difficult time, except for Joe and the people who worked here, made it even worse. Trevor didn't have kids yet, but he couldn't imagine ever abandoning one. Planned or unplanned.

Trevor shared a little about himself and his time in the military. Then, without giving any specific details or breaking client confidentiality, he explained the basics of R.I.S.C. and what he and the rest of Alpha Team did.

He figured it was best to lay it all out there from the start. That way, if his job was a deal-breaker, they'd both know from the get-go and be able to part ways as friends before any real feelings got involved. *Too late for that, buddy.*

Thankfully, Lexi seemed more intrigued than turned off by it all. Of course, she looked concerned when he spoke of some of the dangers involved with going after a high-value target and such, but thankfully, her only response was to make him promise to do everything he could to stay safe.

An image flashed before him. Him, walking into the diner after being away on an op. Lexi would be standing at one of the booths taking someone's order, her hair in the same, messy bun it was in now. She'd turn her head and smile, and begin running toward him. She'd jump into his arms, press her lips to his. They'd…

"You okay?"

"Huh?" Trevor's head snapped up. He cleared his throat. "Yeah. I'm good. And that was delicious, Lexi. Thank you."

Still propped up on the counter, she smiled down at him. "Thank you."

Trevor shook his head. "Not just being nice here, Lex. Anyone who can cook like this on the fly shouldn't be holed up serving tables in some run-down diner."

"Hey, now," she warned. "Don't go hatin' on Joe's like that. He hears you talking smack on his place, he'll likely ban you for life." With a teasing tone, she added, "Then, you'd have to find somewhere else to get your patty melts."

He laughed, loving how playful she was. "I'm just saying

you've got talent, angel. I hate to see it go to waste in a place like this."

Though, the corners of her lips turned up slightly, his compliment seemed to fall flat. "Yeah, well"—she slid off the counter and headed to the opposite side of the room where the sink was located—"we don't all have the luxury of being picky about where we work."

"I get that," Trevor said cautiously as he stood and carried his dishes to where she stood.

Lexi continued talking while she got the hot water running and began washing her bowl and fork. "Opening a restaurant takes a lot of time and money. Not to mention real estate. So, until I have those things, I'll be holed up, waiting tables, in this run-down diner."

She gave him another forced smile as she took the dishes from his hands. Without asking, he turned the faucet attached to the second sink and began rinsing as she washed.

Damn. Until now, things had been going so well. He'd clearly said something to upset her, and his chest tightened as he tried to figure out a way to fix it.

Trevor walked back over and grabbed their wine glasses and brought them to her. "I'm sorry, Lexi. I didn't mean to upset you."

She took the glasses from his hands and began washing them. He picked up a towel and began drying the dishes he'd placed in the rack, but she stopped him.

"I appreciate the help," she said quietly. "But the health department requires all the dishes to air dry."

Trevor stopped what he was doing and sat the towel back down onto the counter. Lexi turned to him and sighed.

"And, you have nothing to apologize for. You paid me a compliment, and I…" she cut herself off and sighed loudly before going to get the pot and pan still on the stove.

A span of silence passed while she finished scrubbing the pans. As hard as it was, Trevor gave her the time she needed before continuing on.

"I was accepted to Kendall College three years ago. It's a prestigious culinary school in Chicago. I had this grand plan of finishing the program and then opening my own restaurant. Nothing too fancy…someplace simple with a touch of elegance. A place people could go for a nice meal, but also afford to bring the whole family, if they wanted."

"Three years ago," Trevor said with thought. "Your mom?"

Lexi nodded. "She got sick. I dropped out of school and moved back here. Mom had insurance, but that only covers so much. She went through her savings pretty quickly, and I paid the remainder of her medical bills with the rest of what I had put aside for school. I got a job as a server at a really nice restaurant downtown but lost it when I kept calling in to take mom to the doctor or stay home with her when she was having a bad day."

"Damn," he muttered beside her.

"Not that I'm complaining," she was quick to say. "I wouldn't give up that last year with my mom for anything, and I'm very thankful I had enough saved up to help cover the costs, but…" Her voice trailed off.

"But?"

She shrugged a shoulder. "With no savings left, and a job that doesn't pay much, my plan became a fantasy."

With the dishes all taken care of, Trevor took a step closer. "I'm sorry, Lex. I shouldn't have said anything."

"No, I'm the one who should be sorry. First, there's the flat tire fiasco, and then I turn our very pleasant dinner conversation into a pity party." She wrinkled her cute-as-hell nose. "Regret asking me out yet?"

"Are you kidding?" He moved in even closer. "I got to rescue a stranded motorist, ate the best meal I've had in a long time, and I shared it with the beautiful chef who prepared it. What's not to love?"

Lexi's cheeks turned red, and damn, if it didn't make his dick stand up and take notice. "Well, I don't know about all that. I mean, I wasn't exactly *stranded*."

Trevor raised a brow. "You had a flat tire and no spare, angel. Pretty sure that qualifies."

Lexi pulled her bottom lip between her teeth, and his heart started to beat a little harder. "Well, lucky for me, I have my very own hero."

Reaching up, he used his fingertips to brush some hair from her forehead. "Yeah," he whispered. "You do."

Leaning down several inches, Trevor brought his lips closer to her. He knew Lexi was on board when she stood on her tiptoes to help close the space between them. His lips had barely brushed against hers when someone started pounding loudly on the diner's door.

Startled, Lexi jumped back, and Trevor's hand instinctively went to his waistband at his lower back. Remembering he'd opted for his boot holster —to keep from freaking Lexi out—he bent down and pulled his pant leg up. Releasing the gun from its sheath, Trevor stood to find Lexi cautiously eyeing the weapon.

"Sorry, angel. I never go anywhere without it."

"O-occupational hazard. No, I get it. But do you really think it's needed now?" She sounded a little shaky, but otherwise fine.

Trevor glanced down at his watch. "It's too late for

someone to just show up here, Lex. Especially since the diner's hours are clearly posted on the door." Plus, the only lights they'd left on were the ones in the kitchen.

"Seems pretty silly to knock on a door like that if you're planning to rob the place."

She wasn't wrong. "It's probably nothing, but people had been known to knock or ring a doorbell before breaking into a place, just to make sure it's actually empty."

More pounding came then.

"What about our cars?" Lexi whispered, as if whoever was out there could hear her. "Surely, they had to see those."

"Sure, but we could've met up with friends and left our cars here."

Every question she'd asked was valid, and since they weren't in any immediate danger, he wasn't upset at her for taking the time to ask. Actually, he was impressed with the way she was calmly thinking the situation through. However, he needed to see who was outside and make sure she wasn't in any actual danger.

"Stay here," he ordered quietly. Thankfully, she did as she was told.

Slowly, Trevor walked toward the swinging doors. With his free hand, he pushed the left one open just enough to be able to see the man standing outside the diner's front door…and the flashing yellow lights on the large truck parked behind him.

Relaxing his shoulders, he turned to Lexi with a smirk. "You forget to cancel the tow service?"

Chapter 4

Lexi's insides were a bowl of nerves as she stood on the small stoop by her front door. "Thanks again for the ride home."

"Of course." Trevor's eyes glanced around at the other houses. "Looks like a pretty nice neighborhood."

"It is. I think I'm the youngest person on the street, but the neighbors are all really nice." Lexi pointed to the small, ranch-style home across the street. "Mrs. Siemens loves to bake, so she'll sometimes make extra and bring it over to share."

"That's nice."

"Yeah." *Gah!* What was the matter with her? Making small talk was practically a job requirement for her, yet she couldn't think of what to say now to save her soul.

After a few beats of awkward silence, Trevor cleared his throat and said, "Well, the guy from the tow company assured me your car would be ready first thing in the morning."

"What time did you say they open?"

"Seven."

"Okay, good. Gina works breakfast shift tomorrow, and she doesn't live too far from here. I'll just have her pick me up before she goes in and drop me off at the garage."

"If she can't, just give me a call, and I'll come get you."

"Thanks. I will. And, I know I've said it about a billion times already, but I'm really sorry about tonight."

"And I've told *you* about a billion times to stop apologizing. I had a great time."

Lexi rolled her eyes, channeling her inner Caleb for a sarcastic "Okay".

"No, really." Trevor stepped in a little closer. "This was the best first date I've had."

Another sarcastic quip was about to fall off her tongue, but then Lexi looked into his eyes and saw that he was being serious. "Really?"

"Promise."

She exhaled softly. "I had a great time, too." *Minus the tow driver's impeccably bad timing.*

"Enjoy it enough to go out with me again?" he asked with a smirk.

Lexi loved how hopeful he sounded. "Well…" She pretended to think on it. "Technically, we didn't actually go *out* this time."

Trevor narrowed his eyes. "You're gonna cause me trouble, aren't you, angel?"

She smiled innocently. "Me? Never." Lexi opened her mouth to say something else, but it was lost when she began to yawn. Embarrassed, she covered her mouth quickly until it was over. She felt herself blush. "Sorry."

Strangely, a heated look flashed across Trevor's face, but then it was gone. "Don't be. It's late, and I should probably get going."

Lexi smiled up at him, determined not to let her disappointment that he was leaving show. "Yeah, and I want to be at the garage early to make sure everything gets taken care of before I have to get to work. Oh, I forgot to ask. Did the guy happen to mention how much the new tire would be?"

Once they'd realized who the person pounding on the diner's door was, Trevor had insisted on going out and talking to the guy alone. Said he didn't want the man to know there was the possibility of a young woman being there late at night. *Such a protector.*

Trevor's eyes skittered to the side then back to hers. "Uh, I don't think he mentioned a price. I wouldn't worry too much, though. Your car takes pretty small tires."

"Thank God for that," she mumbled more to herself than him.

There were a few more seconds of awkward silence before Trevor leaned down and kissed her on the cheek. "Thanks for dinner, Lex," he whispered softly.

"You're welcome," she returned the whisper, desperate to touch the spot where his lips had just been.

Lexi had read about that special 'spark' some couples had from the start, but she never actually believed it was real. Until now.

Despite the jolt she'd felt, Trevor simply told her, "Goodnight, angel. I'll call you tomorrow."

She watched as he walked off the stoop and down the sidewalk to his car.

"Night handsome," Lexi whispered back, knowing he wouldn't be able to hear her. Turning away, she unlocked the door and went inside.

He hadn't kissed her goodnight. Not really. She hated how disappointed she felt, but she couldn't help it. He'd claimed it was a great date, despite the whole flat tire debacle. So, if that were true, then why didn't he kiss her?

Lexi pulled a loose curl to her nose and inhaled. Maybe it had something to do with the fact that she still smelled like the diner's fried food. Of course, he did say he'd call tomorrow, so she'd just have to wait and see.

Refusing to work herself up over nothing, Lexi headed for the stairs. She needed a shower, and sleep. First, however, she was going to get on her computer and pull up her bank account.

Trevor had said the tire shouldn't be that much, but she didn't *have* that much to begin with. She hated the idea of digging into her money jar, but she would, if she had to. Wouldn't be the first time, and the way her luck went, it probably wouldn't be the last.

With a loud sigh, Lexi had just started up the steps when her doorbell rang. She spun around, surprised to see Trevor's blurred figure through the door's decorative glass window.

Afraid something was wrong, Lexi quickly made her way across the open area to unlock and open her door. The intense look on his face scared her.

"Trevor? Is something wrong?"

His Adam's apple bobbed up and down as he swallowed hard. "Yes."

That was it. He didn't offer any other explanation for why he'd come back to her door. So, she decided to ask.

"Are you going to tell me what it is, or am I supposed to guess?"

His dark brows turned inward and he spoke low. "That kiss I gave you…on the cheek."

Her heart thumped against her ribs. "W-what about it?"

"That's what's wrong," he gritted out, sounding upset.

Looking up at him questioningly, Lexi prayed she wasn't misunderstanding where this was headed.

His gaze burning into hers, Trevor shook his head. "That shouldn't have been our first kiss."

Before she could even think of a response, he grabbed the back of her neck and brought his lips to hers.

The tiny spark from before had nothing on the explosion of electricity she felt now. Fireworks ignited throughout her system as he finally kissed her the way she'd been craving.

Even on her tiptoes, Trevor towered over her. Wanting to make it easier on him, she closed what little space separated them and wrapped one hand around the back of his neck for support. Her short nails inadvertently dug into his tanned skin, which seemed to trigger something inside him.

Trevor took more control then, wrapping his free arm around her waist and pressing her body against his. Lexi could feel his erection through his jeans, her own sex becoming heavy and swollen with arousal.

She opened her mouth and Trevor wasted no time accepting the invitation. His tongue slipped inside and began to expertly dance with hers. Like him, his movements were powerful; their tongues thrusting together with a fierce and wild need.

Before she could stop it, a tiny mewling sound escaped the back of her throat. Her hips moved instinctively forward, her body seeking out the release it knew this man's touch could provide.

Trevor growled in appreciation, but then ended the kiss as quickly as he'd started it. With his hand still holding the back of her head and his other arm wrapped loosely around her waist, he rested his forehead against hers.

"*That*"—he spoke between heaving breaths—"should've been our first kiss."

"I forgive you," Lexi whispered teasingly.

His warm breath hit her chin when he exhaled on a silent laugh. "You're constantly surprising me, angel."

Right back at ya, soldier. Lexi wanted to say the words, but she was still having a hard time catching her breath.

"I've wanted to kiss you like that since I first saw you," he said with a low rumble.

All she managed to say was, "Same."

"I want to kiss you again."

"Okay." Lexi nodded shamelessly, uncaring of how quickly she'd agreed.

His smile widened with appreciation. "Okay."

Leaning down again, Trevor kept the pace slow this time. Sensual. It was even more arousing than the first, which was something Lexi wouldn't have thought possible.

Once again, when he pulled his lips away, Trevor leaned his forehead against hers. "I need to go."

Lexi had never had a one-night stand before. To her, the idea had just always seemed wrong. However, standing here, now…wrapped in Trevor's arms…she was seriously considering inviting him in.

"Why?" The question was out before she could stop it.

Trevor gave her a low chuckle before taking in a deep breath and letting it out slowly. "I think you know what'll happen if I don't."

And that's a problem because…

As if he could read her mind, he cupped one side of her face and said, "I don't want to push things too far, too fast."

Okay, there seriously had to be something wrong with this guy. Some major flaw he was hiding. No man was that considerate. At least none she'd ever met. Especially not one as devastatingly handsome as Trevor Matthews.

Again, he seemed to know exactly what she was thinking.

Brushing a wayward curl from her eye, he explained.

"I know we barely know each other, but…I like you, Alexis. A lot." He leaned in and gave her a sweet, chaste kiss before whispering, "I don't want to be something you regret in the morning."

From the way he kissed and the impressive erection she'd felt against her belly just a few minutes before, Lexi had a feeling she wouldn't regret a damn thing. Still, she couldn't help but appreciate his way of thinking.

"Okay. And, for the record"—because she needed him to know— "I like you, too."

His dark eyes lit up with the tilt of his lips. "Good. Now, I really do have to go before I do something lame, like invite myself in for a cup of coffee or something."

Lexi laughed. "Well, you'd be out of luck, anyway. I'm all out of coffee."

"You are, huh?"

"Yep. It's been a while since I've gone grocery shopping. I'm at the diner most days, and I guess I figure eating there with other people is less depressing than eating here alone after work."

With his thumb, Trevor gently caressed her bottom lip. "Maybe we can do something to change that. You eating here alone, that is."

The sincerity in his voice was so powerful Lexi barely whispered back, "Maybe."

With one more short, gentle kiss Trevor said, "Sweet dreams, angel."

Through the glass in her door, Lexi watched as he got into his truck and drove away. She brought a fingertip to her lips, loving that she could still taste him there.

****

He watched the silver truck drive off. Could see Alexis—Lexi—Hamilton moving away from the doorway and disappearing into the shadows of her home. At first, he'd thought the two were just friends.

He'd thought about moving on, taking on a different route to achieve his goal. But, there'd been something about the way Lexi and Soldier Boy had been looking at each other lately. That and the way Soldier Boy and his shaggy-haired sidekick had so valiantly come to her rescue yesterday.

The fact that Lexi and Soldier Boy were seeing each other didn't deter him. In fact, it made his plan that much more rewarding.

He'd damn near decided to go after Lexi tonight. From the trees, he'd watched as the other two employees left. Thirty minutes later, he'd stood behind the cover of trees and watched as she walked to her car. Alone.

The opportunity couldn't have been more perfect. Unfortunately for him, it was too soon. As much as he'd wanted to take her right then, he'd waited. Needing to be certain before he made his move.

The longer he gave them, the more devastating his end game would be. And, it would be devastating. For both of them.

Seeing Soldier Boy practically run back to her porch and go at her the way he had…right there, on her front stoop, for all to see…yeah, friends didn't kiss like that. He would know.

The fiery rage he felt every time he thought about it threatened to consume him. He glanced at the Craftsman-style home again, just as the upstairs light went off. He wanted to go in now. Knew he could break in easily enough.

He'd tried it earlier this evening, while the bitch and her new lover were probably back fucking in the diner's kitchen. The waitress and the soldier. It sounded like a cheesy romantic comedy.

Laughing silently to himself, he turned his car on and put it in drive. As he drove down the quiet street, he thought about what he had planned for little Miss Lexi. He wasn't quite ready for his big move, but he needed to do something soon. He wouldn't kill her. That would come later. For now, he'd keep it simple. Just enough to show the bubbly blonde and her Soldier Boy he could get to her whenever he wanted.

His smile grew as he pulled his car onto the interstate, knowing this story would have anything but a happy ending.

****

Lexi picked up the two paper sacks full of groceries and walked toward the set of large, automatic doors. Most people didn't use paper anymore, but she liked them.

For one thing, she didn't feel as though her fingers were going to be sliced in half by the time she carried them into her house like with the plastics. However, the real reason Lexi usually asked for paper instead of plastic was that they reminded her of when she was younger and would go to the store with her mom.

Blinking back her tears, she stepped outside and inhaled, breathing in the cool, night air. After two years, you'd think she'd quit getting weepy-eyed with every thought of her mom. Time didn't seem to matter, though. Not when it came to missing her.

Tonight wasn't about that, though. Trevor would be at her house in an hour, and she needed to hurry and get home.

After the fiasco of their first date the night before, Lexi was determined to make this one go smoothly.

Gina had called last night, right after Trevor left, and asked if Lexi would switch shifts with her. Apparently, she'd taken a second job to help with her bills, and they needed her that morning. Knowing it would free up her evening, Lexi had jumped at the chance to work the early shift.

This morning, after being dropped off at the garage and getting her car, she'd texted Trevor to see if he was free for dinner, more than excited when he accepted. She hadn't mentioned his buying her four new tires. She was waiting to have that conversation in person.

Lex had tried to get the guy to take all but the one off and put her old ones back on, but he'd told her he couldn't. Apparently, once they were securely placed on the car, they were no longer considered 'new' tires, and they'd have to sell them as used. In turn, the garage would lose money on them.

She wasn't sure if that was true, or if Trevor had just made sure the guy didn't take no for an answer. Either way, she intended to have a discussion about boundaries with him tonight.

Lexi liked Trevor. More than she'd liked a man in probably forever. But, she needed him to know that, even though the gesture was amazingly sweet, it was too much. She didn't want him thinking she was a charity case, but an independent woman capable of taking care of herself.

Her heels clicked against the smooth pavement, focused on not rolling her ankle as she made her way to her car. Normally, she would have waited to get ready until closer to the time Trevor was supposed to arrive, but after the way she'd looked during their date last night, Lexi was determined to look more presentable, this time.

Using the few hours she had after work to pamper herself—something she very rarely did—she'd splurged and gotten her brows waxed. After that, she went home and indulged in a relaxing, well-deserved bath.

Surrounded by bubbles, Lexi took her time re-reading a few chapters of a book by her favorite romance author before getting into the shower to shave and wash her hair.

She then gave herself an at-home mani-pedi, got dressed, and did her hair and makeup. When she was finished, Lexi felt pretty and refreshed, which had been her goal. However, time had gone by faster than she'd thought, and now she was rushing to make it home to get dinner prepped and in the oven on time.

Finally to her car, Lexi leaned her hip against the back bumper and shifted both sacks into in her left arm. Then, lifting that same knee, she propped the bottoms of the sacks onto her leg so she could use her right hand to dig into her pocket for her keys. Not an easy task, considering she was in a dress and heels.

Pulling her keys free, Lexi had just found the right button and was about to pop her trunk open when a man's loud voice came from right behind her.

"Fancy meeting you here."

"Oh!" Startled, Lexi jumped and turned quickly, dropping one of the bags in the process.

The sound of glass shattering hit her ears, and Lexi cringed, knowing the bottle of wine she'd just bought to go with dinner had broken. When she looked up and saw who the man was, she became even more frustrated.

"*Rob?* W-what are you doing? You scared the crap out of me!"

Bending down, Lexi sat the bag she'd been holding onto

the ground and quickly scooted the other one away from the growing puddle of spilled wine. Swiftly, she began to transfer the groceries out of the ruined sack and piling them into the other one as best she could.

Ignoring her question, Rob asked, "What's the wine for? Hot date?"

Thinking he'd back off if he knew she was seeing someone, Lexi answered, "As a matter of fact, yes. Well, it *was*."

"With who? Oh, wait!" He snapped his fingers. "I bet it's that tall asshole from the diner. What was his name…Trevor?"

Lexi hated the way Rob said Trevor's name. She stood to face him. "That's none of your business."

Just then, a mom with a shopping cart and two young kids in tow walked by. Rob waited until they'd passed before inching his way closer. "See, that's where you're wrong, Lexi-Loo."

He smelled of whiskey and was starting to slur his words. Alarm bells went off inside her head, and Lexi glanced over to where the mom had walked. Maybe, if she could make eye contact with her, the other woman would call for help. Unfortunately for her, the mom was leaning into her minivan's open side door, buckling the youngest child into his car seat.

She quickly scanned the rest of the parking lot for someone else. Regrettably, it was a small, neighborhood market. A handful of other cars were in the lot, but Lexi didn't see any people around.

Her breathing picked up, and her heart felt like it would pound straight out of her chest, but she stood her ground. "No, I'm not wrong." She tried to go around him, but he slid over, blocking her path.

"Like hell, you're not. I've been asking you out for a month and a half. Then, this guy walks in and you're practically spreading your legs for him right there in the middle of the fucking diner. Now, you're dressed like a whore, wearing all that makeup and those fuck-me heels. The guy must be a damn good tipper."

Having lost her patience with the imbecile, Lexi slapped her palms against Rob's chest and pushed him hard enough he stumbled back a few steps. Then, she let loose with everything she'd wanted to say since he'd started coming into the diner, but couldn't.

"I am *not* dressed like a whore, and for the past month and a half, I've been telling you no! I know you think you're God's gift to women, but the reality is, no woman with a lick of common sense would even *think* about dating someone like you. So, take a freaking hint, Rob. I don't want to go out with you. Not now, not ever. Got it?"

Stepping past him, Lexi made a beeline for her door. Remembering she still hadn't unlocked the car yet, she hastily pressed the button and reached for the handle. She'd just started to open her door when a large hand flew past her head and slammed it shut.

"Where do you think you're going?"

Lexi's entire body jolted as if she'd been shocked. Brushing against her from behind, Rob moved in even closer, essentially trapping her between him and her car.

Desperate for help—and praying someone would hear and intervene, she shouted, "Leave me alone!"

Then, bucking backward, she tried to make enough space she could open her door and get into her car. Only, this time, Rob stood his ground.

Growling next to her ear, he said, "You don't turn your back on me, bitch."

Ready to dial 911, Lexi slid a shaking hand into her purse to get her phone, but Rob grabbed hold of her right forearm and twisted it behind her back before she could get it.

He spun her around and pushed his torso against hers. Lexi cried out when he slammed her back into the car.

Oh, God. Where is everyone? With her right arm now trapped behind her, she started punching and shoving at him with her left. "Let me go," she gritted out, still trying to wrench her arm free. "I'm serious, Rob. You're hurting me."

"Yeah?" He pressed against her even more, causing her car door to painfully dig into her lower back. With his nose nearly touching hers, he yelled, "Well, maybe I wouldn't have to if you weren't such a fucking cock tease!"

Lexi managed to turn her head to the side, just before whiskey-infused spittle hit her cheek. She barely kept from gagging at the smell of his breath.

Strong fingers wrapped around the upper portion of her left arm as Rob attempted to control its flailing. His grip tightened, ripping the sleeve of her dress.

"Quit playing games, Lexi-Loo," Rob softened his tone and ran the tip of his nose along the side of her face. "You know you want this."

No, she didn't. She wanted to be as far away from this man as she possibly could. She wanted…Trevor.

Lexi thought about the date they were supposed to have. One that was now ruined, thanks to this asshole. Anger began overriding her fear. Doing her best to clear her mind, she thought of her options. Only one came to mind.

Not waiting a second longer, Lexi brought her right knee upward with as much force and speed as she could muster.

Thanks to the way he was standing, she had a clear shot straight to his crotch. She hit her target with perfection.

Bellowing out a loud groan, Rob dropped like a stone onto the hard pavement. "You stupid bitch!" he moaned as he curled up into the fetal position.

Wasting no time, Lexi swung her door open, leapt into her car, and slammed the door shut. She took a precious second to secure the locks. After two attempts, her trembling fingers managed to insert the key into the ignition and start the car.

She could hear Rob's muffled curses coming from outside, and in her peripheral, she saw him trying to stand back up. He was still yelling and calling her names as she spun her tires and drove to the nearest police station.

Chapter 5

"Are you sure?" Trevor asked the guy from the garage for the second time.

"Dude. I've been doing this shit for ten years. I'm tellin' ya, there's nothing wrong with the tire or the valve stem. Somebody had to have let the air out of it on purpose. Probably some dumbass kids playing a prank."

"Yeah, maybe," Trevor mumbled, though his gut told him otherwise.

"So, you want it back, or not?"

"Yeah, I'll take it back. If there's nothing wrong with it, she can use it as a spare." He looked at his watch. "I don't have time to get it tonight. Can I swing by in the morning and pick it up?"

"Sounds good. I'll mark it sold so no one messes with it."

"Thanks, man."

"Sorry I didn't know about it sooner. When I talked to you last night, you seemed more concerned with making sure your girl got all new tires, and we got our asses handed to us today. To be honest, I almost forgot to even check it."

"No worries."

"Well, like I said. It was probably just some stupid prank, but the way the world is these days, you never can be too careful. Your girl seemed nice enough. I'd hate to think of someone messing with her like that."

If they are, I'll find them. "I appreciate you letting me know."

"Any time, man."

Ending the call, Trevor sat his phone down onto his desk. With his elbows resting on its edge, he brought his fists together and thought about what he'd just learned.

"Whoa, who pissed in your Cheerios?"

His eyes snapped up to find Derek standing in his office doorway. Tipping his chin toward the folder D was holding, Trevor asked, "What's up?"

"Nuh uh. You first. What's got you lookin' like you're ready for a fight?"

Trevor shook his head. "Remember I told you about Lex's flat tire?"

"Yeah."

"The garage just called. She didn't run over a nail, like I'd thought. Someone intentionally let the air out of it."

Derek's brows turned inward. "Who would mess with a sweetheart like Lex?" Then, a look of awareness crossed his face. "I bet it was that fucknut, Rob."

Trevor leaned back in his expensive leather chair and ran a hand over his jaw. Sighing, he agreed. "That was my first thought, too." He thought for a moment and then, "I don't suppose you could find out more about this guy, could you?"

Narrowing his eyes, D said, "I cannot believe you just asked me that."

Trevor grinned. "Find out what you can and get back to me ASAP."

Derek's brows rose. "Is that an official order? Because, I'm not sure Jake would approve the use of company time and resources for a personal favor."

Trevor rolled his eyes. "Just shut the hell up and do it." Then, belatedly, he added, "please."

Derek snorted. "I'm just fuckin' with ya. Of course, I'll do it. Even if he wasn't the one who jacked with Lex's tires, that guy had bad news written all over him." Then, as if he just remembered the folder in his hands, D said, "Oh, yeah." He walked over to Trevor's desk and held it out for him. "Almost forgot to give this to you."

"What is it?"

"Me and the guys and Mac went through that list of applicants you gave us the other day. Those are our picks for Bravo Team."

"Bravo Team?"

"Makes sense. We're Alpha Team. We all thought Bravo was a natural choice for the next R.I.S.C. team name."

Trevor couldn't argue with the guy's logic. Taking the folder, he quickly skimmed through its contents. "I'll check these over more thoroughly tomorrow, but from what I can tell, it looks like you chose the same ones I did. I'll scan and email them to Jake to look over." When Derek looked at him expectantly, he sighed. "And I will pass along the suggestion to name the new team Bravo."

"That's why we're such a good team." With his index finger, he tapped his temple and made a clicking sound with his tongue. "Great minds, baby."

Trevor smiled and shook his head. "I'll see you tomorrow. Let me know if you find anything out about Rob."

"I'll do it now, before I leave." Derek threw his thumb over his shoulder toward the door. "Then, Coop and I are gonna head down to The Ranch for a couple drinks. Wanna come?"

The Ranch was a bar not far from where their office was

located. It was smaller, since it was a higher-end place, it didn't carry the rambunctious, college crowd like a lot of the other bars did.

"Can't. I'm having dinner with Lexi."

Derek smiled wide. "Two nights in a row. Way to go, you stud muffin', you." Cracking himself up, he laughed and started for the door. From over his shoulder, he said, "Enjoy your date. Tell Lex 'Hey'." Just when Trevor thought he was gone, Derek peeked his head back around the corner to add, "And I expect details."

Trevor unceremoniously flipped him the bird before glancing down at his watch again. He had just enough time to pick up a bottle of wine before heading to Lexi's house.

His heart rate sped up at the thought of seeing her again, and Trevor smiled to himself. He'd almost forgotten what that type of anticipation felt like.

After Lisa, Trevor pretty much closed himself off to that part of his life. He made the conscious decision to minimize the risk of experiencing any sort of personal loss like that, again. He didn't want to be responsible for the life of someone he cared about romantically.

This explained why Derek was unaware of any dates or casual encounters Trevor had since the start of R.I.S.C. That and Trevor was always very careful to keep his private life completely separate from his work.

Hell, one of the biggest reasons their boss had kept things platonic with his new wife for as long as he had was to protect her. Like the rest of the team, Jake McQueen knew how easily it would be for an enemy to use a loved one in order to extract their revenge.

However, Jake learned the hard way that sometimes, even the best protection still isn't enough. They came damn close to losing Olivia a few months ago, but thankfully, the team got to her before it was too late.

They all learned a lesson that day. If evil wants someone bad enough, it'll find them. No matter how hard you try to keep them safe.

After seeing Jake and Olivia survive the horrific hurdles life had thrown their way to finally achieving their happy ending, Trevor had started to think. Maybe, just maybe, he could find someone to be happy with, too.

Lexi's beautiful, smiling face flashed before him, making his dick twitch. He hadn't lied about it being his best first date ever. Though he hated the trouble she'd been put through with the flat tire, he loved the way she'd been herself.

She was so down to Earth. Even opened up to him about her mom and the struggles she'd faced financially. Everything about Lexi was just so…real. Genuine. It was one of the things that first drew him to her.

She hadn't been embarrassed to share her dreams with him. Had called them a fantasy, but if he had anything to say about it, they'd become so much more. *I'll make her dreams come true.*

Most women had a tendency to be fake with him, and he hated it. Trevor wasn't blind. He knew he was a good-looking guy. He saw the way women's eyes lit up when he walked past. But when he took one on a date, they seemed to think they needed to look and act a certain way.

They'd laugh a little too loudly at his jokes. Make sure their hair and makeup was just so, as if they had to be perfect in order for him to like them. That couldn't be farther from the truth.

As a result, he'd pretty much given up the whole dating scene and just took care of things himself. It wasn't hard, no pun intended. All he had to do was picture a certain blonde with a set of gorgeous, blue eyes and the most adorable dimples he'd ever seen, and…

Trevor's cock began to swell behind his zipper. Jesus, he needed to focus on something else before he completely embarrassed himself. Derek would never let him live it down if he walked out of the office sporting a massive hard-on.

To help, he grabbed his jacket from the back of the chair and draped it casually over his left forearm. Holding it in front of his waist, Trevor checked to make sure he had his keys and walked around the edge of his desk.

He was halfway to the door when Derek burst through the doorway again, holding a single paper. This time, he wasn't smiling.

"What is it?"

"I was diggin' for dirt on our guy. Cross referencin' any credit cards with the name of Rob or Robert attached to them that had been used at Joe's in the past six months."

"Okay…" Trevor's voice trailed off.

"There were only two. One belongs to a seventy-seven year old man who goes there every morning for breakfast and coffee."

An uneasy feeling began to churn in Trevor's gut. "And the other?"

"The second belongs to a guy named Robert Lockwood." Derek handed him the sheet. "It's him. It's our guy. Has a record for battery, assault, resisting. It's all there."

"Damn," Trevor muttered as he scanned over the man's rap sheet. He hated the thought of this guy being anywhere near Lexi. "Guess we were right about him, huh?"

"That's not all, Trev."

Hearing the worried tone in his friend's voice, Trevor

glanced back up. The level of concern in the other man's eyes left him holding his breath.

"While I was lookin' into Lockwood, a new arrest warrant notification popped up on my screen." Derek swallowed before continuing. "The charge is assault. It was time stamped fifteen minutes ago, and…"

Trevor's heart dropped, terrified of what he was about to hear. "Tell me."

Sympathy filled Derek's eyes. "Trevor, Lockwood just attacked Lexi."

****

"Are you sure I can't get you somethin' else? A coffee or soda?" Detective West asked for the second time.

The man spoke with a slight southern accent. Tall with light brown hair and green eyes, he wore navy pants, a white dress shirt, and a powder blue tie. A shiny, gold badge was clipped to his belt near his right hip, and his gun was securely fastened in the holster at his left.

He's a lefty. The thought was random, but if she kept her mind focused on random facts like that, she wouldn't have to think about how scared she'd been in that parking lot. So, Lexi tried to focus on everything but the fear still making its way through her veins.

Like, despite the fact that Detective West's long sleeves covered his arms, she could easily tell he was in excellent shape. With no wedding ring and as handsome as he was, he'd no doubt had many women drop their panties for him. Maybe more than one at a time.

Not that she was interested in becoming one of them. There was only one man who held her interest in that way.

Of course, after tonight, Trevor was probably a lost cause.

With her elbows resting on the table, Lexi held the water bottle in front of her with both hands, mindlessly rubbing her thumb up and down its smooth ridges. She gave the detective a small smile.

"I'm good. Thank you."

He tilted his head slightly." It won't be much longer, Miss Hamilton. Your statement is being typed up right now. Once that's done, you'll just need to look it over to make sure everything is accurate, sign it, and you'll be free to leave."

"Thank you," she repeated quietly.

"We're going to find Lockwood. Officers are out looking for him as we speak. I promise I'll call you the second he's brought in."

"Thanks. I appreciate that."

Sincerity filled the man's eyes when he kindly asked, "Would you like for me to call someone to come get you?"

Yes, please. His name is Trevor Matthews. "No, thank you. I drove myself here."

This time, when Detective West smiled back at her, she was hit with a strange feeling of familiarity.

"Look, I'm not tryin' to be pushy here, but...what happened to you...somethin' like that can really shake a person up." He shrugged a shoulder. "Might be best if someone else drove you home."

Lexi licked her dry lips. "I'm fine, detective. I don't need anyone else."

At least that's what she told herself when she'd texted Trevor to cancel their date. No guy like that would stick around after she'd flaked on not one, but two dates. Back to back.

Thankfully, a few minutes after he'd taken her statement,

Detective West had stepped out into the hallway to take a phone call. Lexi had used that opportunity to send Trevor a text canceling their date, thankful she was able to do so without an audience. With every letter she'd typed, her tears had been closer and closer to falling.

Not wanting to send the details of what had happened over text, Lexi had simply told Trevor something had unexpectedly come up, and she could no longer do dinner. She'd ended it with an apology for the short notice and a promise to call when she could.

She hadn't received a response, which told her everything she needed to know. Most likely, Trevor had decided she wasn't worth the trouble. Not that she could blame him.

No man liked a girl surrounded by drama. First, she gets a flat because she can't afford proper maintenance for her car, and now this. Though, the whole tire thing may not technically count as drama, tonight most definitely qualified.

The detective's phone vibrated. He glanced down at its screen, then quickly back to her. "I, uh…I need to go check on something. I'll be right back."

With him gone, Lexi went back to focusing on her water bottle. A couple minutes later, she heard muffled voices coming from the hallway just before the door to the room she was in flew open. Lexi's head whipped up, and she nearly gasped when she saw who'd just stepped in.

"*Trevor?* W-what are you doing here?"

"Apparently, tryin' to get my ass in trouble." Detective West shook his head as he pushed his way into the room. Derek was hot on his heels.

"Derek? What's going on?" She looked at all three men, then back to Trevor. "Why are you two here?"

"I think the better question is, why the hell didn't you call me?"

Shocked at his harsh tone, Lexi took a second to really look at Trevor. He was dressed in a black suit with a white shirt and black tie. A definite change from the jeans he usually wore when he came into the diner. But it wasn't his attire that grabbed her attention, so much as the murderous expression filling his handsome face.

Gone was the easy-going man from last night. Instead, he'd been replaced by a sexy, suit-wearing beast. One who appeared ready to fight to the death. Oh, yeah. The guy was definitely pissed.

"I-I'm sorry," her voice shook. Despite her efforts to stop them, unshed tears welled in her eyes. "I was planning on calling you after I got home. Things just"—she looked at the detective, and then back to Trevor—"things got a little crazy tonight, that's all." Her voice broke, and she blinked quickly, sending two silver streaks running down her cheeks. She quickly swiped them away.

With a muttered curse, Trevor was at her side in an instant. Squatting next to her chair, he shook his head. "I'm sorry, angel. I didn't mean to snap at you. I was just so damn worried when I heard about what happened."

He brought a hand to her face, but froze when she moved away from it on reflex. He started to lower it, the pain in his eyes gutting her.

Quickly grabbing hold of his thick wrist, Lexi brought his hand back up to her cheek. She leaned into his touch and whispered, "Sorry. I guess I'm still a little jumpy."

"Don't do that," he ordered softly.

"Do what?"

"Apologize for being scared. Not after what that bastard did to you."

It was probably wrong of her, but Lexi's heart swelled, knowing he cared. "I'm fine, Trevor. I promise."

Being careful not to startle her again, he slowly removed his hand and stretched her arm out between them. A muscle in his jaw bulged when he spotted the new bruises Rob's fingers had left on her forearm when he'd twisted it behind her back.

With almost clinical eyes, he assessed the rest of what he could see. A low growl came from deep in his throat when he noticed her torn sleeve. With the gentlest of touches, Trevor's thumb brushed by a small scratch Rob had left on her shoulder.

Bringing his eyes back to hers, he asked, "Where else are you hurt?"

"Nowhere." When he didn't look convinced, she cupped his strong jaw. The bit of scruff there tickled her sensitive skin, but she couldn't bring herself to pull away. "I'm fine, Trevor. I promise."

He covered the back of her hand with his. Trevor then closed his eyes and turned, pressing his soft lips against her palm. Lexi's heart tripped over itself at the sweet gesture.

A few seconds later, those dark chocolate eyes found hers once more. "Okay, angel. If you say you're okay, then I believe you."

Relieved, she was about to ask again why he was there when Detective West purposely—and very loudly—cleared his throat.

Lexi's head turned to where he and Derek were both still standing. For a moment, she'd completely forgotten they were even there.

"If you're done with your...professional medical examination, Matthews, I'd like to get Miss Hamilton's signature so she can go home."

Something about the way the man said Trevor's last name gave her pause. "Wait," Lexi looked to Trevor, then back to the detective. "You know each other?"

"What?" Derek slapped the detective on the back. "You don't see the resemblance?"

It took all of three seconds for Lexi to finally realize who Detective West reminded her of. Another second passed and she remembered Derek's last name.

"West," she mumbled more to herself than anyone else. She looked at both men again. "You're brothers."

"Give the lady a prize." With his hand on his brother's shoulder, Derek grinned from ear to ear. "Lex, I'd like you to meet Eric. My baby brother."

"I'm only younger by two minutes, dumbass," Detective West—Eric—shrugged Derek's hand from his shoulder.

Lexi made a tiny snorting sound and smiled. "You're *twins*? And your parents named you Derek and Eric. Really?" She giggled as she turned and glanced at Trevor.

"There she is," he whispered softly, some of the concern finally dissipating from his eyes.

Lexi no longer felt like laughing. She felt like...

"Take me home."

Detective West spoke up, "I offered to call Miss. Hamilton a ride earlier, but she refused."

"Lexi."

The man looked at her questioningly.

"You can call me Lexi."

"Whoa, she must like you, bro." Derek nudged his brother. "Only her *friends* get to call her that."

Eric rolled his eyes, but Derek gave her a wink and a smile, helping to calm her nerves even more. Being around these guys, she could almost forget about what had happened with Rob. Almost.

Her chest started to get tight as memories worked their way through. Of course, Trevor noticed.

"Come on, angel." He stood, one corner of his mouth tilting up. "Let's get you out of here."

Leaving her statement on the table, she stood and scooted the chair back some, its metal legs screeching against the tile floor. Trevor offered his hand, which she took without hesitation.

They were almost to the police station's entrance when he said, "Why don't you give Derek your keys. He can follow us in your car."

"I'm okay to drive myself, Trevor."

"I know," he agreed, but kept walking.

Assuming he wanted her to ride with him so they could talk about what happened, Lexi released Trevor's hand and dug her keys from her purse. Handing them to Derek she asked, "Don't you need my address? You know, in case we get separated in traffic or something?"

Trevor spoke up before Derek could answer. "We're not going to your house, angel."

This surprised her. "Then, where are we going?"

Rather than answer right away, Trevor took her hand again and led her outside. They'd just started to go down the concrete steps when he casually threw out, "My place."

Lexi immediately stopped walking. "Your place?" Pulling on his hand, Trevor made it two more steps before he turned around.

With her hand still in his, she shook her head. "I can't stay at your place, Trevor."

"Why not?"

With him being a few steps below her, they were nearly at eye level. "Why not? We've been on *one* date. I can't spend the night with someone after just one—"

"That's not what this is about, angel." Trevor cut her refusal short.

Lexi bit her lip. Despite the words she'd just given him, a sprig of disappointment grew inside her. "Then, what's it about?"

Looking her square in the eye, he sounded anything but casual when he told her, "You. Being safe."

Lexi's muscles tensed. His words should have brought comfort, but instead they were a reminder that Rob was still out there, somewhere.

"Do you"—she licked her lips and swallowed nervously—"do you really think he'd show up at my house?"

Reaching for her other hand, Trevor gave them both a little squeeze. "The cops are going to find him, Lex. But, until they do, I won't get a wink of sleep knowing he's still out there and you're in that house all alone. My apartment is in a secure building, and I have a state-of-the-art security system. But, if it'll make you feel more comfortable, we can stay at your place."

A few seconds of silence passed as Lexi mulled it all over. When she still didn't say anything, Trevor said, "Either way, I'll be sleeping on the couch." He cupped her face, "Please, angel. For my peace of mind…stay with me tonight."

Chapter 6

Trevor stepped into his living room. The thick, luscious carpet swallowed his footfalls as he walked. He paused when he saw the woman standing in front of the large, floor-to-ceiling window. With her arms wrapped around her center, Lexi stared at the bustling city below.

Her gaze lifted, their eyes meeting in his reflection. "You have a great view." She turned to face him. A set of beautiful, wary eyes glanced at the blanket and pillow cradled in his arms.

Walking over to his couch, Trevor set them down onto the cushion. "I put clean sheets on the bed and laid a clean towel and an extra toothbrush on the sink in the master bathroom." Eyeing her torn sleeve, he did his best to control the anger still brewing inside. "I also set a t-shirt and some sweats on the bed. Thought you might feel better if you had a shower and some different clothes."

Reaching for the tattered material, Lexi gave him a small smile. One that didn't show her dimples. *I want to see them. I want a real smile.*

"Thank you. You really didn't have to go to all this trouble."

Trevor slowly closed the distance between them. "Yes, I

did." He traced the scratch on her upper arm, as he'd done at the station. "I hate what he did to you, angel. And I know neither one of us would have gotten any sleep tonight if I'd taken you home and left."

Trevor needed the worry in her eyes to go away. Taking care to move slowly, he tucked some hair behind her ear. "You're safe, Alexis. You'll always be safe with me."

Placing her hand on his chest, Lexi looked up into his eyes and whispered, "I know." She almost looked embarrassed when she confessed, "We barely know each other, but…I always feel safe when you're around."

Trevor covered her small hand with his, knowing she couldn't miss the forceful beating of his heart beneath her palm. "Good," he whispered back.

Their eyes remained locked. God, he wanted to kiss her. So, he took a step back, hating the void he felt from losing her touch. Lexi's own disappointment flared behind her eyes, but then it was gone.

She wanted me to kiss her.

Stuffing his hands into his pockets, Trevor cleared his throat and asked, "Would you like something to drink? I have beer, or I could make some coffee or…"

"Actually…" She wrapped her arms around herself again. "I think I'd like to take that shower first."

Trevor nodded. "Take your time."

Fifteen minutes later, Trevor had ordered some dinner and called Jake to check in. After finally convincing him there was no need to end his honeymoon early, Trevor ended the call.

Leaning against his kitchen counter, he listened to the muffled sound of running water. Did his best to ignore the images that refused to stay hidden.

Lexi…wet. Naked. Running her delicate hands over all

those sexy, petite curves.

Trevor's dick began to swell as he imagined *his* hands touching her. Spreading the lathered soap across her soft, flawless skin. Taking her small, but perfect breasts into his hands, before moving lower between her thighs. His fingers sliding into her—"

The doorbell rang, snapping him back to reality. Only then, did he realize the running water had stopped. *Jesus.*

Adjusting himself, Trevor made his way to the door. He was more than thankful Lexi hadn't walked in while he'd been lost in his naked-with-her fantasy.

Checking the peephole to verify his visitor, Trevor entered his security code before unlocking and opening the door. After signing the receipt and thanking the delivery boy, he reengaged the locks and alarm system and carried the two pizzas to the kitchen.

He'd just slid the boxes onto the countertop when he heard her soft voice from behind.

"That smells delicious."

Trevor turned, nearly losing his breath. *I seem to do that a lot around her.* He didn't hide his smile. "Hey."

She'd cuffed the bottom of the sweats several times. He assumed she'd done the same to the elastic waistband. The shirt was one of his old service T's, gray with faded black letters spelling ARMY across the front. Falling to just above her knees, she nearly swam in the thing.

Seeing her in his clothes did something to him he couldn't explain. With her damp hair hanging loose around her shoulders and not a trace of makeup on, she was still the most beautiful woman he'd ever seen.

"Trevor? Is everything okay?"

Shit. Like an idiot, he'd just been standing there, staring.

"Yeah. I, uh…I ordered pizza."

She smiled, her dimples making their first appearance of the night.

"I can see that."

"Right." Trevor shook his head at himself and tried to recover. "I wasn't sure what kind you'd liked, so I got one with just pepperoni, and one with everything. I figured if you don't like pepperoni, we can just pick it off."

Smiling a little wider, she slid onto one of the barstools. "Supreme is my favorite, actually."

Trevor grabbed two plates and some napkins and sat down next to her. Flipping the supreme box open, he gave her a slice before taking one for himself.

"Thanks again, Trevor. You didn't need to do all this for me, but I really appreciate it." She took a bite.

"There wasn't much to it, Lex. I called, made the order, and the guy showed up with the food."

Laughing, she quickly covered her mouth until she'd finished chewing and swallowing her food. She playfully slapped his bicep. "Smart ass. I wasn't just talking about the pizza."

Hearing her laugh made his chest swell and his half-hard dick twitch. "I know." He watched her take another bite. "Trust me. This was as much for me as it was for you."

Her brows turned inward, and her eyes narrowed. She swallowed, and then, "Speaking of doing things for me—"

Trevor stopped her with a raised palm. "I know what you're going to say, and you'd be right. I crossed a line with the tires."

His confession seemed to surprise her. "Oh. Um, yeah. You did." She sighed. "It's not that I don't appreciate the gesture. I do, but…four tires is a lot, Trevor." Lexi pointed her tiny finger at him. "And I am going to pay you back every penny."

Trevor smiled. "I apologize for overstepping, but honestly, it really didn't cost that much. You don't need to pay me—"

"Yes," she interrupted him. "I do. Look, I know I shared a lot last night, but I can and *will* pay for those tires. I may not be rich by any stretch of the imagination, but I'm not some charity case, either."

"Never thought you were, angel."

She stared back at him for a moment, as if she were trying to figure him out. Sounding a bit flustered, she said, "Okay, well…good. Because I'm not."

A corner of Trevor's mouth tilted up. "I got that."

Lexi blushed, and his cock began to swell even more. *Damn.* He didn't know what it was, but seeing her cheeks become rosy and flush like that got him instantly hard. Every. Single. Time.

"Look, Lex." Trevor swiveled his bar stool to face her better. "I don't mean this to come off as bragging or pretentious, so please don't take it that way." He licked his lips and dove in. "I have some money saved up. Quite a bit, actually. I've never been married and don't have any kids, so my expenses over the years have been minimal. I put back as much as I could while in the service, and I make a damn good living working for R.I.S.C. So, four tires for your car didn't do any damage to my finances."

Lexi's eyes left his to focus on her half-eaten slice of pizza. Shifting uncomfortably in her seat, she mumbled, "I'd still feel a lot better if I paid you back."

"If you feel the need to, that's fine. I just wanted you to know there's no rush." Trevor smiled when she glanced back up at him. "The way I see it, it makes up for all the times you've gotten gypped on your tips."

She let out a soft laugh but didn't say anything. Though he hated to, Trevor knew he needed to tell her the rest.

"The garage called me tonight. Someone purposely let the air out of your tire."

Her brows shot up. "What?"

"It could have been a prank. Some kids messing around the diner."

She studied him a minute. "Do you think that's all it was? Just someone out looking for kicks?"

"No," he answered honestly. "Which is another reason I wanted you here, where I knew you'd be safe. Just in case."

Picking at her pizza, she asked, "Why do you care so much, Trevor? We barely know each other." Lexi glanced over at him as she waited for his answer.

"The truth?"

"Always," she grinned.

Trevor shook his head. "I don't know."

He couldn't read her expression, so he tried to better explain himself. "I've always been protective, Lexi. It's who I am." He shrugged. "It's…what I do."

"Have you ever been hurt on the job?"

"I have," he laid it all out for her. "Between my time in the Army and then with R.I.S.C., I've been shot twice. Stabbed once. Had some broken ribs and a couple minor concussions. And more bruises and scrapes than I could ever keep track of. Nothing a couple stitches and a few days' rest didn't cure."

Trevor held his breath as he waited for her response.

Lexi's eyes widened. "Wow." She blinked a couple times and let a out slow breath. "And here, I thought having to deal with guys like Rob once in a while was bad."

Hearing the other man's name, Trevor reflexively squeezed her knee a bit more. She looked down to where he was touching her, making him realize he needed to ease the hell up.

"Sorry." He loosened his hold. "I just can't stand the thought of you being treated that way."

Her expression softened, and Lexi laid her hand over his. "I know. I still don't quite understand it, but I get it. And I'm okay. Really."

"Tell me what happened, Lex."

After a few seconds, she did. "I was at the grocery store buying stuff for our dinner. I'd just made it to my car and was trying to get my keys out when Rob walked up behind me. He startled me and I dropped one of the bags. The bottle of wine I'd bought broke, and I was trying to save what I could…" she paused, lost in the memory.

"What happened next?" Trevor asked calmly.

"He started giving me a hard time. Asking about the wine and if it was for a hot date…that sort of thing. I thought"—she licked her lips and swallowed—"I thought maybe if I told him I was seeing someone, he'd finally take the hint, you know?"

"But, he didn't."

Lexi shook her head. "It just made him more belligerent. He basically tried to make me feel guilty for going out with you and not him." She quickly added, "I didn't tell him it was you, I swear. He just assumed."

He realized she was worried he'd be upset. "It's okay, Lex. He probably saw us talking at the diner." His thumb caressed her knee through his sweats. Nodding to her arm, he asked, "How'd you get the bruises?"

Trevor watched as Lexi swallowed hard before answering.

"Rob made a crude comment about the two of us. It made me really mad, so I yelled at him. When I tried to leave, he got in my way, so I pushed him. Just to get past. He got really angry then and grabbed my arm. He twisted it behind my back, then he pushed me up against my car, and…"

Her breathing picked up and the fear in her eyes was back. *To hell with this.*

"It's okay, angel. You can stop."

One corner of her mouth raised, her smirk surprising him. "If I stop now, you'll miss the best part."

"Yeah?"

Lexi nodded. "I kicked him in the balls as hard as I could. He dropped to the ground like a sack of potatoes, and I got into my car and drove to the police station."

Trevor barked out a laugh. "You're right. That's most definitely the best part of that story." After a few seconds of silence, his smile faded as he asked, "Why didn't you call me?"

Sitting a little straighter Lexi sighed. "I hate drama, Trevor. Always have. The whole junior high, mean girls scene? Yeah, I stayed as far away from that as I possibly could."

He started to say something, but she cut him off at the pass. "I'd already screwed up our first date with the flat tire and then forgetting to call and cancel the tow truck. I didn't want to have to explain that I was breaking our *second* date because some idiot couldn't take no for an answer."

Lexi took a deep breath before exhaling slowly. "Honestly, I was afraid if I made that phone call to you, then you'd decide I wasn't worth the trouble. I mean, what if Rob does come after me again? You can't sit there and tell me *this* is how you want to spend your nights with someone you just started seeing. I'm still shocked you even came to the police station in the first place, let alone invited me to stay here tonight."

Part of Trevor wanted to tell her she was right. He probably should run…far and fast. Just not for the reasons she was thinking.

The last time Trevor let himself begin to care about a woman, he ended up getting her killed. Since then, he made sure there were no strings or romantic attachment of any kind. Not because he didn't love the idea of having a woman in his life to come home to. To share his life with.

Trevor couldn't bear the thought of another woman he cared about getting hurt because he couldn't protect them. The overseas and weeks-long jobs R.I.S.C. took on only made that possibility worse. So, for the past few years, he'd steered clear of any serious relationship.

Then one day he just happened to walk into Joe's Diner, and there she was. Though he hadn't known it at first, it was the very moment this tiny little waitress had begun wriggling her way past his defenses.

Trevor didn't know why or how. He only knew the choice was no longer his to make. He had to do everything in his power to keep this woman safe.

"Are you done?" he asked, his voice low and calm.

With downcast eyes, Lexi drew her bottom lip between her teeth and nodded. Needing to set some things straight, Trevor took both hands from her lap and held them in his.

"Look at me, angel," he whispered the order. Reluctant eyes found his again. "I want to make a couple things clear. First of all, what Rob did to you was his fault, not yours. And I promise you, he will never lay his hands on you again. Got it?"

Uncertainty still shone in her eyes, but she gave a little

nod. "Got it."

"Good. Second, and this is just as important… I like you, angel. I told you that last night, and I meant it."

Their eyes remained locked, and for what felt like the longest time, they both just sat there, staring. Trevor had just started to lean in, but Lexi's soft-spoken words stopped him short.

"You said you'd never been married but"—she licked her lips—"what about a girlfriend?"

Trevor moved his thumb across the back of her hand in a gentle caress. "If I had a girlfriend, Lex, last night's date wouldn't have happened. And I damn sure wouldn't have kissed you like I did."

Relief swirled in the set of brilliantly blue eyes staring back at him. He felt pissed, wondering what kind of assholes she'd dated in the past that would make her think he'd say the things he'd said and acted the way he had if he already had someone else in his life.

Desire filled her eyes as she continued to stare back at him. Trevor noticed the way her chest rose and fell more rapidly, and that damn flush crept from her neck and into her cheeks. In an instant, the crotch of his pants became painfully tight.

Trevor was teetering on the edge of giving in to the need he felt for this woman, but the last thing he wanted was for Lexi to think he was taking advantage of the situation. Knowing he'd probably regret it, Trevor cleared his throat and let go of her hands.

"It's getting late." He stood a bit too quickly and began picking up the dinner mess. "You've had a long day and should probably get some rest."

Lexi blinked, clearly taken off guard. "Oh. Um…okay." A

look of confusion and disappointment filled her eyes as she slowly slid off the bar stool.

Guilt settled in his gut, but Trevor knew he was making the right call. It had been a long damn time since he'd liked anyone as much as he did Lexi, and he'd be damned if he let his deprived hormones screw it up.

"Here, let me help." She started to reach for her plate, but he picked it up before she had the chance to.

"No, it's okay." Trevor put their plates into the sink and started the water. Facing the sink, he said, "You go on to bed. I've got this."

"Okay," she drew the word out a bit. "Well…goodnight."

He offered her a smile from over his shoulder. "Goodnight."

Lexi looked at him for half a second longer before turning and heading down the hallway. Trevor held his breath until he heard the soft click of his bedroom door closing.

Exhaling loudly, he looked down at his tented crotch and muttered a curse. This was quickly followed by a silent prayer of thanks that, once again, he'd been able to keep his massive hard-on hidden.

He washed their two plates and put the leftover pizza away. When he was finished, Trevor headed for the guest bathroom where he proceeded to take the coldest shower he could stand.

****

Lexi was still lying in Trevor's bed, awake and restless, when she'd heard the water from the other shower come on. A picture of his nude, muscular form flashed before her eyes. As hard as she tried, she couldn't make it go away.

She didn't mean to be inappropriate with her thoughts, but damn…the man was mouth-watering. Knowing he was only a room away—wet and naked—left her more wound up than when she first lay down.

When the bathroom door opened and then closed again, Lexi listened closely. She ignored the feeling of disappointment that hit when she heard him walk back down the hallway. Away from the room she was in.

Not that she actually expected him to come join her. *Hoped*, maybe, but hadn't expected it.

Trevor had claimed the drama with the tire and Rob weren't an issue. He'd looked and sounded sincere when he told her he liked her, and there was no mistaking the heat in his eyes when he'd been staring back at her.

Lexi had been certain he was about to kiss her. Instead, he'd acted as if someone had drenched him with a splash of cold water by standing abruptly and practically ordered her to go to bed.

For the next hour, she lay there, tossing and turning. Wondering what she'd done wrong. Until it hit her.

He was protecting me. That had to be it. After what happened with Rob, Trevor hadn't wanted to come off as a pushy, uncaring asshole. So, he'd sent her to bed, and he'd taken the couch.

Though, she'd rather he be snuggled up next to her, Lexi couldn't help but smile. She fell asleep thinking chivalry was alive and well after all.

The next morning, Lexi shuffled her feet across the carpet as she walked into the bathroom. She'd slept all night, but it had been a restless sleep. One filled with wonderful dreams of love and laughter, as well as some not-so-good dreams of Rob and his manhandling ways.

After taking care of her teeth and other necessities, Lexi decided a quick shower would help wash the grogginess away.

A few minutes later, she felt refreshed and ready for the day. She put Trevor's shirt back on but decided to forgo the sweats for now. The water had felt amazing, but her legs were still pink from its heat. After all, the t-shirt was just as long as her dress was.

And, it's not torn.

Shaking those thoughts away, Lexi ran her fingers through her damp hair one last time before turning off the light and heading to the kitchen. She smelled coffee as soon as she'd woken, so she knew Trevor was already up. When she saw him, Lexi froze in place.

He was standing at the stove, stirring what smelled like some sort of delicious bacon and egg concoction. He had on a black t-shirt and a pair of faded jeans that made his tight ass appear even more grab-worthy than the dress pants he'd had on last night.

Lexi watched the muscles move beneath the fabric of the shirt as he efficiently worked the food in the skillet. The man was stunningly gorgeous, was sweeter than any she'd ever met, and he cooked.

In a word, he was…"Perfect."

She hadn't meant to whisper it out loud, but Trevor must have heard something because he turned then and gave her the sexiest grin she'd ever seen.

"Morning, angel."

Then, he blinked and his eyes widened slightly before sliding down the length of her bare legs. When his gaze found hers again, there was no mistaking the heat there.

Trying to pretend an embarrassing blush wasn't currently crawling up her neck and into her cheeks, Lexi smiled back and walked into the room.

"Good morning. What smells so good?"

"Scrambled eggs with crumbled bacon, chopped onion, and American cheese." He looked adorable when he shrugged a little and added, "My grandma used to make eggs like this when I was little."

Feeling much more like herself than the night before, Lexi used her hands to hoist herself up on the island behind him. From there, she watched as he worked his culinary magic.

"Smells delicious."

"Well, I'm sure you could come up with something a lot better, but I figured I'd let you rest while I cooked."

See? Perfect.

"Did you sleep well?"

It took her a second to realize he'd asked her a question. "Uh, yeah. I did." She wasn't about to share her dreams with him…the good or the bad. "What about you?"

"Great."

"Great? You slept on the couch, Trevor. I'm sure it wasn't great."

His shoulders shook with a silent laughter. "Okay, so maybe it wasn't *great*. But it wasn't too bad. Trust me"—he grinned from over his shoulder—"I've slept on much worse."

Lexi opened her mouth to tell him they could share the bed tonight but stopped herself before she could make such an enormous blunder. Of course, they wouldn't be sharing a bed tonight. She'd be back at her place, where she belonged.

Ignoring the pang of disappointment that thought created, Lexi grabbed a piece of crisp bacon from the plate sitting next to her. Trevor turned the burner off and slid the pan to one that was cool before facing her, right as she took a bite.

"Hey"! He pretended to chastise her. "You can't have that

until breakfast is ready."

Lexi tilted her head to the side and eyed the cooling pan. "Looks done to me."

With a smirk, he came closer, stopping directly in front of her. Wrapping his fingers gently around her wrist, he brought the piece of bacon she was holding to his mouth and bit down.

"You could have gotten your own piece, you know." She glanced at the plate. "You made enough for an army."

"I know."

She loved this playful side of him. Last night, he'd acted as if he were walking on eggshells. This morning, he was acting more like the Trevor she'd come to know from his many visits to the diner.

His eyes remained glued to hers and soon, all traces of teasing were gone. In a low, sexy rumble, he surprised her by saying, "God, you're beautiful, angel."

His words left her nearly speechless, but she managed to ask, "Why do you call me 'angel'?"

A corner of his delectable mouth turned up. "That's what you reminded me of the first time I saw you."

Lexi considered this for a moment. "The first time you saw me was at the diner. You came in with Derek and another man."

"Coop," Trevor offered.

"It was afternoon. The dinner rush had just started, and I'd been working all day."

Now, both corners of his mouth rose. "Glad to see that day stuck in your mind, too."

She let out a very unattractive half-laugh, half-snort. "That's because after having already worked nearly nine hours, I smelled like fried food; my hair was falling out of its bun, and I had zero makeup left on my face..." She shook her head. "I was a complete mess. Then, you walked in looking like sex on a stick, and I wanted to crawl into a hole somewhere."

Trevor looked as though he wanted to laugh, but instead, he sounded sincere when he said, "That's not how I remember it."

"Oh, really? And how, exactly, do you remember it?

He stepped closer, his thighs touching her bare knees.

"I remember walking through that door, seeing you, and completely losing my ability to breathe. That's never happened to me before, but with you...it did. Messy bun and all." In a sweet gesture she was quickly growing to love, he tucked a curl behind her ear.

Okay, now she really *was* speechless. Not one funny quip or smart-ass comment came to mind. Her only thought was how much she wanted to kiss him again.

As if reading her mind, he traced her jawline and whispered, "I really want to kiss you right now."

Lexi's heart pounded deep within her chest. In a bold move, she opened her legs, inviting him to come closer. Licking her lips, she asked softly, "So, what's stopping you?"

Then, she waited.

Just as she'd hoped, Trevor stepped between her thighs. The rough denim covering his legs was oddly tantalizing as it brushed against her bare skin. In a surprising move, he put an arm around her waist and pulled her to the edge of the slick, granite countertop.

Gasping, Lexi dropped the rest of her bacon and grabbed hold of his wide shoulders to steady herself. Their bodies were aligned perfectly, allowing her to feel the large bulge between his legs as it pressed against her core.

"I wanted to do this last night, but I was afraid you'd think I was taking advantage of you. You have to know, I would never—"

Lexi cut off whatever he was going to say when she cupped his face and pulled his mouth down to hers. She traced his lips with the tip of her tongue, hoping he'd understand. Thankfully, he did.

After taking half a second to catch up, Trevor parted his lips and let her in. Their tongues met in a seductive duel, twirling and dancing around each other's in the most amazing dance.

As they continued feeding from one another, Trevor slowly moved his fingers down to her hips and pulled his mouth from hers.

Lexi started to protest, but stayed quiet when he began leaving tiny, wet kisses along her jawline. She tilted her head to give him more access, gasping when he reached the pulse point on her neck.

Using his teeth, Trevor gently nibbled the sensitive spot. She moaned loudly, not even bothering to hold back her reaction.

He slid his hands beneath the shirt's hem, his fingertips finding the soft, smooth skin of her tiny waist. Moving upward, he reached the bottom swell of her breasts.

Trevor's touch was electrifying, but she needed more. Lexi arched her back, pushing her breasts toward him. Large, strong hands cupped the firm mounds, but it still wasn't enough.

The shirt was so big and bulky…and it was getting in the way. Lexi decided it needed to go.

Without a word, she pulled back. Beautiful, brown eyes locked on hers as she raised her arms into the air.

Knowing exactly what she wanted, Trevor lifted the shirt up and over her head, setting it on the counter beside her. His eyes slid down to her chest.

Lexi's small but proportional breasts moved up and down with the steady rhythm of her heaving breaths. She knew they weren't huge, so if he was a boob man…

"They're not very big, but—"

Her words vanished when he gave her a swift kiss. His lips brushed against hers as he ended the kiss just long enough to say, "They're perfect, angel." He kissed her again, slowly this time. When he was finished, he whispered, "*You're* perfect."

They may have only had one sort-of date, but in that moment, she didn't care. Trevor wasn't just throwing out lines to get laid. The truth was there, in his eyes. She could hear them in his words.

Lexi couldn't explain it, but the connection she felt with this man was unlike any she'd ever known. If her mother's death taught her anything, it was that life was short. Sometimes you just had to close your eyes, take a leap, and pray you landed safely.

With that in mind, Lexi brushed her lips against his and whispered back, "Take me to bed."

Chapter 7

Trevor waited all of two seconds before he grabbed Lexi's hips and hoisted her off the island. She smiled wide as she wrapped her legs around his waist and her arms around his neck.

With careful but quick steps, he carried her to his bedroom. Gently, as if she were made of the most fragile glass, he laid her down onto the mattress.

His heart was pounding with anticipation and his dick was hard as a hammer. But as he glanced at the bruises Rob had left on her arm, Trevor couldn't help but question if he was making a mistake.

"I need you to be sure, Lex."

Despite the massive case of blue balls it would cause, Trevor would stop this whole thing, right now, if he even suspected she wasn't.

Lucky for him—and his balls—she whispered, "I'm sure."

With her blond curls splayed out beside her head, she truly looked like an angel. *My angel.*

Lexi glanced down at his jeans then back up at him.

"You're overdressed," she teased.

Trevor grinned. "And unless you want this to be over before it even starts, I'm gonna stay that way for a bit."

Humor gleamed in her eyes as Trevor rested a knee on the mattress and looked at the offering before him. There wasn't much of the coarse, blond hair…only a tiny bit at the top, giving him a perfect view of the bare slit below.

With her knees raised, he could see the shimmer from her arousal. His dick was already so full he thought he'd lose it just from catching that first glimpse.

I have to taste her. Unable to hold back any longer, Trevor put his head between her thighs to finally take what he'd been craving.

Wanting to savor her, he slowly ran the tip of his tongue along the length of her slit. Lexi gasped, her body jerking beneath his mouth. The musky scent of her arousal filled his nostrils as he lapped up her juices for the very first time.

He'd never tasted anything like her. She was all sweet and salty and…something else. Something so delicious Trevor couldn't even begin to describe it.

Her moans of pleasure echoed his own as he took more of what he wanted. Moving upward, he found her stiff and swollen clit. It was peeking out from beneath its protective hood, begging for his attention.

He gave it a quick flick of his tongue. Lexi cried out as her hips shot forward again, more forcefully this time. He repeated the move, loving the way her body reacted to his every touch.

"Oh, God, Trevor."

He raised his head slightly, in awe at the sight before him.

Eyes closed, Lexi's head was lying flat on the mattress. Her mouth was open slightly and her hands were clenching the comforter at her sides.

"You like that?" he asked, already knowing the answer.

Keeping her eyes closed, she nodded quickly. "Oh, yeah."

She sounded breathless, and Trevor couldn't help but love that it was because of what he'd been doing to her.

"Don't worry, baby. I'm just getting started."

She nodded again. "Okay."

She was naked with her legs spread and her sex less than an inch from his face, and she still managed to make him chuckle.

Getting back to business, Trevor gave her clit a quick kiss, and then slowly ran his tongue over it again. And again.

He increased the pressure slightly, but not enough to push her over the edge. He didn't want to make her come. Not yet.

The soft, keening sounds coming from Lexi while he made love to her with his mouth nearly set him off. She was so receptive to everything he was doing, and damn if that wasn't a turn-on.

Sensing she needed more, Trevor ran a fingertip down her slit to her entrance. He continued rubbing her clit with his tongue while he slowly inserted his index finger into her heated core.

Her inner muscles instantly clamped down. Jesus, she was tight. Trevor felt his cock jerk in his pants. It knew exactly what it wanted, but he forced himself to wait.

Lexi would always come first. Literally and figuratively.

Adding another finger, Trevor worked her pussy with his hand while he licked and sucked her clit. With a little more force, he kept thrusting the digits in and out of her soaked flesh. Soon, her thighs began to tremble against his face. He moved his fingers even harder. Faster.

Sounds of wet sex filled the morning air. It was erotic and arousing, but nothing compared to the sounds Lexi was making.

Between her moaning and whispered affirmations, Trevor

had no doubt she loved what he was doing to her body. The fact that she wasn't afraid to show her enjoyment turned him on even more.

"I'm close, Trevor. God, I'm so close. Please don't stop."

His lips moved against her sensitive flesh as he promised, "Not stopping, angel. Not until I make you come against my mouth."

"I'm almost there. Please, Trevor…Please, make me come."

With his fingers still inside her body, Trevor took one last look at her clit. It had become even more swollen, and he knew exactly what he needed to do.

He took the bundle of nerves between his lips and began to suck, determined to give her the release she was begging for. The combined sensation of that and his hand was all she needed.

"Trevor!"

Lexi cried out his name as she came. Her entire lower body shot up off the mattress, and Trevor could feel her inner muscles fluttering around his fingers.

When the contractions subsided, he quickly pulled them out and brought his lips to her core. He licked and sucked, feasting on her release as if it were his last meal.

Not my last. He wanted this again and again. Over and over. No matter how many times he had her, Trevor already knew he'd never get enough of this woman.

****

Lexi was flying. It was the only way she could describe what had just happened. She'd just experienced the most intense orgasm of her life, and it was all thanks to the man standing at the edge of the bed.

She watched as he grabbed the hem of his T-shirt and pulled it up and over his head and had to force herself not to gasp aloud.

As a chef-in-training, Lexi was very familiar with the term 'mouthwatering'. She'd experienced the sensation numerous times when the aroma of a delicious new dish filled her kitchen.

However, her body had never reacted in such a way by simply looking at another human being. Until now. Between his physique and gorgeous face, the guy could seriously be a model.

Trevor wasn't just fit. He was *cut.* Strong shoulders connected with a set of defined biceps. Large enough to show his strength, but not overly huge like some guys she'd seen. And his washboard abs…those were a thing of beauty.

He stood there, not appearing to be bothered at the way she was staring. As her eyes took him in, Lexi noticed a few areas of dark, puckered skin. *Scars.* She remembered the injuries he'd shared, and her heart ached at the thought of this man being hurt in any way.

The markings on his tan skin did nothing to diminish his appeal. If anything, they made him appear even stronger than before. A survivor. *My protector.*

Lexi's eyes were drawn back to the tattoo positioned along his ribs on the left side of his torso. It was an ornate cross with a sword running down its center and two dog tags hanging from its outstretched arms.

Lexi opened her mouth to ask him about it, but her question vanished when he reached into his night stand and grabbed a box of condoms. A brand *new* box of condoms.

He turned it over and began studying the back of the box.

Trevor smiled, blowing out what sounded like a breath of relief. "Still good."

A look of confusion must have crossed her face, because as he tossed the box on the bed and began to unbutton his jeans, he explained.

"I wasn't lying when I told you it had been a long time. I don't sleep around, Lex. You need to know that before this happens."

She nodded. "I haven't been with anyone in over two years."

This surprised him. "Two years?"

"My mom."

"Right. Sorry."

"If you're really sorry, you'll take those pants off."

Laughing, Trevor obliged. He pushed his jeans and boxer briefs down together and kicked them to the side. She thought he was beautiful before, but that was *nothing* compared to him totally nude.

Lexi licked her lips as her eyes followed the V in his muscles. It was as if its sole purpose was to guide her straight to his cock. And mercy, what a treasure it was.

Trevor was big. Bigger than any of the men she'd previously been with. There'd been less than a handful, and none were this impressive.

Between his size and her extended dry spell, that worried her a little. She was small to begin with. Sure, his fingers had just been inside her, but those alone had made her feel full.

Trevor opened the box and pulled out a foil packet. Sensing her trepidation, he gave her a lopsided smile. "Don't worry, it'll fit."

Embarrassed, she felt herself blush. A ridiculous reaction given what had just happened between them. Thankfully, this didn't seem to bother Trevor. In fact, he looked even more turned on than he had a second ago.

Lexi watched as he rolled the protection over his solid erection. Jutting out from his body, it bobbled as he crawled back onto the bed.

She couldn't wait to feel it. Leaning up, Lexi started to reach between his legs, but Trevor stopped her.

"You touch it right now, it'll explode."

Giggling, Lexi lay back down, more than willing to let him take the lead, this time. Trevor moved his body up and over hers. Using an arm to keep from crushing her, he reached between them and positioned the blunt tip against her opening.

Locking his gorgeous eyes on hers, he whispered, "You ready, angel?"

Cupping one side of his face, Lexi brushed her thumb against the slight stubble there. "I want this, Trevor. I want you."

He glanced at the scratch on her arm and the discolored skin around it. The guilt reflected in Trevor's eyes had her fearing he would put a stop to things. Instead, he simply leaned down and gently kissed the injured area.

Then, with their eyes locked, Trevor gave her a whispered promise. "I'll take care of you, Lex. Always."

Lexi's heart swelled as he eased his body forward, taking his time as he worked his way in. Once he was fully seated, they both moaned in unison. She'd thought his fingers had filled her, but that was nothing compared to this.

His body stretched hers, but it wasn't painful. The opposite, actually. It was as if he'd truly become a part of her. Having Trevor inside her made her feel…whole.

Don't get ahead of yourself, Lex.

"You okay? Am I hurting you?"

Trevor's concern had his brow wrinkling.

"No," she was quick to assure him. "It feels good." She licked her lips. "More than good."

A corner of his mouth raised. "Yeah?"

"Oh, yeah."

"How about this?" He eased part of himself out then slowly pushed back again. "That feel more than good?"

"God, yes."

He smiled and thrust in and out again. "Good. 'Cause it feels amazing to me." He leaned down and pressed his lips to hers.

Soon, their bodies were moving together in a slow, steady rhythm. Their breathing picked up and Lex could see sweat beginning to bead on Trevor's forehead.

When his brow creased, she panted, "What's wrong?"

He shook his head. "I'm not going to last long this first time. I'm almost there, already."

This made Lexi smile. She couldn't help but enjoy the fact that she had such a strong effect on him.

Suddenly, she *wanted* him to come. She wanted her body to be the reason he fell over the edge. Lexi needed to give him as much pleasure as he'd just given to her.

Tilting her hips, Lexi angled her lower body and began meeting him thrust for thrust.

An intense look crossed over his face. The veins in his corded neck bulged, and she knew it wouldn't be much longer.

"Ah, shit, Lex. You're gonna make me come."

That's kind of the idea.

She leaned up and pressed her lips to his. She slid her tongue between his lips and took the kiss deeper. Their mouths began to mimic the rest of their bodies, and just as she'd hoped, Trevor began to move faster.

His movements became more powerful. Erratic. He tore his lips away from hers, grunting as he spoke between thrusts.

"Can't…stop…*Alexis!*"

Lexi loved the way Trevor grunted her full name as he pushed into her one last time, his entire body stiffening from the powerful surge. Hot bursts of air hit her neck from his panted breaths. Their hearts beating to a synchronized rhythm.

She felt him kiss her shoulder just before he raised his head and lifted his chest from hers. Propped on his elbows, he looked down at her with a satiated gaze.

"Damn, angel. That was incredible."

Lexi smiled. "Glad you enjoyed yourself."

One of his dark brows lifted. "I sure hope I'm not the only one."

Giggling, Lexi leaned up and softly pressed her lips to his. "You're not. Trust me."

"Yeah?"

"Oh, yeah. I'm so glad we didn't wait to do that. In fact, I could do it again"—she kissed the corner of his mouth.—"and again"—another kiss on his chin—"and again." This time, she gave him a kiss on his neck before nibbling and then running her tongue across his skin there.

Trevor moaned. "I like the way you think, angel. You'll have to give me some time to reload, though. I'm not a teenager anymore."

Lexi laughed and brought her gaze back to his. "That's okay. It's still early, and we don't have to go anywhere for a while, right?"

Heat flashed in his beautiful eyes. "Right."

Trevor leaned down and began to kiss her again. Slowly, as if they had all the time in the world. Despite what he'd just said, she could feel him already becoming hard again. She was about to suggest he replace the used condom with a new one when his phone began to ring.

"Do you need to get that?"

He shook his head. "It's Derek. He'll call back if it's important."

Fine by me. The kiss grew more intense, and before long, his cock had become fully erect again.

Lexi pushed her hips upward. "I think you underestimated your reloading time."

He smiled against her lips. "You seem to have a unique effect on my body."

With a smug look, she gently pulled his bottom lip between her teeth. "Good to know."

Trevor's hips surged forward in reaction, and he groaned. "I think I pegged you all wrong."

"Yeah? How so?"

He smirked. "You're no angel." He leaned down and put his mouth to her ear. "You're the devil in disguise."

For some reason, his words sent a shot of arousal through her already-sensitive system. Lexi had always been a good girl, but she had to admit…the thought of being bad felt oh, so good.

With a quick kiss to her cheek, Trevor said, "Need another condom. I'll be right back."

He slowly slid from her body, and she immediately missed the fullness of his cock. The only thing that kept her from moaning out in protest was the fact that he was coming back to finish round two.

She enjoyed the view as he walked into the bathroom.

Less than two minutes later, he was crawling back in bed. Anticipation matching her own filled his eyes as he reached for another condom.

Putting the foil packet between his teeth, he was about to rip it open when his phone began to ring again. He looked at her regretfully.

"Sorry. I need to answer that."

"You don't have to apologize. Like you said, he'd call back if it's important. So, it must be."

Affection spread across his face as he got off the bed and bent to get the phone from his jeans. Feeling a little weird just sitting there, naked and waiting for him to have a conversation with someone else, Lexi reached for the sheet to cover herself.

"This had better be good, D."

Lexi watched as he listened to whatever Derek's response was. Trevor looked to her.

"Yeah, she's still here. Why?"

Clearly frustrated with his friend, Trevor rolled his lips between his teeth before gritting out, "If you don't have something important to share, I'm hanging up." The look of confusion falling across his face made her curious about the other guy's response. "Only if you promise to behave." Rolling his eyes at whatever else Derek was saying, Trevor held the phone away from his ear and tapped the screen. "Okay. You're on speaker."

"Hey, Lex. It's Derek. How are ya this mornin'?"

Lexi couldn't help but smile. "I'm good, Derek," she spoke a little louder than normal. "How are you?"

"I'm fine as wine, darlin'. Is Trev treatin' you okay? If not, you can always come over to my place."

"D," Trevor warned.

Laughing, Lexi looked Trevor straight in the eye and said, "Don't worry, Derek. Trevor's treating me just fine."

One corner of his delicious mouth turned up, and she knew he was thinking the same thing she was. Unfortunately, Derek's next words put a damper on the mood.

"So, I've been trackin' Robert Lockwood's credit card activity. He's made some purchases in a couple towns in California."

"California?" Lexi asked, surprised.

"He's in the wind, Lex," Derek offered.

"Meaning?"

"Meaning"—Trevor answered for Derek—"he's putting a safe distance between himself and the DPD. His charges are non-extraditable, which means—"

"They won't go across state lines to find him and bring him back."

"Right," Derek's voice chimed in. "But, if he's picked up for somethin' else while he's there, the California authorities will get ahold of the DPD. Between the two departments, they can decide whether or not to bring him back here or keep him locked up there."

"Well, at least we know he's far away from here, I guess."

"That, he is. And I don't foresee him comin' back to Texas any time soon. I'd say you're safe, darlin'."

Lexi sighed in relief. She'd love to stay another night with Trevor, but knowing Rob wasn't coming after her took a huge weight from her shoulders.

"That's good news, D. Keep watching him, just in case."

"I'd planned to. And Lex?"

"Yeah?"

"I mean what I said. My door will always open for you, sugar."

Sounding serious, Trevor said, "I'm hanging up now."

Lexi chuckled. "Bye, Derek." She barely got the words out before Trevor tapped his screen again and tossed the phone onto the mattress beside her.

"Now, where were we?"

He started to open the condom wrapper again, but again, his phone began to ring. It was a different ringtone, this time.

Clearly frustrated, Trevor cursed under his breath. With that same look of regret he'd gotten when Derek called, he said, "I'm sorry. That's Jake. He's my boss. He's on his honeymoon, so if he's calling me now, it must be for a good reason."

For some reason, Lexi found both his frustration and his need to explain adorable. "It's seriously fine, Trevor."

He grinned, then answered with, "Aren't you supposed to be enjoying that new wife of yours?" Trevor paused to listen to his boss. His brows turned in. "Now? I just checked in with Ryker this morning. He told me there weren't any active jobs on the books for us."

Suddenly, every muscle in his body became tense as Trevor's entire demeanor changed. He gave her a quick glance before asking the man on the phone, "Are you sure?"

Trevor waited, listening to the other man's response before he made his way to his clothes. Using his shoulder to hold the phone to his ear, he continued to talk in short, vague phrases while he swiftly put his clothes back on.

Something was clearly wrong. Not wanting to appear as though she were trying to eavesdrop, Lexi gathered the sheet around her and got out of bed. Grabbing her panties from the floor, she went to the kitchen to retrieve the shirt she'd been wearing earlier.

Trevor was so distracted by whatever his boss was telling

him, she didn't think he even noticed when she'd stepped out of the room.

Feeling a bit awkward, she dropped the sheet onto the floor near the island and put Trevor's T-shirt back on. By the time she walked back into his bedroom, Trevor was off the phone and fully dressed.

Checking the contents a black duffle bag he'd placed on the mattress, his head swiveled to face her. "I'm sorry, Lexi, but I have to go."

She walked over to his dresser where she picked up the pair of sweats she'd neatly folded and placed there the night before.

"Is everything okay?"

He gave her a tight smile. "Everything's fine. It's just work."

His words told her one thing, but the tone of his voice and the haunted look in his eyes said differently.

"I don't know how long I'll be gone." He continued to look through his bag. "I'd really like to take you out when I get back." Trevor gave her a tiny smirk. "A real date, this time."

"Third time's a charm?" Lexi teased.

Trevor gave her a real smile, making her feel more at ease. "Something like that."

She took a step closer. Still trying to ease some of the stress that phone call had obviously caused, she suggested, "Maybe we can pick up where we left off."

Zipping the bag closed, Trevor closed the distance between them and cupped her face with one hand. "This thing with us…it's not just about that." He tilted his head toward the bed behind him. Raising his other hand, Trevor now held her face with both. "Please tell me we're on the same page, angel."

Vulnerability shone behind his dark chocolate eyes as they searched hers, making her oddly happy. Knowing this strong, courageous man was worried she didn't want more than just a casual fling was exhilarating.

Raising onto her tiptoes, Lexi pressed her lips against his. "Definitely the same page."

He started to smile, but it faded quickly. "I hate leaving you. Especially now." His thumb caressed her cheek. "Promise you'll be careful while I'm gone."

Lexi leaned into his touch. "I'll be fine. Don't worry about me, Trev."

"Not possible, angel."

Standing a little taller, she took his hands into hers. "I'm serious, Trevor. I don't know what's going on, but I could tell from the look on your face it's not good. So, whatever it is…whatever you have to do…you need to stay focused on that. Not me. Besides, you heard what Derek said. Rob's in California. He's not going to risk getting arrested by coming back here. It's not like he's obsessed with me or anything. He was drunk, and his ego was bruised. That was it."

"He has a record, Lex. Including previous assault charges."

"Even more reason for him to stay away." Desperate to take the worry from his eyes, Lexi looked down at the clothes she was wearing. "I hope you're okay with me wearing this home. I'll wash them and have them ready for you when you get back."

His lips curved. "Tell you what"—Trevor placed his hands on her hips and pulled her closer to him—"how about you just keep those. You can put them on when you get to missing me."

"Keep them? They're huge on me!"

Trevor chuckled. "And you look sexy as hell in them."

Lexi shook her head. "You're crazy." She leaned up and gave him another quick kiss. "I'll sleep in them every night until you get back."

Groaning, Trevor tilted his head back. "Damn, you make it really hard to leave. But..." He checked his watch. "I really do have to get going. Derek is on his way over, and I'd rather you be gone before he gets here."

Unable to hide the hurt from her face, Lexi started to pull away. Trevor easily held her where she stood.

"That came out wrong. I don't want you here when Derek gets here, but only because I don't want you to have to deal with him and his razzing."

Her muscles loosened with relief. "I like Derek."

"Trust me, angel. The guy has no tact. He'll bombard you with questions about us. I just didn't want him making you uncomfortable. That's all."

"Oh."

Pulling her flush against his chest, he assured her, "You're special, Lex. Any man would be proud to show you off. Myself included."

He leaned down and kissed her slowly. This wasn't like the short, chaste kisses she'd given him. Trevor took it slowly, letting them both say goodbye in the most delicious way.

When it was over, Lexi laid a hand on his chest and whispered, "Stay safe, Trevor. Do what you have to do and then come back to me."

An emotion she couldn't quite put a name to filled his eyes. He shook his head, almost in disbelief and said, "That's the plan, angel."

Chapter 8

"Listen up."

All eyes turned to the front of the plane where Jake McQueen, owner of R.I.S.C. and Alpha Team's leader, stood. The cabin's interior lights reflected off the guy's shiny new wedding band as he stood with his hands resting low on his hips.

"I assume you've all had a chance to look through the files Ryker put together for us. I'd like to go over the highlights before we land to make sure we're all on the same page."

The sound of papers rustling filled the air, and their boss waited a few seconds for everyone to gather the files they'd been handed as they boarded the plane.

"According to Homeland's intel, Omar Hamid was sighted two weeks ago, then again three days ago in Guettara, Algeria. He's believed to be hiding out in the desert just outside the city."

"Why Algeria?" Coop asked from across the aisle.

Trevor swiveled his head to the young sniper who was sitting across the aisle from him. "What do you mean?"

Coop's green eyes moved from Jake's to Trevor's. "From what I read here"—the young sniper tapped the manila folder in his lap—"this Hadim guy seriously pissed off a lot of our country's higher-ups several years ago and has been hiding out ever since."

"And?" Trevor asked.

"*And*, the U.S. has a pretty good relationship with Algeria. From what I understand, their law enforcement and security channels all support us."

"What's your point, Coop?" Jake asked.

"My point is this asshole's been hiding out for nearly a decade. There's been no sign of him, and there's been no chatter of any kind. Then, all of a sudden, he's spotted in a country where we're not only welcomed but supported?" The guy shrugged one of his broad shoulders. "Just seems odd to me, that's all."

"He's gone home," Trevor mumbled the words more to himself than the others. But the private jet was small and everyone was within earshot.

"Home?" McKenna "Mac" Kelly asked from the seat facing Coop's. As was typical for an op, her blond hair was pulled back into a tight ponytail. Like Trevor and the others, she was dressed in desert camo.

"Omar Hadim grew up in Guettara," Trevor informed the group. "His mother still lives there."

Mac's gaze became quizzical. "That information wasn't included in the file I was given."

There were several murmurs of agreement, and Trevor understood why. Only he and Jake had been given Hadim's entire file.

Rather than answer her immediately, Trevor shifted his gaze to the front of the cabin. He and Jake shared a look before Jake gave him a slight nod.

Filling his lungs, Trevor did his best to push his emotions aside as he filled the rest of Alpha Team in on what he and

Jake—and of course, Derek—already knew.

"A little over nine years ago, a CIA liaison was assigned to our Delta Force team. Her job was to assist us in capturing a guy we'd been after for several months. The CIA had intel, and we had the means and the manpower."

"Sounds like a win-win," Coop exclaimed.

Trevor looked over at him again. "Should've been."

Seated beside him, Derek leaned closely and whispered into his ear. "Dude. You don't have to go into the details. All they need to know is that Hadim is a major fuckwad who needs to be taken down."

But Trevor wanted them to know. They needed to understand how important this opportunity was. Not only for him and Jake, but also for those killed as a result of Hadim's betrayal.

Drawing in a deep breath, Trevor shared with his team the cliff notes version of what happened in Syria.

"The short of it is, Hadim had been a CIA asset for years. He'd helped put several high-value targets away, so when he provided us intel on the guy we were after..."

"You trusted him," Mac finished for him.

Trevor nodded, his internal struggle to keep it together becoming harder and harder.

"What happened?" The low-spoken question came from the seat behind his. Grant Hill, Alpha Team's explosives expert, remained quiet as he waited for a response.

Swallowing hard, Trevor stalled while trying to figure out the words to describe the worst day of his life. Thankfully, he didn't have to.

"Hadim set us up," Jake answered for him.

Mac's pretty blue eyes zeroed in on Jake's. "These files tell us the guy was an enemy of the United States, but they didn't go into detail."

Jake looked to Trevor for another nod before continuing. "The intel he gave us was false. Our target and his men were waiting for us. We lost two team members and Lisa, the CIA liaison. Hadim and the man we were after got away."

"Was the original target ever neutralized?"

"A year later. A team of SEALs cornered him. He fired on them, and they responded by filling him full of holes. And before anyone asks, yes...DNA, fingerprints, and facial rec were all performed after his death to confirm his identity."

"Damn," Coop sighed. "Hearing all this shit makes me want to bring this Hadim guy down even more.

"Good," Jake responded. "Use it. Now, let's go over the plan so everyone knows what the hell they're supposed to do once we land."

Four hours later, the team was suited up and in position. Using the night sky to their advantage, they remained in the shadows as they surrounded the tiny, run-down shack.

The entire, wooden structure was roughly about ten by eight with a window on each side of its door. Through his night vision goggles, Trevor could tell the wood was mismatched and ill-fitted. The person who'd built it was clearly more concerned with utility than appearance.

"Any movement?" Jake's voice made its way through the coms.

"Negative, boss," Coop answered first. He and Mac were positioned on opposite ends of the shack. While Coop kept his rifle pointed at the front door, Mac was watching the back.

"I got nothin'," Derek said from the east side.

"Same here, boss," Grant agreed. "If our guy is in there, he ain't moving."

Crouched beside each other, Jake turned to Trevor and asked, "So, how do you want to play this?"

The question caught Trevor off guard. "You're the one in charge, not me."

"You are tonight."

Trevor opened his mouth to protest, but Jake stopped him. Turning his com volume down, he spoke low. "The men we lost that day were good men. And Lisa…she was yours, man. Now, I know you weren't in love with her, but she was as close as you've ever gotten. And there's a good chance the bastard who led her to her death is in there, right now. So, I need to know…you good with the plan as-is, or you wanna switch it up?"

Jake's words stirred up a whirlwind of emotions, and Trevor waited a moment for them to settle before responding. Part of him wanted to be the first one through the door, their original plan was the safest for the team.

Trevor stared back at the shack. "Those men we lost weren't good. They were the best. And Lisa…" He shook his head. "She was a great agent and a good friend. I want to give them the justice they all deserve, but…" After a blowing out a long, slow breath, he looked back at Jake. "I'm not losing another teammate to this asshole. We stick with the plan."

With one, sharp nod, Jake returned the volume on his com to its usual setting and gave the order. "All right, boys and girl…it's show time. Mac…keep your eyes out back. D and Coop, either of you see Hadim, take his ass out. Trevor and I will have cover Hill. Grant, you ready?"

"Been ready, boss."

"Go."

Switching from goggles to the night vision scope mounted on his Colt AR-15, Trevor watched and waited as Hill made his way to the front door. Adrenaline itched through his veins, but his hands remained steady.

At the door, Grant silently attached the blast strip before easing himself from the building. Squatting down a safe distance away, his deep voice travelled through the team's coms. "Ready when you are, boss."

Jake's eyes remained forward as he spoke to Trevor. "Your call, Matthews."

Trevor ignored the memories threatening to assault him. A different time. Different team. As he gave the go-ahead, he prayed history wouldn't repeat itself.

With his chin tipped down, he spoke clearly into the mic attached to his vest. "Light it up, Hill."

"Fire in the hole." Grant's warning came only seconds before the door was blown from its shoddy hinges. A cloud of dust blew toward them.

"Go, go, go!" Trevor yelled loudly.

Swarming the shack from all sides, the members of Alpha Team were at the door and entering the structure within seconds. Guns raised and ready to fire, they moved as one, their boots stomping on top of the fallen door as they made their way inside. It was a lethal dance they'd long-ago perfected.

The smell nearly knocked them over the instant they were inside. It was one Trevor and the others recognized instantly.

"Holy shit." Coop lowered his weapon and used his other arm to cover his mouth.

Mac did the same, her arm muffling her voice. "Jesus Christ, that's nasty."

Pushing past the need to vomit, Trevor blinked against his watering eyes and stared at the source of the odor. There, in the center of the room, was a dead man.

With a medic's eye, he quickly assessed the visible injuries. Wearing nothing but a pair of shorts, Trevor could easily see his wrists and ankles were tied to a wooden chair. And the man had clearly been tortured.

Dried blood encircled his skin from his struggles against the rough rope. All ten fingers had been broken, as well as the man's nose and jaw. Shallow cuts that would never heal had been made all over the man's body. Trevor's experience told him they'd been made to inflict maximum pain with minimal risk. All made prior to the deep, open gash running along the front of the man's neck.

Moving his eyes around the rest of the single-room shack, he noticed a large, metal bucket tipped on the floor near a crude, wooden table. A blood-stained towel was in a heap beside it, and Trevor instantly knew what it all meant.

He was waterboarded.

The same memories he'd fought against a few minutes before came barreling in. This man, whoever he was, had been tortured in almost the exact same way Lisa had been before she was killed.

"Check his prints," Trevor ordered roughly.

Knowing the directive was meant for him, Derek slid his backpack from his shoulders and swiftly removed a small tablet.

Clearly trying to hold his breath, Derek approached the chair and grimaced as he lifted one of the dead man's disfigured digit. Pressing the fingertip to the screen, they only had to wait a few seconds before the device beeped with recognition.

He stood straight and turned to Trevor and Jake. Lifting the tablet, he turned the screen in their direction. "It's Omar Hadim."

"Well, that's unfortunate," Coop said, sounding genuinely disappointed. Trevor could sure as hell relate.

"Pretty anti-fucking-climactic, if you ask me," Grant grumbled. "I'll keep an eye on things outside." Then, the big guy unceremoniously left the small space.

Looking like he was about to lose his lunch, Coop spoke up a little too quickly. "Uh, yeah. That's a good idea. I should probably go with him. You know, just in case."

Shaking her head, Mac rolled her eyes and mumbled, "Pussies."

She then unzipped one of her thigh pockets and pulled out her work phone. Knowing Ryker would want as much evidence as they could gather for his final report, she began taking pictures of both Hadim and the room.

"Well, I don't know who did this to him"—Derek drawled—"but it sure seems like Karma finally caught up with the bastard."

Trevor was still standing in the same spot he'd stopped in after entering the structure. From beside him, Jake said, "I'd say you're right, D." Facing Trevor, he added, "You wanted Lisa and the others to get their justice. Looks like they finally got it. I'm just sorry someone else handed it down before you got the chance to do it yourself."

"That's enough pics," Jake directed Mac. "I'm sure Ryker will have plenty to work with." Turning to leave, he stopped and slapped Trevor on the shoulder. "Let's go home."

"Wait," Derek called out. He tilted his head toward Hadim. "What about him?"

Jake's eyes connected with Trevor's. "That's his call." Then, with one final nod, Jake stepped past Trevor and joined the other two men outside.

"Leave him," Trevor ordered.

Nodding, Mac pocketed her phone and left. When Derek started out, he paused just long enough to say, "It's finally over."

And just like that, Trevor found himself alone with the man who'd invaded his nightmares for years. Despite the smell of decaying flesh, he remained standing there for a few minutes longer.

"She trusted you," he whispered to the dead man. "She stood up for you every single time" —he stepped closer— "Lisa believed in you, and you…" His throat tightened, and the image he faced blurred. "You were a lying, murdering sonofabitch who got exactly what you deserved."

With a sudden, unplanned move, Trevor lifted his gun and blasted three bullets into Hadim's chest. Two for the men they'd lost that day, and one for Lisa.

Ready to put the final ghost from his past behind him, he turned and walked away. Less than two hours later, they were all back on the jet and not one team member had made mention of the gunshots they'd heard coming from the cabin.

As the plane took off over the expansive, dry land, Derek nudged his shoulder from the seat beside him. "Cheer up. I know you wanted to be the one to send the bastard straight to Hell, but look at it this way. With him already taken care of, you can see your girl even sooner than you'd expected."

"Your girl?" Jake asked, facing him. "Wait, there's a girl?"

"Oh, yeah." Derek grinned. "And she's a looker, too." The man wagged his brows up and down at Jake.

"What the hell, Trev?" Jake actually looked a little hurt. "I'm gone for what, two weeks, and you found a girl? Why the fuck am I just now hearing about this?"

Trevor felt as though he were spinning as his thoughts shifted from Hadim to Lexi. With things still so new between him, Trevor wasn't ready to share too much about their relationship just yet.

"As you just pointed out, you've been gone. You really wanted me to call and interrupt your honeymoon to tell you I started seeing someone? Olivia would've had my ass."

"Bullshit," Jake blurted out from across the small table separating them. "My wife will be over the moon when she hears you're dating someone. Hell, she's been talking about trying to set you up with one of the nurses she works with."

Despite the day's events, Trevor smiled. "Your *wife*. That sounds…weird. But great."

Jake's smile was even wider. "I know."

With a sincere look, Trevor told his friend, "I'm happy for you, brother. Really."

"Thanks. Now, stop trying to change the subject and tell me about this girl of yours. What's her name?"

"Alexis," Derek answered for him. "She's a waitress at that shitty-ass diner we've been goin' to. She's five-foot nothin'. Blonde, blue-eyed. And she's as sweet as apple pie on a Sunday mornin'."

Trevor gave Derek a look. "Anything else you'd like to tell him about my…about Lex?"

His friend apologized. "Sorry, man. Go ahead. You tell him."

"Gee, thanks, D. But I think you pretty much covered it."

"So," Jake prompted, ending the childish tiff the two were about to get into. "Is it serious?"

Cursing under his breath, Trevor ran a hand over his jaw. "Jesus, I feel like I'm talking to a couple of teenage girls at a sleepover."

"Been to a lot of those, have you?" Derek taunted.

Not giving Trevor the chance to fire back, Jake said, "I'm

just asking about your girl because I know *Liv's* gonna ask. And if I come home with this news but didn't bother to get the details, she's gonna be pissed."

"And then, what? She'll make you wait a whole five minutes before tearing off your clothes?" Trevor asked with feigned horror.

"Not my fault my wife loves this body." After a few chuckles from the group, Jake relented. "Fine. You don't want to kiss and tell, I get it. And I respect it. Just answer this one question, and I promise I'll leave you alone."

"What?" Trevor groaned.

"She make you happy?"

Recent memories flashed through his mind. Lexi smiling. Laughing. Those dimples and that damn blush.

"Yeah," Trevor admitted. "She does."

"Then, I'm happy for you, man. It's about fucking time."

His friend was right. With Hadim dead, Trevor was finally free to close that chapter of his life and start looking at his future. Hopefully, that future would include Lexi.

Just thinking about seeing her again made his stomach bubble with anticipation. He felt like a damn teenager, but he couldn't help it. She *did* make him happy. Happier than he'd been in a very long time, and he couldn't wait to see her again.

****

Lexi, Joe, Caleb, and Gina all walked across the vacant parking lot to their cars. It had been an especially busy day, and Lexi was ready for a hot bath and a glass of wine.

"When's your man coming back?" Gina lit a cigarette as they walked.

Though they were the same age, the other woman looked nearly ten years older than Lexi did. Gina's dark hair was kept pixie-short, and the lines and creases on her face told much of her story.

Years of living hard and playing even harder had taken its toll on Gina's youthful skin. But she was nice, and Lexi genuinely enjoyed working with her.

"I don't know," Lexi answered. She didn't bother to deny that Trevor was her man. Mainly, because she already felt as though he was. "Most of what he does is confidential, so he can't really tell me much. But, he promised to call as soon as he got back."

Taking a drag, Gina inhaled deeply before releasing a stream of smoke between her ruby red lips. "Well, honey. For your sake, I hope he does."

"Oh, he'll call," Caleb spoke up from behind them.

"Yeah?" Gina asked, turning her head. "How can you be so sure?"

Caleb snickered. "Trust me. He's nowhere near done with our little Lexi."

"You think he's just stickin' around 'till he gets tired of her, or is he in for the long haul?"

"That guy's playing for keeps."

"Keeps, huh? Wow." Gina shouldered Lexi's arm. "Way to go, Lex."

"Um, hello…" Lexi drew out the word and waved her hand. "I'm right here, you know. And ya'll can stop talking about my love life anytime, now."

"What?" Gina asked. "We're happy for you. Aren't we, Caleb?"

"Hell, yeah. We've been talking all week about how much more you've been smilin', lately."

"Gee…I didn't realize I was such a miserable hag before," Lexi teased. "Someone should've said something."

"Ah, come on, Lex. You know what we mean." Sincerity filled Caleb's young eyes. "You just seem…happier. That's all."

Lexi blushed, but couldn't hide her smile.

"See?" Gina pointed at her with the hand that held her cigarette. "That's exactly what we're talkin' about."

Rolling her eyes, Lexi laughed silently. "Well, maybe you'd look this happy, too, if you'd asked that one guy for his number."

"What guy?" asked Caleb.

"Some customer who came in tonight. He's come in a few times lately."

"So…why didn't you ask for his number?" Caleb prodded.

"I don't know," Gina shrugged. "I mean, the guy is pretty hot."

"See," Lexi pushed Gina's shoulder playfully.

"Fine." Gina rolled her eyes. "If he comes in again, I'll see if he's interested."

"Good. Then maybe you'll find something else to focus on besides me and my love life."

Laughing, both Gina and Caleb said their goodbyes.

"They're not wrong, you know," Joe looked at her pointedly after the other two had gotten in their cars. "I know it's only been a short time with this Trevor fella, but you *are* different. It's like there's an extra little bounce in your step. And I, for one, am tickled to see it."

Lexi's cheeks became warm as she grinned and gave Joe a big hug. "Thanks, Joe. You know"—she pulled back—"It's not too late for you, either. You're a handsome, successful man. You should find yourself a nice woman to settle down with."

Joe's eyes lit up with his smile. "I did find a nice woman. Was with her for forty-two years before the Good Lord took her to be with Him, instead. My Helen's up there waiting for me, and when my time comes, I want to be the same man I was when she left me. With a heart that belongs to only her."

It was one of the sweetest things she'd ever heard. Blinking quickly, Lexi hugged Joe again. "Your wife was a very lucky woman."

"We were both lucky." Joe hugged her back and then broke away. "Now, go on home and get some rest. From the way those two talked you're gonna need it when that boy of yours comes callin'."

Lexi gasped. "Joe!"

"What? You think I don't know what sex is? Let me assure you, little lady. This old man had the moves back in the day."

When he began to swivel his hips and dance around, Lexi nearly lost it. "Goodnight, Joe," she chuckled, shaking her head as she got into her car.

The entire drive home, Lexi thought about what the others had said. She knew they were right. She *was* happier. More so than she'd been in a very long time.

Butterflies danced around in her belly as she wondered when Trevor would come back home. Though, he'd only been gone for four days, she'd missed him terribly.

At first, that worried her. Was she getting too attached, too quickly? Then, she realized it didn't matter. The fact was, she already cared about him more than any other man she'd ever dated. Crazy or not, she couldn't help how she felt.

Finally home, she couldn't wait to wash the stink of the diner from her hair and skin. After indulging in a long, hot shower, Lexi dried off and threw on a tank top and some loose pajama shorts. She was half-way through blow-drying her hair when the power went out and the whole house went dark.

"Great," she groaned, knowing she'd tripped a breaker. The house was old, and this usually happened about once a month.

Stumbling her way to her nightstand, Lexi pulled a small flashlight from the top drawer and carefully went downstairs. She went to the utility closet just off the kitchen and began searching the black, rectangular switches.

"That's odd," she whispered to herself. None of the breakers were out of position. If she hadn't tripped one, then why were the lights out?

She didn't remember any storms being in the forecast, and the skies had been clear when she'd left the diner. Maybe there was a downed line somewhere, and the whole neighborhood was without power.

Deciding to check and see, Lexi made her way to the living room. She stood in front of the oversized window near her front door and looked across the street at Mrs. Siemens' house. The older woman's porch light shone brightly. A quick glance at the other houses told Lexi the power was working just fine. All except for hers.

A strange, gnawing feeling settled deep in her gut. Nervous now, she quickly double-checked the locks on her front door. Thankfully, they were still locked.

Knowing she'd never get to sleep if she didn't check the back door, too, Lexi turned and started for the kitchen. She'd made it half-way between her front door and the other room's entryway when a large shadow stepped into her view.

A man was in her house. A man wearing all black,

including a stocking cap and gloves. It took her brain about half a second to process what that meant.

With her eyes locked on the threat standing before her, Lexi screamed and turned to run. She'd almost made it to the door when a pair of strong arms wrapped around her from behind.

She screamed again, praying a neighbor would hear, but the sound was cut short when a large hand was pressed painfully against her lips. *Oh, God!*

Bucking as hard as she could, Lexi kicked and fought with all she had. Unfortunately, she was much smaller and not nearly as strong as her attacker. That meant, she had to be smarter.

Think, Lexi! Think! She needed a target, and her short stature against his tall frame gave her just the one she needed.

He'd wrapped his left arm around her center, trapping her left arm against her own body in the process. His right hand was still covering her mouth, which left her right arm free.

Praying her plan would work, Lexi twisted her body to the left and at the same time, jabbed her right elbow back as hard as she could…right into the man's crotch.

He grunted and his hold on her loosened just enough for her tiny body to slip through. Ducking her head beneath the arm that had held her mouth closed, Lexi ran as fast as she could toward the kitchen. If she could get to the back door, she might have a fighting chance.

Unfortunately, the man's long legs allowed him to eat up a lot more space than her short ones. He was on her in mere seconds. Tackling her from behind, Lexi was sure at least one of her ribs had broken as the man's muscular body landed on top of hers, slamming her against the unforgiving wood floor.

Struggling to breathe, she was unable to fight back. He

flipped her over and held her wrists above her head. With nothing else to do, Lexi let out another loud cry for help.

Through the opening in the stocking cap, she watched as his lips curved upward into the most sinister smile she'd ever seen.

"I didn't expect you to be such a fighter. But, you really should save your energy. You're going to need it."

"Go to hell," Lexi gritted between her teeth, not allowing herself to think about what his words meant. She tried to push against the thick fingers wrapped around each wrist, but it was no use.

A loud, piercing cry escaped her throat, and her attacker started to smile again. A sudden rage fell over her, and for a second, she became more pissed than frightened. Driven by an overwhelming anger toward this man, this intruder, Lexi used the only weapon she had left.

Filling her mouth with as much saliva she could, she spit directly in the man's face. The majority splattered against his right eye.

He drew his head back in surprise, squinting that eye shut. Transferring both wrists into one of his fists, he used the other to wipe her spit from his face.

Glaring down at her, he shouted, "You bitch!" Then he reared his free hand back and swung it toward her face.

Fire erupted painfully in her cheekbone as her head flung to one side. Momentarily stunned, she barely registered the fact that she was being yanked to her feet. Swaying, she was still trying to find her bearings when the man whispered into her ear.

"You're going to pay for that."

****

Trevor pulled onto Lexi's street. He probably should have called before coming over, but he wanted to see her. As crazy as it seemed, he wanted her to know he was already falling for her.

He was pretty sure she felt the same for him, but even if she didn't, that was okay. He'd give her all the time she needed to get there, because whether it made sense or not, she was it for him. Trevor knew it as surely as he knew his own name.

With Hadim dead, he could finally put the past to rest, where it belonged. Feeling lighter than he had in years, Trevor was too amped up to sleep. He knew Lex might be in bed by now, but he simply couldn't wait until tomorrow to see her.

A twinge of guilt filled his belly as he parked his truck behind hers. Every light in her house was off. Even the porch light. *Damn.* Trevor considered leaving, but his selfish need to see her overrode his guilt about waking her.

He glanced up at the darkened porch light and made a mental note to talk with her about getting better security. Maybe a motion light and some cameras like the ones Jake had installed at his wife's old house not long before she'd been attacked and abducted. Those cameras had been instrumental in catching the bastard and saving Olivia's life.

Stepping up onto the small stoop in front of her door, he raised his hand to knock. Trevor stopped mid-motion when he heard voices coming from inside the house. Tilting his head, his heart dropped into his stomach when he realized the person talking was male.

Trevor felt sick as he tried to think of a plausible reason Lexi would have another man inside her house at this hour, especially with the lights off. She didn't seem like the type of woman to screw a guy around. Not after the moments they'd shared.

He thought of the way she'd kissed him before he left for Algeria. The emotion behind her eyes as she'd stared up at him and made him promise to come home to her. *Jesus, could I really have been that wrong about her?*

No! He wasn't wrong about her. Which meant whoever was in that house with his woman, shouldn't be there.

Trevor had just tried to open the locked door when he heard a sound he'd never forget for as long as he lived.

Despite the walls separating them, the shrill from Lexi's terrified scream reached his ears clearly. He didn't think of his training, or whether or not it was safe for him to enter her house. His only thought was to get to Lexi.

Drawing his weapon from his waistband—thank God he'd decided to keep it on and not leave it in the truck—Trevor raised his booted foot and kicked the door just above the lock.

The deadbolt didn't completely give way, so he gave it everything he had and kicked it one more time. Wood splintered as the door flew inward, and Trevor stepped into a nightmare.

Lexi was standing in the middle of her small living room. A man in head-to-toe black was holding her against his chest, one arm wrapped around her waist, his other beneath her chin.

Though the room was dark, Trevor could see the fear in Lexi's eyes. It shook him to the core. His training finally kicking in, he pushed his emotions aside and quickly assessed the situation.

The man's forearm was pressing against her throat, and it was clear she was struggling to breathe. She was doing her best to find purchase with her tiptoes, but the bastard was damn near holding her off the floor.

"Get your hands off her!" Trevor ordered as he moved farther into the room. Of course, it couldn't be that easy.

Rather than respond with words, the other man simply held a struggling Lexi in place and stared. Trevor tried again.

"I said let her go."

"T-Trev-or."

Lexi's broken voice was barely a whisper, but it still managed to reach his ears.

"I'm here, angel. I'm right here. Everything's going to be okay." To her attacker he warned, "I'm not going to tell you again. Let her go, or I will shoot you where you stand."

Oddly, the man's mouth slowly began to spread into a smile. Moving lightning-fast, he picked Lexi completely off her feet and threw her bodily toward Trevor.

His need to protect was instant and reactive. Dropping his gun, Trevor reached out for Lexi, his arms wrapping around her flailing body. He screamed her name as they both went flying backward…crashing right through the large, picture window he'd been standing in front of.

Chapter 9

Trevor's heart felt as though it would fly out of his chest when he lifted his head and saw Lexi's motionless form in the grass a few feet away.

He scrambled across the short distance to where she lay. With heavy amounts of fear and adrenaline rushing through his veins, he didn't even feel the bits of glass cutting into his palms and knees as he moved. *She's too still.*

"Lexi!" he shouted as he reached her. She was on her left side, her blond hair blanketed across her face. "Alexis, look at me!"

She moaned, the sound bringing with it a wave of relief. "Baby, I need you to look at me. I need to know you're okay."

Another moan escaped her throat just before her eyes flew open with a gasp. She sat straight up and began fighting him.

"Lexi, stop! It's me…Trevor. You're okay, now. He's gone, and you're safe."

Her muscles froze as his words sank in. "H-he's gone? Are you sure?"

Unfortunately, he was. Trevor had seen the bastard running out the back just as they'd crashed through the glass.

"Yeah, baby. I'm sure."

Her face crumbled. "Thank God!"

Lexi threw herself in his arms and Trevor held on tightly. He could physically feel her fear as her entire body shook against his.

"I was s-so s-scared. I thought he w-was going to k-kill me."

"I know, baby," Trevor crooned as he rubbed her back. "I'm so sorry."

"W-why?" She hiccupped as she pulled back, wiping her tears with her palms. "It's not l-like you knew this w-would happen."

Trevor shook his head. "Still. I could have had someone watching you while I was away. I could have—"

"You get away from her right this minute!"

A loud, shrill voice coming from the direction of the road had both their heads turning. A slender, silver-haired woman was barreling toward them wearing a light blue bathrobe that buttoned up the front and a matching pair of house slippers.

"Alexis?" The elderly woman's eyes were wide, and she was clearly alarmed. "Good heavens, are you okay? What happened?" Without giving her a chance to answer, she turned her attention back on Trevor. With one fist raised, she yelled, "What have you done to my sweet Alexis? You get away from her right now, you hear? The police are on their way, and when they get here, they're going to arrest you!"

Trevor seriously thought the woman was going to try to wallop him, until…

"Mrs. Siemens, no!" Lexi pushed against Trevor's chest to stand. When he tried to stop her for fear she was injured, she quickly assured him she was fine and stood. "This is Trevor," she laid a hand on the old woman's frail shoulder. "He's my…" Clearly unsure what she should call him, Lexi hesitated, her eyes sliding back to his.

Trevor decided to help her out. Now standing beside her, he held his hand out to Mrs. Siemens. "I'm Lexi's boyfriend, Mrs. Siemens. Trevor Matthews."

"Boyfriend?" She sounded shocked, but shook his hand, anyway. "Alexis, you never told me about any boyfriend."

"It's…new."

As if she'd just noticed her neighbor's busted door and window, Mrs. Siemens gasped. "My stars, what happened here?"

"A man broke into Lexi's house tonight and tried to hurt Lexi." Trevor swallowed hard and did his best not to show the fear he still felt from seeing her with that man. "Did you see or hear anything suspicious?"

"A man broke into your house?" She swiveled her head toward Lexi. "Are you okay? Did he hurt you?"

"I-I'm a little bruised and shaken up, but I'm okay. Thanks to Trevor." To him, Lexi whispered. "If you hadn't come along when you did…"

Unable to keep from touching her, Trevor grabbed her hand and gently pulled her to his side. He was barely keeping his shit together, but kissed the top of her head and forced himself to sound calm when he said, "I'm just glad I showed up when I did."

"From the looks of things, I am, too," Mrs. Siemens exclaimed as she surveyed the damage once more. "And to answer your question, no. I was about to go to bed when I heard a loud crashing sound. That's when I looked out my window and saw you two on the ground."

Just then, several sets of flashing lights turned onto Lexi's street as the emergency vehicles made their way to them. Two

DPD patrol cars, an unmarked car, and an ambulance parked in front of where they stood.

The two paramedics—a younger man and a woman who appeared to be in her late forties—made their way to them first. "Police dispatched an ambulance. Is someone hurt?"

Before she could protest, Trevor pointed toward Lexi. "She needs to be checked out. A man attacked her and then tossed her through what used to be that window." The young, male paramedic's eyes grew wide when he saw what Trevor had been referring to.

"Trevor, I told you. I'm sore, but I'm…"

"This isn't an argument you're going to win, angel." He looked down at her pointedly. "You either let them check you out here, or they're taking you to the hospital. Your choice."

Lexi's brows turned slightly inward, and he could tell she didn't care much for the directive. Trevor couldn't bring himself to feel bad about it. He came damn close to losing her tonight. Hell, his hands were still shaking, though he was doing a good job at hiding it.

"I like him," Mrs. Siemens smirked. Then, she leaned around the paramedic and whispered none-too-softly, "And he's sure easy on the eyes. You did a good job picking this one, Alexis."

Despite the seriousness of the situation, Lexi looked up and gave him a tiny smile. "Yeah," she whispered. "I did."

Trevor let her hand go so she could walk over to the ambulance to be seen. He was thankful when Mrs. Siemens followed.

As Lexi walked, he assessed her from behind, checking the gate of her walk to make sure she didn't limp or appear to have any neck or back injuries. He breathed a little easier when she appeared to move with relative ease.

"Damn, man. I must have really pissed someone off to have to deal with your ass twice in one week."

Trevor looked over to where Eric West was walking toward him with two uniformed officers. The detective had the same, smartass smirk his brother typically wore.

"He's back," Trevor stated bluntly. "Lockwood's back, and tonight he broke into her home and tried to hurt her. Threw her through the fucking window."

"Whoa. Trevor Matthews just threw out an f-bomb. Shit must be getting real."

"I'm serious, Eric."

"So, am I. Been around you long enough to know that language comin' from you only happens when you're severely pissed off. From the way that vein in your neck is popping out right now, I'd say you're there."

"I almost missed it. The team just got back in town, and I almost went home instead of coming here."

"But, you didn't. You came here, and you stopped the bastard."

Trevor clenched his teeth. "He got away. I heard her scream, so I busted the door down. The asshole had her in a choke hold. I threatened to shoot if he didn't let her go. I…I never dreamed he'd pick her up and throw her like he did. I caught her, but her momentum pushed me backward, and we both went through the glass."

One of the officers whistled through his teeth. "Damn, man. You're lucky neither of you were seriously hurt."

Trevor glanced over to the ambulance. Its back doors were open and the interior lights were on. The paramedics' shadows were moving around inside as they worked, and Trevor felt a slight relief that she was being taken care of.

Eric put a comforting hand on Trevor's shoulder. "The

good news is, she's going to be okay. I do have to ask, though…how certain are you that Robert Lockwood was Lexi's attacker?"

Trevor looked at him like he'd lost his damn mind. "Who else would it be? The guy assaults her a few days ago, vanishes, and now this? Come on, West. You can't seriously tell me you think it's all one big coincidence."

"Easy." The detective held a palm up. "I had to ask. It's not uncommon for neighborhoods like this one to be a target for burglars or sexual deviants. Speaking of…did the guy take anything? Was anything missing or out of place? Did he touch her in a sexual manner at all?"

Suddenly, Trevor became extremely nauseated. The thought of someone hurting Lexi was bad enough. Hurting her in *that* way? He couldn't even let his mind go there.

"I don't think he was there to rob her. You'll have to ask her, but when I came through the door, his entire focus was on her. My gut's telling me it wasn't about that. As far as the other"—he inhaled deeply to keep from puking all over her grass—"you'll need to ask her that, as well."

Eric nodded silently as he took notes in his small, spiral-bound notebook. "What time did you first get here?"

Trevor looked at his watch. He was surprised that it actually hadn't been all that long since he'd first pulled into her drive. "About ten minutes ago, give or take. You should ask her neighbor, Mrs. Siemens, what time she heard the big crash."

"That the older lady over there with Lexi?"

Mrs. Siemens was standing by the ambulance doors barking orders at the paramedics and Lexi. Trevor almost smiled. He could see why Lexi liked her so much.

"Yeah. Lex says she's a good neighbor."

"And you think she may have seen something?"

"I have no idea. I just know she heard us crash through the window and came running to see what happened."

Eric shook his head as he wrote. "Not smart."

"No, but she's sure brave. About took me out when she thought I was hurting Lex."

Derek's brother raised his brows. "Seriously?"

"Dead serious. That woman may be old, but she's a spitfire."

"You say the team just got back?"

Trevor nodded. "A few hours ago. We debriefed with Ryker then went our separate ways. Far as I know, everyone else went home."

Just then, the sound of a loud engine and squealing tires filled the air. Eric cursed under his breath and shook his head. "Not everyone, apparently."

The four men watched as Derek's gunmetal grey Challenger Hellcat raced down the street, stopping just short of slamming into Eric's department-issued car.

"Trevor!" Derek yelled across the lawn as he jogged toward them. "You okay, man?" One of the officers stepped aside to make room in their little group. Derek's gaze went to the busted door and window behind Trevor. "Holy shit. What the fuck happened?" His head swung toward the ambulance. "Is Lex okay?"

"Take a fuckin' breath and calm your shit," Eric ordered. "And how the hell did you even know somethin' happened?"

Derek gave his brother an exacerbated look. "I put Lexi's address into my system before the team left town." He looked at Trevor and shrugged a shoulder. "So we'd know if something happened while we were gone."

Trevor hadn't known Derek had done that, but

appreciated his friend's concern for Lexi's safety. "Thanks, man."

"Yeah, sure." He blew his appreciation off. "You gonna tell me what happened? Is Lexi okay?" Derek looked him over quickly. "Are *you* okay?"

While Trevor talked, Eric sent the officers inside the house to start processing the scene. Another pair of officers showed up and Eric sent them to check out the issue with the power. He jotted down a few more notes as Trevor went through the entire story again.

"Goddamn Lockwood," Derek gritted through his teeth. To his brother he asked, "I thought your people were looking for him."

Clearly frustrated, Eric assured him, "We are, D. But we don't even know for sure this *was* Lockwood. Hell, even Trevor couldn't give a positive I.D. on the guy, and he had his damn gun pointed at the man's head."

Anger flooded Trevor's system, but not toward Eric. He was pissed at himself. He should have paid closer attention to detail. While the bastard was holding Lexi, he should have studied the man's eyes and mouth so he could match the description with Lockwood. Instead, he'd been focused on Lexi.

"Knock that shit off, Matthews. This isn't on you."

Trevor blinked and realized Derek was talking to him. "I lost focus."

Derek looked at Trevor as if he were stupid. "Of course you lost fuckin' focus. Some jagoff had his hands on your woman. Any one of us would've reacted the same way."

"Not Jake," Trevor argued. "When all that shit went down with Olivia, he was focused on the task. Not her."

"Bullshit. I was there, too, remember? And I seem to recall

Jake losing it a couple different times after Olivia was taken. A woman you care about was in danger, Trev. Only natural, you bein' focused on her. Especially after the shit we just got done dealin' with."

Hadim's tortured body flashed behind his eyes. Almost seamlessly, a different face replaced his. One that was beaten and broken in nearly the exact same way as Hadim's. *Lisa.*

His heart ached for his dead friend, but it wasn't until another woman's image filled his thoughts that Trevor blinked and shook his head. He couldn't even begin to imagine something like that happening to his Lexi.

His eyes flew to the ambulance just as she was guided out the back. The paramedics had given her a blanket, which she'd wrapped around her shoulders and was clutching together with her small, precious hands.

"See?" Derek crossed his arms at his chest and gave Trevor a smug look. "You're thinkin' of all that shit right now, aren't you?" Trevor shook his head in denial, but his teammate wasn't buying it. "Dude, it's all over your face. You gotta remember…Lexi isn't Lisa."

Trevor was about to lay into him when Lexi got within earshot. Derek gave him a look that said he needed to cool it, and damn it…he knew his friend was right. But his immediate reaction was to protect this woman any way he knew how.

He didn't know why, but every time Trevor was around Lexi, every one of his primal instincts kicked into high gear. *You know why, you just don't want to admit it yet.* Finally, Lexi was back by his side, where she belonged.

"Hey, angel." He forced a smile, doing his best to pretend he had it all together. "What'd they say? You okay?"

Lexi nodded. "I'm fine."

Trevor wished her porch light was working so he could get a better look for himself. His eyes moved to the paramedics standing behind her. The woman spoke up.

"We offered to take her to the hospital for x-rays, just to be sure, but she signed the refusal. There are a few minor scrapes on her left arm from landing on the broken glass, and her ribs are probably going to be sore for a few days. We advised her to ice the bruise on her cheek, but other than that, she's going to be fine."

"Just like I told you," she muttered to him.

Trevor was relieved to hear the bite in her tone. Carefully, he put his arm around her shoulders and pulled her to him. He kissed the top of her head, then rested his cheek there.

"I just needed to be sure."

"I know." Lexi's voice softened as she leaned into his embrace.

The paramedics were walking back to the ambulance when light suddenly illuminated Lexi's front yard. Everyone's focus turned to where her porch light, along with a few others inside the house, were now working. Everyone's except Trevor's.

Not caring about the lights, he took the opportunity to get a better look at Lexi's condition. Her hair was bedraggled and her eyes were red-rimmed from crying. He saw the bruise on her right cheek the paramedic had mentioned and wanted to put his own fist through her attacker's front teeth.

"Found the issue with the lights," a voice called from the side of the house, pulling his attention away. They all waited as one of the officers came walking out from the shadows, flashlight in his hand.

"Someone cut somethin'?" Derek asked.

The older officer shook his head. "The main disconnect

from the outer box was pulled."

****

"That explains why none of the breakers were tripped," Lexi said quietly.

When Trevor looked down at her, she answered his unspoken question. "I'd just gotten out of the shower when the power went out. I grabbed a flashlight from my nightstand and went downstairs to check the breakers." She shrugged a shoulder. "It's an old house, and sometimes when I blow dry my hair, one flips and I have to go reset it."

"What happened after you checked the breakers, Lexi?" Eric asked, pen in hand.

Only then did she notice it and the notepad in Eric's hands. "Right. You still need my statement." She gave him a small smirk and added, "Seems like we just did this, Detective."

Derek's brother responded with a sympathetic smile. "Yeah, we really need to break this habit of yours."

Taking a deep breath, Lexi began to tell them all what happened. "So, I came downstairs and checked the breaker. When I realized none had been tripped, I walked over to the window…"

Her voice trailed off for a second as she glanced at the gaping hole where her window used to be. The memory of her being lifted and flying toward Trevor had her heart racing again.

"Can we just do this tomorrow, Eric?" Trevor grumbled. "I'll bring her down to the station, and…"

"No!" Lexi snapped out of it. "I'd rather do it now, and then just forget it ever happened."

Trevor looked down at her, his dark brows turned inward. "You sure?"

She nodded and began speaking to Eric again. "I checked the breaker then went to the window. I wanted to see if the neighbors' lights were off, too. I thought maybe there was a power line down somewhere, or something. I noticed Mrs. Siemens' porch light on and then glanced down both sides of the street to the other houses. That's when I started to get an uneasy feeling."

"What did you do, then," Eric asked quietly.

"I checked to make sure the front door was still locked, which it was, and then turned and started to go into the kitchen to check the back door. That's when I saw him."

"Can you describe him for me?"

"He was tall. Much taller than me." She gave a silent chuckle. "Of course, *everyone's* much taller than me." Eric smiled back at her, and so did Trevor and Derek. Trevor's seemed forced, though, and she hated that.

"Anyway, he wasn't quite as tall as Trevor…I'd say he was more about your height," she motioned to Eric. "He was dressed in all black and had on gloves and a stocking cap. And he was strong. I remember thinking how solid his muscles felt as I tried to fight him off. A shiver raced down her spine and Trevor drew her closer to him.

"Okay," Eric said softly. "Let's back up a minute. Tell me what happened after you saw him."

"I screamed. At least, I think I did. I spun around and ran for the front door. He grabbed me from behind, and I began to fight." She tilted her head up so she could see Trevor better. "I fought as hard as I could. I even got loose at one point."

Trevor's mouth tilted up a little as he began gently rubbing his hand up and down her arm for comfort.

"Tell me about that. How did you get loose, and what happened after?"

"I took advantage of being short and rammed my elbow back into his crotch as hard as I could."

Derek groaned and grimaced, and Eric's brows creased slightly at the thought. Pride filled Trevor's expression, which put her slightly at ease.

"The man's hold loosened and I managed to duck underneath his arm and slide out from his grasp."

"Smart," Eric nodded with approval.

"Yeah, except he was a lot faster than I was. He caught back up to me quickly and tackled me to the ground. Then, he flipped me over onto my back. He had my hands trapped above my head, and I wasn't strong enough to fight like before. I got desperate, so I spit in his face. I thought maybe he'd get distracted or something and I'd have a chance to get away. Instead, it just made him really mad. That's when he hit me."

Trevor's entire body tensed to the point she could actually feel his muscles tighten against hers. "He hit you?" he growled.

"That's how I got this." She let go of one corner of the blanket to touch her right cheek, wincing when she pushed against the tender skin a bit too hard.

A muscle in Trevor's handsome face bulged, and she knew he was clenching his teeth to hold back his anger. "I thought you got that from when we landed on the ground."

Unsure of what else to say, Lexi simply shook her head.

Eric cleared his throat, "What happened next, Lexi?"

She broke eye contact with Trevor and looked back at Eric. "Um, he yanked me to my feet and held me from behind. I remember thinking I was going to choke because he was almost lifting me clear off the ground and his arm was pressing against my throat. Then, Trevor burst through the door with his gun and yelled at the man to let me go."

"After that was when he threw you toward Trevor?"

"Yeah." She nodded. "Trevor told him several times to let me go, but the guy never even acted like he'd heard him. Then, all of a sudden, I went flying toward Trevor, and we both went through the window. The next thing I knew, Trevor was yelling my name, and the guy was gone. Then, Mrs. Siemens came over, and you guys showed up."

Eric looked around. "Where did your neighbor go?"

"Home." Lexi pointed to the house across the street. "She wanted to stay, but I finally convinced her to go back home where she'd be more comfortable. She's expecting a visit from you."

Eric closed his notepad and clicked his pen closed. Shoving both into his back pocket, he said, "I'll head over there now." He looked behind Lexi to her house. "I'm sure you're aware that your house is now a crime scene. I can escort you in to grab a few things, but you can't stay here tonight."

Lexi responded with a wry smile. "Well, given that I have no door or window anymore, I wouldn't want to stay here, anyway."

"Right." Eric smiled back.

"I can take her in to get her things if you want to go talk with the neighbor," Trevor offered.

"I guess that'd be all right," Eric agreed. "Thanks."

It was the first time she'd ever been afraid to go back into her mother's house. Stepping through the broken door was like walking right back into her attacker's arms. Large splinters of wood were scattered on the decorative welcome mat and floor just inside the door, and shards of glass covered the windowsill and the area beneath.

Large, jagged pieces of the window remained stuck in place, their pointed edges like large teeth surrounding the gaping hole their bodies had made. *It's a wonder we weren't sliced to bits.*

"Hey," Trevor rubbed his hand against her lower back. "I can do this while you wait outside."

My sweet, sweet hero. "I'm good." She swallowed hard. "I just didn't realize how hard it would be to come back in here and see all this."

She took a deep breath and forged on, Trevor following her as she made her way upstairs and to her bedroom. By the time they got back outside, Eric was back from across the street, and another man she didn't recognize was standing with him and Derek. All three men stopped talking at once and looked their direction.

The one she didn't know approached Trevor directly and slapped a hand to Trevor's shoulder. "Glad to see you're both okay."

"Thanks, man. You didn't have to come all this way, but I appreciate it."

"Of course I did."

"Olivia?" Trevor smirked.

The other man rubbed the dark scruff on his jaw. "She may have mentioned something about wanting me to check on you."

Trevor chuckled. "Well, I can see who'll be wearing the pants in your marriage."

"Only on some things, brother." Smiling, he turned to Lexi, then. His brilliant, blue eyes shining back at hers. "I'm

Jake. You must be Alexis."

"Lexi." She shook his hand tentatively."

"Lex, this is Jake McQueen. He owns R.I.S.C.."

"Oh," she said with understanding. "So, he's your boss."

"Well, he has to be somebody's, since his wife is clearly the boss at home."

"Funny, asshole," Jake narrowed his eyes at Derek.

"For once, I have to agree with my brother," Eric joined in on the razzing.

"Don't you have a job to do?" Jake spouted back.

All four men laughed. It was the first real smile she'd seen on Trevor's face tonight. Not that they'd had much to smile about.

In a more serious tone, Jake spoke to Trevor again. "You need anything?"

"Just to find the bastard who did this."

Jake gave him an understanding nod. "Derek said you already have someone who looks good for it. Robert Lockwood?"

Lexi let out a slight gasp. "You think it was Rob who did this?"

"You don't?" Trevor asked, sounding surprised.

"I…I don't know. I hadn't thought about it being him." Addressing Derek, she challenged, "You said he was in California."

"He was."

"And as far as we know"—Eric spoke up—"he still is."

"That would be a pretty big fuckin' coincidence," Derek offered his two cents. "Lockwood assaults her a few days ago, and then someone else just happens to break into her home tonight? I mean, no offense, Lex"—he glanced at her briefly, and then back to his brother—"but she'd have to have some pretty damn bad luck for that shit to happen."

Lexi didn't bother telling him that was *exactly* the kind of luck she had. She also noticed Derek hadn't bothered to censor himself the way he had at the diner the other day. Not that it bothered her in the least. She had a few curse words flying through her brain, too.

"Let's not forget her tire," Trevor reminded Eric.

"Tire?" Jake echoed.

"Someone purposely let the air out of one of my tires while I was at work last week," Lexi answered for Trevor. After all, it was her shitty luck they were discussing.

"I'm with Trev on this one, Eric," Jake said pointedly. "Sounds to me like someone has a personal beef with Lexi."

"I don't know." She shook her head. "I can't be sure, but I don't think he sounded like Rob."

Four sets of surprised, intense eyes shot to hers.

"He spoke to you?" Trevor asked. His tone became sharp as he began to interrogate her. "Did he sound like Lockwood? Was his voice familiar in any way? What exactly did he say, Lex?"

"Calm down, man," Jake suggested quietly. "Let the woman talk."

"Think hard, Lex," Trevor's low voice rumbled with the order. "What did he say…exactly?"

Lexi paused to think. "Um…he said something about me fighting him. 'I didn't expect you to be such a fighter.'" She looked directly at Trevor. "Those were his exact words. Then, he said something about how I needed to save my energy, because I was going to need it. I don't know." She shook her head. "I can't remember exactly how he worded that part, but it was something like that."

The testosterone level skyrocketed then, and Lexi could

have sworn all three men inched closer. Almost as if they were instinctively protecting her.

Jake and Trevor shared a look, as did the two brothers.

"You thinkin' what I'm thinkin'?" Derek asked Eric.

"This wasn't a simple robbery," the handsome detective answered honestly.

Lexi definitely didn't like the sound of that. "What does that mean?" she whispered to Trevor.

He looked down at her, his expression fierce and dangerous. "It means I'm not letting you out of my site until the sonofabitch is caught."

Chapter 10

For the second time in just a few days, Lexi found herself in the comfort and protection of Trevor's upscale apartment. Not because he'd simply wanted her there, but because someone had tried to hurt her. Possibly kill her.

As she stood beneath his shower's hot, running water, she wondered how her life had taken such a turn. On one hand, she'd met Trevor. A man who, for all intents and purposes, was perfect. A man she was falling for much faster than she had the right to. On the other, it seemed as though Rob was more of a threat than she'd ever imagined.

Shivering, even though she was far from cold, Lexi was finishing rinsing her hair when Trevor's voice traveled over the rush of the water.

"Lex?"

"Yeah?"

"You doing okay?"

Despite the night's events, she smiled. "Yeah. I'm almost finished."

"No rush, but I wanted to let you know, Jake's here with his wife."

That seemed odd. "Okay."

"She's a nurse, and she…she wanted to talk with you for a minute."

Lexi rolled her lips inward. She'd already been checked out and cleared by the paramedics on the scene, and after the night she'd had, she really didn't feel like being poked and prodded by another stranger.

She did her best not to sound irritated or ungrateful when she answered, "Okay. I'll be right out."

"Like I said, take your time."

Lexi waited until she heard the click of the door latch before blowing out a frustrated breath, then immediately felt bad. She knew Trevor meant well and should be thankful he cared enough to have his nurse friend stop by.

By the time she dried off and had thrown on some sweats and a t-shirt, she felt slightly less irritated. Steam billowed out around her as she opened the door and stepped into Trevor's bedroom. She jumped when someone knocked softly on the door.

A woman not much taller than her peaked her head in. "Lexi?" She smiled. "I'm Olivia. Trevor's friend. You mind if I come in?"

"Sure."

Olivia was beautiful. She had chestnut brown hair and beautiful hazel eyes. Dressed in jeans and a white t-shirt, Lexi noticed she also had a very kind smile. One that she was very familiar with.

Holy crap! Jake's married to Olivia Bradshaw!

The woman made her way around the foot of the bed and held out her hand. "It's nice to meet you."

"Alexis. But, you can call me Lexi," she added quickly, returning the gesture and shaking Olivia's hand.

"Hi, Lexi. I'm sorry we're meeting under these circumstances."

She sounded so nice and genuine in person. Having followed the story of her supposed death and then her miraculous rescue, Lexi knew this woman would understand her fears better than anyone else. Oddly, that helped her relax some.

"Yeah, it's been a crazy week, for sure."

Olivia smiled wider. "Sounds like it." She tilted her head toward the bed. "You want to sit and talk for a bit?"

"Okay." Lexi felt silly for being so scared about tonight after everything *this* woman had endured.

Sitting on the edge of the bed. Lexi clasped her hands nervously in her lap. She wasn't used to feeling this way, and wasn't quite sure how to handle it. Even during the worst times with her mom, she'd never felt as though she were weak…until tonight.

Before her mom died, Lexi had no doubt the faithful, God-fearing woman would be going to a better place once she left this earth. Lexi had also been confident enough to believe she'd be okay on her own. Before this past week, she had been.

It hadn't always been easy, but she'd kept herself afloat without anyone else's help. Now, after everything that had happened, she was beginning to doubt herself…and she hated it.

"I hope you aren't upset with Trevor for letting me come here," Olivia said softly. "I didn't really give him much of a choice." The other woman smiled.

"Really? Why?"

"I was with my husband when Derek called earlier. After Jake got home from your place, I called Trevor. When he told me more about you and what all had happened, I had to make sure you were both okay."

Lexi wasn't quite sure how she was supposed to respond to that, so she stayed quiet.

"Trevor's one of my husband's best friends. During the past two years, he's become one of mine, as well. He's like a second brother to me."

"Oh," Lexi said quietly. And because she felt like she was being deceitful, even though she really wasn't, she admitted, "I…I know who you are. I mean, I recognize you from when you were on the news a few months ago."

Olivia simply smiled. "I figured you did. People get a certain look in their eye when they figure out I'm *that* Olivia."

"I'm sorry. I didn't mean to…"

"Oh, no," Olivia interrupted her. "There's nothing to be sorry for. I just didn't want you feeling like you couldn't mention it or anything. It was a major event in my life, and even though it was beyond horrible, what happened to me brought Jake and I closer together. So, I try to focus on that," she said with a smile.

A few seconds of silence passed before Olivia laughed. "Well, now that the superbly awkward introductions have been made…Trevor told me you work in a diner, but hope to own your own restaurant someday."

"Someday, yeah." Lexi nodded, though she was beginning to accept that particular dream would never come true.

"Well, let's see. What should I tell you about myself that you don't already know? I'm a nurse…wait, you probably know that, right?" When Lexi nodded, Olivia went on to explain she no longer worked in the public hospital system. "I work at a private medical facility owned by Homeland Security now."

"Oh, wow. That sounds exciting."

Olivia shrugged a shoulder. "It is. Except when they bring in someone from Alpha Team. That's the one part of my husband's job I hate."

Lexi could understand that. She'd been on edge the entire time Trevor had been gone. "How do you deal with it. The fear of something happening to him while he's on an op?"

The other woman gave her a sad smile. "After everything I went through, I guess I learned that life is short for us all, no matter what our jobs are. I mean, don't get me wrong…I can't imagine my life without Jake. But, if something happened to him while he was away on a job, I'd like to think I could at least find comfort in knowing he died doing what he loved…helping those who need it most."

"Wow."

Olivia wrinkled her cute, button nose. "Too cheesy?"

Lexi chuckled. "Not at all. Actually, it's a great way to look at it." Biting her bottom lip, she started to ask something else, but wasn't quite sure how to word it. Apparently, she didn't hide her thoughts very well.

"It's okay, Lexi." Olivia rested her hand on Lexi's shoulder. "You can ask me anything. I'm pretty much an open book."

In that case…

"Do you know what their last job was?"

Olivia groaned. "Okay, so you can ask me anything but *that*."

"Oh," Lexi bit her lip again.

"Not because I don't want to tell you. It's because I can't. I have no idea what their last job was. Or most jobs, for that matter."

"Oh," she said again. "I figured since you were married..."

"Nope." Then the other woman rolled her eyes exaggeratedly and used air quotes when she said, "It's classified."

Lexi laughed. She could totally see Olivia as someone she could be good friends with.

Feeling more at ease than she had all night, Lexi said, "He just seemed a little different after he got the call to go, that's all." Lexi thought for a moment and then, "Okay, fine. You can't tell me about his job. What about his love life."

"Oh, that I would *totally* dish on...if the man had one. Of course, I guess he does, now...with you, I mean."

"So, it really has been a long time since he's dated someone?"

"As far as I know, you're the first woman he's dated since I met him. I know for a fact, you're the first woman he's cared enough about to introduce to the team."

"Well, I wouldn't say he actually introduced us because he *wanted* to. I met Derek when he came with Trevor to eat at the diner where I work. They've been coming there somewhat regularly, lately."

"Uh huh." Olivia looked at her knowingly. "And why do you think that is?"

Lexi thought for a moment, then blushed. "Oh."

"Yeah, *oh*."

"So, why is he still single?" Lexi's blurted question made Olivia laugh, but Lexi said, "I'm serious. The guy is drop dead gorgeous. He has a steady—albeit dangerous—well-paying job. He's funny and nice...what am I not seeing?"

Olivia grinned. "There's nothing wrong with Trevor. He's one of the sweetest, most caring men I've ever known." She patted Lexi's knee and zeroed in on her gaze. "Honestly." Then, Olivia inhaled deeply, her smile turning a bit sad. "His story's not mine to tell. All I can say is that he's ready to start a future with someone. And"—Olivia nudged Lexi's shoulder—"from the way it looked and sounded when he was telling me about you, *you're* that someone."

Lexi wasn't quite sure why, but she found herself wanting Olivia to know she felt the same for the man who was her friend. "I like him a lot, too. More than a lot, actually."

The other woman smiled wide. "I wish we could have met before tonight. Of course, I didn't really find out about you until tonight. Still want to choke out that husband of mine for keeping me in the dark."

Lexi chuckled. "Well, with the shitstorm that's been my life lately, we haven't really had a chance for introductions before now. Or to even go out on a real date yet."

Olivia smiled sadly. "I'm sorry you've been having such a hard time. I can honestly say I understand exactly what you're going through."

"Oh, I can't even compare my situation to yours. What that man did to you was…I can't even think of a word bad enough to describe it."

"Thanks. Someday, I'll tell you about what happened after I came home." When Lexi's brows turned inward with confusion, she said, "That part didn't make the news."

"How did you cope…after."

"Honestly, it was hard at first. And you should be prepared, just in case. This is a close-knit area, and what happened tonight is probably already on the news. Luckily, yours won't make the national news like mine did. That was a nightmare in and of itself," Olivia shook her head. "But, you could have reporters approach you, so just be aware of that.

Although, with Trevor by your side, I doubt it will be an issue for you."

"What do you mean?"

"R.I.S.C.'s Alpha Team guys are all the same. They may have the hearts of saints, but they're all a bunch of overprotective bulls when it comes to keeping their women safe. I don't see Trevor letting anyone you don't know getting within ten feet of you."

Lexi started to deny the claim that she was Trevor's woman, but Olivia wouldn't let her.

"Don't bother, sweetie. I saw the way he looked when he was talking to me about you before I came in here. Trust me. I know that man well, and if there's one thing you can believe, it's that his heart already belongs to you."

Swallowing hard, Lexi blinked against the rush of emotions Olivia's words brought forth. She knew how she felt about Trevor, but had been wondering if he felt the same. She prayed Olivia was right.

"Also, don't be afraid to lean on Trevor…or me, for that matter…if you need us. Being attacked like that, twice, would make anyone nervous and jumpy. If you start to feel scared or overwhelmed, talk to Trev. He's a great listener. Or, you can call me. I'll use any excuse to go out for a good cup of coffee and some girl time." Olivia smiled.

After talking for a few minutes longer, the two women had just started for the bedroom door when there was a quick knock and then it opened. Trevor peaked his head inside.

"You two doing okay?"

Olivia grinned over her shoulder at Lexi before reaching for the doorknob and opening it the rest of the way. "Yes, Trevor. I'm fine and so is your girl, here."

"Yeah?" he asked, sounding genuinely relieved. He looked to Lexi.

"I told you before. I'm all right."

His broad shoulders relaxed and he smiled that handsome smile. "Good."

How can I be mad at him for caring so much?

Olivia looked at Trevor, then to Lexi, then back at Trevor. "All right, then. I'd say my job here is done." She gave Lexi a hug, telling her Trevor had her number. Her new friend made her promise to call if she needed anything. Then, going to her tiptoes, she gave Trevor a kiss on the cheek and a hug.

"I'm glad you're okay, too."

"I'm fine, Liv. Thanks for coming by."

"Anytime."

"Your hubby's waiting for you in the living room."

Lexi couldn't help but notice how Olivia's smile grew from hearing that. The love she felt for Jake was inspiring.

Once those two were gone, it was just Trevor and Lexi, once again.

Trevor took a tentative step toward her. "I hope you aren't too upset that she came over. I know I probably should have asked you first, but she called, and you were in the shower…"

"It's fine, Trevor. Really."

He didn't come any closer, which she found disappointing. He'd been different with her since the attack. Distant.

Lexi moved closer to him. "Are you okay? You took the brunt of the fall."

"I'm good. Just pissed that the guy got away." He lifted his hand slowly, as if he were afraid to touch her. His fingertips lightly caressed the sore spot on her cheek. "Pissed that you were hurt again. I'm so sorry, Lex."

"For what? You saved my life."

"You were hurt because I wasn't here to protect you. I should have been here, with you…not chasing some damn ghost—" He cut himself off, the look on his face telling her he'd almost said too much.

"You're not the reason I was attacked, Trevor. You're the reason I'm still alive. I don't even want to think about what would have happened if you hadn't shown up when you did."

His eyes bore into hers. "There's something else I want to talk about. I was going to wait, but after tonight, I realized I needed to say it…before I miss my chance."

"Okay." Lexi waited nervously. No good conversation ever started out that way.

"I don't want to see anyone else. I know we haven't really set any ground rules for this thing between us, but I want us to be exclusive."

Lexi exhaled; relieved to hear that's what he wanted to discuss. "I want the same thing. I don't date more than one person at a time, Trevor. I never have. That's just how I am."

Trevor looked deep into Lexi's eyes. "Good." He stepped a bit closer. "You're all I thought about on the plane ride home."

Butterflies danced around inside her. "I didn't stop thinking about you the entire time you were gone."

His perfect mouth tilted up at both corners. "I'm glad we got that settled." Trevor leaned down and gave her a soft, sweet kiss. Lexi wanted more, and she could swear he did, too. But his eyes slid to her bruise, and he suddenly pulled back before she could even try to do more.

In an almost startled manner, he turned and began walking down the hallway. "Are you hungry? I can fix us something or order in."

"I-I'm really not that hungry," she said, her short legs

trying to catch up to him. Why was he walking away so quickly?

She followed him into the kitchen where he went to the fridge and pulled out a couple bottles of water. Handing her one, he then went to a cabinet and pulled out a bottle of ibuprofen. Opening the lid, he dropped two pills into his palm and handed her those, as well.

"Here. These will help with your sore muscles."

"Thanks," she muttered, taking the pills from him. Using the water he'd just given her, she swallowed them quickly. "I really don't feel too badly, though."

"You might later. Hopefully, those will help head it off at the pass."

Lexi nodded. "I'll probably take some before I go into work tomorrow, too. Just in case."

Trevor looked at her as if she'd suddenly grown six heads. "Work? You're not going to work tomorrow."

"Um, yes…I am. I work the early shift tomorrow."

"Well, call Joe and tell him you can't come in. Better yet, give me his number, and I'll talk to him. I know he'll understand if I—"

Now, it was her turn to look at him as if he'd lost a few marbles. "You're not calling Joe, and neither am I."

Setting his water bottle down onto the kitchen counter, Trevor looked at her pointedly and said, "One of us is calling him, because you're not working while this guy's still running loose. End of discussion."

Then, as though he'd just declared Marshall Law, Trevor stepped around her and walked into the living room.

End of discussion? Oh, I don't think so, mister.

Following him, Lexi decided to let him know exactly what she thought about his little plan. "That most definitely is *not* the end of this discussion. I can't just call in, Trevor. I have responsibilities."

"Yeah?" He turned around to face her. "So do I. It's called keeping you alive."

Lexi rolled her eyes. "It's not like I'll be walking down some dark alley by myself at night. I'll be at the diner surrounded by people the entire time I'm there."

Trevor rested his hands on his hips, and she should *not* be thinking about how sexy and powerful he looked. Not when she was so mad at him.

"Lockwood has escalated, Alexis. Do you understand what that means?"

Okay, now that was just insulting. "Of course, I do. I'm not stupid, Trevor."

He closed his eyes and drew in a deep breath. "I'm sorry, Lex. I'm not trying to imply that you are. It's just...with guys like this, once they start taking things to the next level, they usually keep going until they get what they want. Even if that means attacking in broad daylight while surrounded by witnesses."

"I understand what you're saying, Trevor. I really do."

Shaking his head, he shocked her by saying, "I don't think you do."

"Excuse me?"

"I do this for a living, Alexis. I know guys like Lockwood."

She threw her hands in the air, her voice raising an octave. "You keep saying his name, but we don't even know for sure it was *him!*"

"It doesn't matter!" Trevor's voice boomed through his apartment, making Lexi jump. Lexi turned away and started for the bedroom when he pleaded with her. "Angel, wait. Just listen to me for a minute. Please."

Damn it. Turning back around, she couldn't help but sound snippy when she asked, "What?"

"I don't know what you know about Olivia, but..."

"I know who she is and what was shared in the news," she interrupted. In a bit calmer voice, she added, "Olivia said something happened to her after she was rescued and came back home. She told me she'd share the rest of the story with me someday."

Trevor nodded. "Olivia and I are good friends, and I know she'd be okay with me sharing a little of that story with you now. Especially if it helped convince you I'm right about this."

Biting her tongue, Lexi waited for him to say whatever it was he thought he needed to say.

"Liv's nightmare followed her home. Long story short, the man who originally abducted her wanted revenge for something that wasn't her fault. He got someone else to try to abduct her...from the hospital where she worked. During the day."

"Oh, my God."

"Now, do you see?"

"Well..." Lexi thought for a moment. "I'm truly sorry for what Olivia went through. I can't even imagine, but Trevor...I *have* to work. I don't have a choice."

"Yes, you do."

"No, I don't. Now, *you're* the one who doesn't understand. The electric company doesn't care whether or not someone's trying to kill me. I have bills I have to pay, and unlike you, I don't have a ton of money stashed away that I can use to live off of until he's caught."

Understanding crossed over his face. His voice softened.

"I'll take care of your bills, Lex."

Getting more frustrated by the minute, Lexi nearly shouted, "I am not going to let you pay my bills, Trevor. I get that you're trying to help, but I am perfectly capable of taking care of my responsibilities."

"Is that why you had a spare ready to go when your other tire was flattened? Because you can take care of yourself?" His sarcastic tone pushed her over the edge.

Fuming, Lexi looked him straight in the eye and said, "Go to hell."

"Damn it, Alexis." He ran a frustrated hand through his gorgeous hair. "If you'd just stop being stubborn for one second and listen to what I'm trying to say, you'd see that I am trying to help you."

"Oh, I heard you loud and clear. Poor little waitress Lexi. Her mom died, she had to give up her dream, and now she can't even afford to take time off work to save herself from some psycho with an ego problem. I get all that, but you know what, Trevor? This isn't just about me. I can't just call Joe and tell him I'm never coming back in. I won't leave him high and dry like that. Not after everything he's done for me."

"Joe can take care of himself."

Lexi gave Trevor a sad smile. "But I can't. That's what you're saying, right? Well, at least your true feelings about me have finally hit the surface."

She turned and stomped down the hallway to the bedroom. She knew Trevor was following her, but that didn't stop her from going in and grabbing her suitcase. She threw it onto the bed and hastily unzipped it.

"It's my own fault, really. I should've known you were too good to be true." And damn, if a tear didn't fall down over her cheek. She swiped it away angrily and picked up the few toiletries she'd brought from the bathroom sink.

"Lexi?" Trevor sounded damn near panicked. "Angel, what are you doing?"

"I'm going to a hotel," she dumped the items into the bag without caring how they landed.

"No, you're not."

She spun around on him. "See? That. *That* right there is the problem. You think you can just order me around without any consideration for *my* feelings. I'm not some client you took on, Trevor. I'm supposed to be someone you care about. Tonight you said you were my boyfriend, but for the past fifteen minutes, you've suddenly started acting more like my boss."

"Because I'm trying to keep you *safe*," he gritted through his perfect teeth.

"You know, sleeping with me one time doesn't give you the right to tell me what I can and cannot do." She paused to take in a deep breath and to try to calm down. She needed to understand how this sweet, gentle man had become so different in a matter of minutes. "Why are you being like this?" she asked quietly.

"Are you kidding me? You were just attacked. We went through a fucking *window*. You could have been killed or worse, and…" He swallowed hard, his voice lowering. "We just found each other, Lex and I can't…I can't lose you, too."

As if suddenly realizing what he'd said, Trevor stopped talking and broke eye contact. The haunted look that came over him terrified her.

"W-who did you lose?"

Trevor blinked and raised his gaze back to hers. "What?"

"Who was she?"

He shook his head and blinked some more. "I…uh…I don't…"

Desperate to understand, Lexi swallowed down the last bit of her anger and whispered, "Please, Trevor. Talk to me."

****

Trevor knew better than to push Lexi the way he had. He never should have ordered her away from working. And, God, the way he'd just talked to her…his mother would be so ashamed. *He* was ashamed.

But he'd panicked. The thought of her going back to work while that bastard was still out here, knowing he could get to her again, had sent a bolt of fear through his system unlike any he'd ever known.

She'd been trying to explain why it was so important for her to continue working, but he hadn't listened. His innate, desperate need to keep her safe had taken over, and he'd acted like a total ass because of it.

He wouldn't have blamed her if she had walked out and never talked to him again. Thankfully, she was still here, those baby blue eyes pleading with him to open up and give her his soul.

Trevor didn't want to tell her. He never wanted Lexi to be touched by his sinful past. He realized now, if he wanted any chance at a future with her, he had to.

Swallowing past the giant lump in his throat, Trevor looked at her and said, "I was Delta Force. I don't know if I ever told you that."

"No," she answered softly. "You told me you were former military, but I had no idea you were special ops."

For some reason, the fact that she knew Delta was spec

ops made him smile. It quickly faded, however, as he continued telling her the one thing he never wanted her to know.

"Several years ago, my Delta team was on an op that went bad."

"You lost someone from your team?"

"Two men…and one woman."

Understanding mixed with her unshed tears. "I'm so sorry."

Trevor cleared his throat. "She and I…" he paused. "It was casual. We cared about each other, but it wasn't like…"

"Us?" she finished for him.

He nodded. "We were friends. Some days…" he paused again, not comfortable discussing this part with Lexi. "Some days, we were more."

"It's okay, Trevor," Lexi offered sincerely. "I know you had a life before we met. I'm glad you had someone you cared about during that time."

"I did care about her."

Lexi gave a little smile. "I can tell. What was her name?"

What was he doing? She didn't need to hear all this. "Lexi, I don't think—"

"If you want me to understand this sudden and fierce need to protect me, then I need to hear more from you than just an order of what I can or cannot do. I need you to *talk* to me, Trevor. Please"—she closed the distance between them and put her hand on his arm—"let me in."

There was no way he could deny her anything when she looked at him the way she was in that very moment. "Lisa. Her name was Lisa. She was a CIA liaison assigned to our group for a specific objective."

"What happened?"

"We got played. Her asset double-crossed the team, and we walked right into a trap. Lisa was taken. They tortured her before they killed her."

"God. That's awful."

"It was my fault, Lex. I made the call that day, and she and those two men were killed because of it. I didn't trust the asset, but Lisa did. I let her talk me into listening to him and going ahead with the plan."

"And because you feel responsible for what happened to her, you're afraid to let me out of your sight for fear of something happening to me."

Her words gave him more relief than he'd ever imagined they could. Not only did she actually seem to understand, she wasn't looking at him with disgust as he'd feared.

Trevor was already half-way there, but in that exact moment, he fell the rest of the way in love with her.

Lexi bit her bottom lip nervously. "I know you can't tell me any details, but…did this last job have something to do with what happened to Lisa and your teammates?"

Her question surprised him. "The details are classified, but yeah. The two were related."

"Your tattoo…you got it for them, didn't you? Two dog tags for the teammates you lost and…"

"The sword down the middle for Lisa," he finished her thought quietly, not at all surprised she'd figured out his tat was related to what happened. "She wasn't military, but she was every bit as much of a warrior as the men we lost. So, instead of the dog tags, I gave her the sword."

"That was really sweet. I'm sure they all would have loved it." Trevor nodded in response, waiting quietly as she thought for a moment. Then, Lexi looked up at him and smiled. "Okay, so how about this. What if we compromise?"

That same panic started to set in, but this time he didn't let it control him. "Lexi..."

She put one of her tiny hands to his chest. "Just hear me out. What if I agree to stay at your place for a week. That will be plenty of time for my window and door to get fixed, and show you and everyone else I just have fantastically crappy luck, and tonight really was just a random home invasion."

Trevor narrowed his eyes at her. "What's the rest of this negotiation?"

She grinned. "I still get to go to work."

He opened his mouth to argue, but she cut him off. "That part is non-negotiable. I've worked my ass off to keep my independence, and whether you like it or not, I can't always rely on you for everything. I need to make my own way. At least for now. Plus, Joe's like family to me. I can't just up and quit on him."

With both hands, Trevor began slowly rubbing up and down her arms. "I hear what you're saying, Lex. I really do. But, surely Joe can find someone to cover your shifts for the next few days. If it makes you feel better, I can lend you the money you'd be making and you can pay me back. With interest."

In a surprise move, Lexi moved back and stepped out of his reach. Crossing her arms in front, she came back with, "I'll stay here for two weeks, and I still work."

Despite his warring emotions, one corner of Trevor's mouth lifted. "You drive a hard bargain, Miss Hamilton."

She raised a brow, looking too damn cute for her own good. "So, you agree to my terms of the deal?

He broke into a full smile then and began slowly walking toward her. Resting his hands low on her hips, he said, "Counter offer."

She raised a brow. "I'm listening."

"You stay with me for two weeks, work your scheduled shifts, but I drive you to and from work every day. And you do not, under any circumstances, go outside the diner while you're at work. No exceptions."

He held his breath as she considered his request. He was sure she was going to agree, but then the skin between her brows crinkled together, and she asked, "What about your schedule? I don't want my mess to interfere with your job. It's too important, and—"

Trevor stopped her with a finger to her lips. "Baby, *you* are my job."

"But," her protest was muffled by his finger.

"No buts. As of now, you're officially under R.I.S.C.'s protection."

Her eyes widened, and she started to shake her head. Good thing he was ready for it. "And before you say anything, Jake takes on a few pro-bono cases every year. He already agreed to give me as much time as I needed to watch over you until we figure this whole thing out."

She reached up and grabbed his wrist, pulling his hand away from her mouth so she could talk. "There has to be more important things you could be doing for R.I.S.C. than this."

Cupping the uninjured side of her face, Trevor locked his eyes with hers. "There's nothing more important to me than you. Nothing." He leaned down and kissed her slowly then pulled away. "That's *my* deal. Take it or leave it."

She pretended to pout. "You kissed me. That's cheating."

"Never claimed to play fair, angel."

She smiled and wrapped her arms around his waist. "Well, I guess there could be worse things than having this body guarding mine."

A sense of relief flooded him. "Thank you, angel. For understanding."

She rose up and pressed her lips to his. "Thank *you*."

"For what?"

"Letting me in."

Trevor's heart swelled with emotion. He reached down and brought her right hand to his chest, just above his heart. "You've been in, baby. Right here, from the moment I first saw you."

He didn't say the words yet. Instead, he spent the night using his hands, his lips, his body to convey how he felt. He didn't care that they'd only started seeing each other. It was right. *She* was right. She was everything.

Chapter 11

Five days later…

"I was going to ask how things are going with you and Lexi, but the way you've been wearing that goofy grin all day pretty much sums it up."

Trevor pulled his attention from the file in his hands to the man sitting behind the large desk. "Pretty much." He smirked, not even bothering to hide how happy he was.

The past few days with Lex had been great. Yeah, it sucked that she was staying at his place because Lockwood hadn't been caught yet, but they'd used the time to get to know each other even more.

It was almost scary how much they actually had in common. They shared the same taste in almost everything…music, movies, books. She even told him she'd always wanted to learn how to shoot a gun.

She was off tomorrow, so he'd planned a little surprise for her. First, he was going to take her out to a nice lunch, then to Jake's ranch. They'd spend the afternoon at the private shooting range there and then go for a ride on Jake's horses.

Olivia and Jake already had things planned so there'd be a

picnic waiting for them on one of the hills overlooking the horizon. It would be their first formal date…and the day he finally told her how he really felt.

"There's that damn grin, again."

Trevor blinked and found Jake staring back at him with a wide, knowing smile. He cleared his throat. "I thought we were supposed to be picking the guys for our new R.I.S.C. team, not sitting around gabbing like a bunch of girls."

"Come on, Trev. Throw me a fucking bone, here. Olivia's chompin' at the bit to find out more. She swears you're planning to propose tomorrow. She thinks that's the reason for the all-day date ending in a romantic picnic at sunset."

"I planned to do all that stuff with her tomorrow because she's worked the past two days. Plus, with all the shit that's been going on, she and I haven't had the chance to really go out as a couple." Jake gave him an understanding look. "And what, you get married and suddenly you have to start gathering intel to take back to your wife?"

Jake shrugged, unashamed. "What can I say? I bring home the goods on you and your girl, and she…delivers payment."

"I get it." Trevor put up a hand. "Olivia's like a sister to me, so please…spare me the details. Speaking of your wife, any word from Mike?"

Mike Bradshaw, Olivia's brother, had recently ended a ten-year stint doing deep undercover work. He came back for Jake and Olivia's wedding, but Trevor hadn't seen or heard from him since.

"He calls Liv about once a week. Doesn't want her thinking he's gone under again." Trevor inhaled deeply. "I was hoping to convince him to be Bravo Team's leader, once we figure out which of these guys we want."

"But?"

Jake shrugged. "Says he's not ready. Can't say I blame him. The guy's more than earned some downtime. Anyway"—Jake closed the file in front of him—"all joking aside, I'm happy for you, man. Lexi seems great. And you"—he gave Trevor an assessing look—"well, you seem happier than I think I've ever seen you. 'Course, it's amazing what having the right woman in your life can do for you."

Just then, Derek came sauntering in. "Geez, I can practically feel my ovaries growin' from all the estrogen in this room."

Jake laughed. "I thought you left."

D shook his head, "Nah, I was checkin' on a possible lead on Lockwood." Then, too serious for Trevor's liking, he added, "You're not gonna like what I found."

This had both men sitting up straight. Trevor's heart beat a little faster than before. "What is it? Did you find him?"

"I did, but..."

"Well, where is he? Did he get picked up?"

"In a manner of speakin', yes. He's currently a patient at a hospital in San Diego. Turns out he didn't take the whole don't drink and drive thing too seriously."

"He was in a wreck?" Trevor asked.

Derek handed Trevor a printout of the accident report. "Single vehicle crash off highway one sixty-three."

"Did you alert the authorities on the charges here?" Jake asked.

"They would've popped up when they ran him. But, Trevor, listen—"

Trevor ran a hand through his hair and sighed loudly. "Thank God. Lexi will be so relieved." He turned to Jake and tilted his chin to the folders on Jake's desk. "Can we finish this later? I want to go to the diner and let her know he's no longer a threat."

"That's what I'm trying to tell you, man." Derek was getting agitated. "Robert Lockwood never was the threat."

The relief Trevor felt quickly began to vanish. "What? What the hell do you mean? He attacked her."

"At the grocery store, sure. But Trev, Lockwood wrecked his car seven days ago. He's been in a coma ever since. He's on life support, and according to the doc's notes, they're not expecting him to wake up anytime soon…if ever."

The realization of his friend's words began to set in. "If he's been in the hospital for the last week, then…"

"He wasn't the one in Lexi's house," Jake finished the terrifying thought.

Fear and worry churned in his gut. "I have to go."

Practically ran from Jake's office, Trevor had just made it to R.I.S.C.'s reception area when Derek came running down the hall, shouting for him to stop.

"Trevor, wait!"

Irritated, Trevor turned and saw both Derek and Jake running toward him. "I *can't* wait. I need to get to her, D. If Lockwood isn't our guy, then someone else is after her. He could be anyone. I need to get to the diner. Now."

He reached for the door, but Derek's next words stopped him cold. "The diner's gonna be gone before you get there."

"What?" That made no sense. "What the hell are you talking about?"

"My brother's on the phone." Derek tapped the screen. "Eric, I've got you on speaker. Trevor's with me. Repeat what you just told me."

Eric West's voice came through the phone, along with the sound of a nearby siren. "Fire and EMS were dispatched to Joe's fifteen minutes ago. Someone set the place on fire, man.

I'm on my way there now."

A lightning bolt of shock went straight through Trevor's system. "Lexi," he whispered, not even realizing he'd said it out loud.

With a hand on his shoulder, Derek said, "Come on, brother. I'll drive you there."

After what felt like hours later, Trevor, Derek, and Jake pulled into the diner's parking lot. Trevor didn't wait for Derek's car to come to a complete stop before he jumped out the passenger side and started running toward the burning building.

"Lexi!"

He screamed her name as loudly as he could, but his voice was swallowed by the whooshing of the flames and the fire trucks' powerful hoses. That didn't stop him from yelling for her again.

A uniformed officer who looked about twenty put herself directly in Trevor's path. "I'm sorry, sir. You can't be here."

Trevor was about two seconds away from laying the kid out flat. He side-stepped the young woman and kept walking.

Moving surprisingly fast, the officer stepped back around Trevor, blocking his way once more.

"Sir, I'm going to have to insist that you turn around and leave immediately."

"My girlfriend works here. I need to see her. I need to know she's okay." Trevor's eyes scanned the scene, but he didn't see her anywhere. This time, he nearly pushed the officer out of his way.

"*Alexis!*" he screamed again.

"That's it," the officer started to take out her cuffs when Eric West walked up and quickly defused the situation.

"It's all right, Hirtler. They're with me." The woman

looked confused, but nodded and took a step back.

Trevor hadn't even realized Derek and Jake had caught up to him, until then. His entire focus was on finding Lexi.

To Trevor, Eric said, "You've got to calm your shit right now, or I'll let Officer Hirtler toss your ass in jail for interfering. You got it?"

Rather than respond, Trevor looked at what was left of Joe's. There was nothing more than a shell of a building, and the flames were nowhere near finished with it yet.

"She's here, Eric. She was working tonight. I was getting ready to come pick her up when you called Derek."

"She's not here, Trev."

His eyes shot to Eric's. "Then, where is she?" He remembered the ambulance they'd passed on the highway. It had been heading the opposite direction as they were…toward the hospital. *Oh, God.* "Was she hurt? Was that her in the ambulance?"

"Listen to me," Eric spoke slowly, as if he were talking to a child. It made Trevor want to punch him in the throat. "Lexi isn't here. The ambulance you saw was transporting the diner's owner to the hospital."

"Joe?" Ah, hell. Lexi was going to be devastated if Joe had been seriously injured.

Eric nodded. "He was the only one found inside the diner when fire and EMS got here. He wasn't burned badly, but he'd inhaled a lot of smoke and wasn't breathing when they got to him."

Trevor's eyes found the flames again. "You're sure she wasn't in there? Tell me you're sure, Eric. Tell me Lexi's not in there somewhere."

"She was the first one I asked about when I arrived on scene. There was no one else in the diner, Trevor. The place isn't that big, and the guys assured me they looked everywhere. Joe was alone."

His head felt like it was spinning. Part of him was relieved beyond words, but the other part…

"If she wasn't in there at the time of the fire, then"—he looked around the lot again—"where is she?"

Eric's eyes slid to the other two men, then back to Trevor. With gut-wrenching sympathy shining in his blue eyes, Derek's brother said, "We don't know."

****

Lexi woke with a piercing headache and something sticky on the side of her face. She was weak and disoriented, but for the life of her, she couldn't figure out why.

As she opened her eyes slowly and looked around the unfamiliar room, she began to remember what happened. Part of her wished she hadn't.

She'd been at the diner. They'd just closed, and she and Joe were finishing the cleanup. Lexi was filling the napkin holders in all the booths while Joe took the trash out back. She remembered walking back into the kitchen and screaming Joe's name when she saw him lying motionless on the floor.

Lexi had just started toward him when a blinding pain exploded in the side of her head. Now, she was here, in this empty, industrial-looking room. A warehouse. Lexi wasn't sure how, but she knew she was in some sort of warehouse.

There was a whole section of new ones being remodeled off the highway just a few miles south of the diner. Maybe this was one of those? But she had no idea which one or how she'd gotten here. Even worse was the fact that no one else knew, either.

A tear slid down her cheek, but she ignored it. She had to focus on finding a way to get out of here. Still in a fog, Lexi tried to stand up to go look for him, realizing then she was bound to the wooden chair she was sitting in. Heavy rope kept her wrists and ankles in place.

Panic set in to the point she nearly hyperventilated. Though, it was useless, she worked as hard as she could to get her arms loose. The only thing she managed to accomplish was cutting her wrists to shreds.

She had to get out of here, but how? Even knowing the results would be the same, Lexi's survival instincts had her fighting against the ropes again. She began to think if she bled enough, she'd be able to slip at least one hand out and get free.

Ignoring the biting pain in her wrists and the throbbing in her head, she spent the next few minutes working on the only plan she could think of. Her blood had begun to drip onto the concrete floor beneath her.

Another thought rolled through her mind. One that left her utterly defeated. She was going to die here. Alone and afraid. The worst part of it all was knowing she'd never see Trevor again.

Trevor. His handsome face flashed through her mind. She thought of last night and the tender, loving way he'd made love to her. Just as he'd done every night since her latest attack.

A hysterical bubble of a laugh escaped before she could stop it. A month ago, her life was boring. Predictable. Then, she met Trevor, and a new and wonderful part of her life began to blossom. Unfortunately, so did an unprecedented amount of danger. *See? Fantastically crappy luck.*

No. She was *not* giving up. Lexi had always seen herself as a fighter and damn it, she was going to fight now. Pushing past the pain, she kept on with the ropes, concentrating only on her right hand. If she could get it loose, she could use it to untie her left, then she could free her ankles and get the hell out of here.

The rope had just started to feel a little looser when the metal door to the room slowly opened. The face on the other side was one she'd seen before, but it wasn't the one she'd been expecting.

Trevor had been certain Rob was the man they'd been after all along. She didn't think he'd go to such extreme measures, and had told Trevor as much. This was one time she hated being right.

If it had been Rob, she may have been able to talk to him. Get him to come to his senses and let her go. She had no freaking clue who this guy was. Just that he'd been a customer of hers a few times the last couple weeks. For some reason, that terrified her even more.

The man was shorter than Trevor's six-four frame. If Lexi had to guess, she'd say he was about five-ten, five-eleven. He wore all black, just as he had the night he broke into her house, except he wasn't wearing the stocking cap.

That couldn't be good. She'd seen enough crime shows to know if the kidnapper let you see their face, they weren't likely planning to let you go.

Funny, he didn't look like what she'd picture a kidnapper to look like. He was actually quite handsome. Gina had even commented on him the first time he came in, and Lexi had actually encouraged her to try to get his number. Thankfully for Gina's sake, the man had shown no interest.

His hair was a lighter brown, his eyes dark like Trevor's. He was clean-shaven, and his features were almost perfectly symmetrical, making him appear more attractive than most.

She remained quiet until he smiled slowly. The look in his eyes was one of madness, which only added to the fear threatening to overtake her.

"You're awake," he said calmly. "Good. We can get started."

Trying not to throw up, Lexi stuttered out, "W-who are y-you. W-what d-do you w-want?"

The man laughed. "What do I want? That's a very good question, Alexis."

"You've been in the diner. That's how you know my name." She was proud that her voice came out a little stronger that time.

"Oh, I know a lot about you, Alexis Ranae Hamilton. The only child of Tarrie Ranae Hamilton. You were an aspiring chef until your mother died, and you had to give up that dream."

Oh, God. She really was going to be sick. "H-how do you know about that?"

"I know *everything!*" Spittle went flying from his mouth as he yelled. "Including the fact that some sins can never be forgiven."

Lexi's mind whirled with thoughts and questions. Who was this guy? What did he want with her? Was he some psycho obsessed with her, or was there more to it?

"W-what did you do to Joe?"

The look of sympathy the man gave her was clearly not genuine. "I'm sorry. Good 'ole Joe didn't make it."

Tears filled her eyes instantly. "You k-killed him?"

"Me? Nah." The man shook his head. "But, I'm sure the fire I set did."

Fire? Oh, God. Poor Joe. Tears slid down both cheeks as

Lexi's chest began to heave to the rhythm of her rapid breaths. "Tell me what you want," she blurted out. "Tell me what you need and…m-maybe…maybe I can help you."

The man laughed, his demeanor changing on a dime. "Oh, don't worry. You're already helping me."

He walked closer to her then, stopping just before he reached the chair. With a shockingly gentle touch, he swiped some hair from her face. Lexi tried to move away from him, but it was impossible given the way she was bound.

"It's time he finally learned what it feels like."

"Who? What are you talking about?"

"You'll find out soon enough."

Lexi opened her mouth to ask something else. She wasn't sure what, but if she could keep him talking, she thought maybe she could buy herself some time to think of a way out of this mess. She never got the chance.

Before she could even make a sound, the same hand that had been so gentle just seconds earlier flew toward her face. The blow snapped her head to the side, and she immediately tasted blood.

If she thought her head hurt before, that was nothing compared to now. "P-please," she started to beg, but it was too late.

The man was on a mission. Apparently his goal was to beat her until she lost consciousness again. Mission accomplished.

****

"Try her phone again."

The other members of the team looked up at him, but no one moved. Grant Hill stood stoically behind the couch, looking over D's shoulder as he typed away on his fancy-assed keyboard. Mac and Coop had each taken a seat in the two recliners Trevor had, and Jake was coming back in from filling his coffee mug for the third time in the past two hours.

The moment they realized Lexi was missing, Jake had called the others in. He'd suggested they set everything up at the office, but Trevor had insisted on coming back here, to his apartment.

For the past few days, this had been Lexi's home. He knew it was a long shot, but if she somehow managed to escape from whoever had taken her, he wanted to be here, just in case.

"I said, try her phone again."

Sitting on Trevor's couch with the coffee table pulled in closely, Derek glanced at the three monitors he'd been using to try and track her down. "Her phone's off. Like I told you before, I can't get a signal if it's not—"

Out of patience, Trevor yelled, "Try the fucking phone again!"

Everyone in the room remained silent. Everyone except Jake.

"I know you're upset, Trevor. Trust me, I get it. But you need to try to stay calm."

Trevor looked at his friend as if he'd lost his damn mind. "Are you serious right now? *You're* telling me to be calm? What, like you were when Liv was taken?" His friend flinched. Trevor knew it was a low blow, but he couldn't seem to stop himself. "It's been over five hours, Jake. You know what can happen in that time."

"Yes, but we don't know anything yet."

"Oh, we know plenty. We know someone besides Robert Lockwood tried to abduct Lexi from her house the other night, and that same bastard has her now. We know whoever it is burned the fucking diner down to the ground, nearly killing Joe in the process. We know I was so stuck on the fact that Lockwood was our guy, this whole time, I didn't open my fucking eyes to the possibility that it could be someone else. She's out there somewhere right now, waiting for me to find her, except I can't, because I don't have a fucking clue where to start. So don't stand there and tell me to calm down!" By the time he was done, Trevor was yelling at the top of his lungs, his voice echoing off his apartment walls.

"We all thought it was Lockwood, Trev," Derek jumped in.

"He's right," Coop agreed. "I know I haven't been as active with this whole thing as Derek, but he and Jake have kept Mac, Grant, and I updated with what's been going on. With the way he acted toward her at the diner, then the flat tire, and what happened at the grocery store that night, it seemed like a logical conclusion to make. We were all on the same page as you with this one, Trevor. We all missed it."

"Yeah? Well I'm the one who was supposed to protect her. I'm the one who let this guy come in right under my nose and take her away from me. I'm the one who never told her…" He stopped himself short.

Without another word, he spun on his heels and flung open the sliding door leading to his private balcony. He then slammed it shut with such force, he was surprised the glass didn't shatter.

Trevor walked over to the balcony's railing and squeezed it between both fists. Despite his angry words just now, he locked his elbows and did his best to calm his racing heart. Inhaling through his nose, he blew out a slow, steady breath and tried to think of anything he'd missed. Something that would give a hint at who had taken Lexi.

Instead, he was flooded with images of her smiling face. He pictured her at the diner, smiling as she took someone's order. He saw her laughing in his kitchen as he stole her bacon, then carried her into his room and made love to her that first time. Trevor pictured her beneath him…moaning and flushed with arousal. Lost in a passion unlike any he'd ever known.

He loved her. Right or wrong, too soon or not…Trevor loved her. And now she was gone, ripped from his hands before he ever got the chance to tell her.

Ah, God. Hanging his head between his shoulders, he squeezed his eyes shut. Two streaks of tears running down his face. He was still standing like that when he heard the door sliding open and then shutting from behind him.

Quickly, he wiped his face dry with his hands as Jake made his way over to him. Without a word, his friend walked up beside him with two open bottles of beer in his hands.

"We're going to find her."

Trevor could tell his friend wholeheartedly believed what he'd just said. Trevor wished he could be just as sure. He took the beer from Jake's outstretched hand and tipped it against his lips. Trevor swallowed a big gulp of the ice cold liquid before speaking.

"How?" he asked almost emotionless. "We don't know where he took her. We don't know what kind of vehicle he was in. Hell, we don't even know which direction they were headed after they left the diner."

"I get that you're frustrated, Trevor," Jake's low voice rumbled. "I really do."

Trevor turned to Jake, trying hard to not sound like a total dick. "Do you? Because you were just inside that room telling me how I needed to calm down. How the fuck am I supposed to be calm knowing that asshole has her? When I have no idea what he's doing to her?"

He didn't wait for an answer. Instead, he turned back around and took another sip of beer as he looked out over the city. "She's out there, Jake. She's out there, and I don't know how to help her." He looked to his friend for guidance. "How did you do this?"

"Do what?"

"How did you not completely fall apart when Olivia was taken? It's like…"—his breath heaved—"I feel like my heart's being ripped from my chest and I can't catch my breath. I can't breathe, Jake." He glanced at his friend, his voice breaking when he asked, "Why can't I breathe?"

"Because you love her."

More tears fell from the corners of his eyes. "I do."

Jake lifted a corner of his mouth. "I know. So, you have to hang on to that. And to answer your question, I got through that time with Liv because I had you and the rest of the team to lean on. Just like you have us now. We're here to help you, Trev. And we aren't going to stop until we find Lexi and bring her home."

Trevor used his free hand to wipe his eyes dry again. "There's got to be something I've missed. I just don't know what it is."

The slider opened, and Derek poked his head outside. "Something just came through." He looked at Trevor. "You're gonna need to see this."

Chapter 12

"I'm going to be sick."

True to his word, Trevor made it to his kitchen trashcan just in time for his stomach's meager contents to come rushing out. When the convulsions stopped, he went to the sink and rinsed out his mouth before walking woodenly back into the living room.

"The good news is she's still alive." Mac offered softly. They'd all seen the pictures that had been sent to Trevor's email account.

"She's been beaten to a fucking pulp!" Trevor nearly gagged as he looked at the picture again.

Lexi was sitting in the middle of an otherwise-empty room. She'd been tied to a chair, and someone had used their fists on her. One of her eyes was nearly swollen shut. She had a bloody nose and lip, and the cheekbone that had already been bruised from before had been struck so hard it was split.

"Anything that gives away where she might be?" Grant asked no one in particular.

Rubbing his hand across his scruff, Trevor did his best to study it as if it were any other case. It was one of the hardest things he'd ever had to do, but he knew he had to at least try to remain objective. He had to stay strong. For Lexi.

When Trevor found the bastard who'd dared to hurt what was his…"I'm going to kill him. I'm going to find the sonofabitch who did this, and I'm going to tear him limb from fucking limb."

"There's not one person here who will stop you." Grant looked at him solemnly.

"I'm assuming you've tried tracing it," Trevor directed the question to Derek, his voice quivering.

"Yeah, with no luck. Whoever sent it has so many encryptions embedded in the fuckin' thing, it could be coming from next door, and I wouldn't know it."

"Damn. That's not good," Coop mumbled under his breath.

All eyes went to Coop, who glanced back at them with confusion. "What? I'm just sayin', when it comes to this shit, D's the smartest man I know. If *he* can't figure where the email came from, we're screwed."

Mac punched him in the arm and muttered something only he could hear. She seemed to do that a lot with Coop. The two reminded Trevor of the way Olivia and her brother, Mike, acted when they were around each other.

"Sean's right about one thing," Derek said, his fingertips still flying across his keyboard. "Whoever is doing this is damn good." He stopped long enough to look up at Trevor and vow, "I'm not giving up, though. There's a way in…I just have to find it."

With a nod, Trevor walked into the kitchen to get a drink of water. He heard a loud ding, followed by Derek hollering for him to come back.

"He sent another one. A typed message."

"What does it say?"

Derek turned one of the screens around to show Trevor

and the others.

Trevor read the message out loud. "The sins of our past always find a way back into our present."

"What the fuck does that mean?" Grant grumbled.

Trevor shook his head. "I have no idea."

"Has she ever mentioned anything about her past that would come back down on her like this? An ex-boyfriend with a major grudge, former co-worker she pissed off…anything?" Jake asked.

"No. Nothing."

"You're sure?" Derek looked at him. "I ran her background and financials, and she's clean on that end, but…"

"But what, D?" Trevor challenged, not liking where Derek was going.

"You two haven't been together all that long. How well do you really know this woman?"

Trevor's hands instinctively fisted at his sides. "Don't. Don't do that."

"There's no reason to get all defensive, Trev. I'm just sayin' that…"

"I know exactly what you're trying to say. And I'm saying, I don't give a shit how long we've been together. I know Lexi better than any other woman I've ever been with, and I'm telling you, this doesn't make any sense."

"It does if it isn't about *Lexi's* past."

All eyes moved to Mac. With her elbows on her knees, the adorable-but-deadly-blonde was scooted to the edge of the recliner cushion. Her blue eyes looked directly into Trevor's. "This could be about you. Someone could be using Lexi to get to you."

Mac's words hit him like a ton of bricks. The thought of

Lexi being used to extract revenge on him was almost unbearable.

"She's right," Grant's deep voice cut through the tense air. "There's always a risk getting involved with guys like us."

"Or *girls.*" Mac gave Grant the stink-eye. To Trevor, she asked, "Why else would this guy take her and then send you that pic and the message?"

Coop added his thoughts. "Could be he's been watching them. Sees them together, finds out who Trevor is and what he does. Hell, you just have to look at where he lives to know he's got money, so this guy could follow you home once and know he'd probably make some quick cash by taking your girl."

Grant countered that with, "That's not what this is about."

"How can you be so sure?" Trevor asked.

"If all this guy wanted was money, he would've asked for it by now. Not send some cryptic-as-fuck message about sins of the past and all that shit."

"Okay, so let's try to think," Jake spoke up in that down to business, leadership tone he had. "What cases have we taken on lately that would garner such a violent act of revenge?"

"Ah, hell. Take your pick, boss," Derek said casually, his southern drawl becoming more prominent as the night went on. "We're always pissin' off somebody somewhere."

Trevor looked down at Lexi's picture on the computer screen again. "If this has happened to her because of me..." his voice broke and he couldn't even bring himself to finish the sentence.

"We don't know that's it, for sure," Jake attempted to reassure him. "Let's just take this one step at a time. Derek, keep doing whatever you can to find this sonofabitch. Hill, get on the phone with Ryker. See if he can do anything to help. Mac, you and Coop go back to the diner and see if Derek's brother's found out anything useful."

"Guys," Derek tried to interrupt, but with Jake dishing out orders and Grant already talking on the phone to Jason Ryker, their Homeland Security handler, no one heard him.

"What can I do?" Trevor asked, feeling more helpless than he ever had in his life.

Jake pulled his keys from his pocket and said, "You and I are going to the office. We're going to pull every file on every case until we figure out who the hell took Lexi."

He and Trevor headed for the door. Derek raised his voice, repeating more loudly this time, "Guys!"

Everyone froze, then turned to the man still sitting on the couch. To Jake, Derek said, "I don't think that's going to be necessary."

"What do you mean?"

"Trevor just got another email. It didn't ding this time because his email thread was already open." He looked at Trevor, the regret in his eyes like a torch to his soul. "I know why Lexi was taken."

Trevor took one, large step back toward their teammate. "Tell me."

"I think it's better if I just show you."

Like before, Derek spun the computer monitor around. A woman's smiling face filled the entire screen. A woman who died over nine years ago. *Lisa.*

Trevor and the rest were still trying to process what they were seeing when the picture began to fade and another one took its place. It was another picture of Lisa, only this time she was tied to a chair. She'd been beaten…just like Lexi.

Below that picture, a new message appeared. This time, it was Derek who read it aloud.

"They gave her six days. Your girlfriend has six hours."

"Oh, God."

The words weren't much more than a whisper, but Trevor felt them to his core. His knees damn near gave out, and he wasn't even sure how he made it back to the couch without falling on his ass.

"This is about what happened in Syria," he said in shock, his voice completely void of emotion. "It all makes sense now."

"What? What makes sense?" Coop asked, clearly frustrated.

"The woman in the picture is Lisa Warren," Jake explained. "She was the CIA liaison assigned to Trevor's and my Delta Force team."

Mac sounded surprised when she asked, "The one Omar Hadim betrayed?"

Jake nodded. "Yeah. That's her."

"Wait," Mac spoke up. "So, someone's pissed about what happened to this Lisa chic, and suddenly decides to use Lexi as a pawn for revenge, nine years after the fact? Who would do that?"

Trevor tore his gaze from the picture and looked at Mac. "Someone who blames me for Lisa's death."

****

Lexi hurt. She could barely see out of her left eye, and every time she tried to move her mouth, the cut in her lip would split back open. Her face was a mixture of fire and throbbing pain, and the worst part was, she still had no idea why this was happening.

The man had continued to hit her until she lost

consciousness, and when she woke back up, he used his phone to take her picture, and then he was gone. He hadn't been back since.

She was going to die. Lexi knew it as surely as she knew her own name. She was going to die, and all she could think of was the fact that she hadn't told Trevor she loved him.

She'd started to the night before while they were making love, but had stopped herself. Afraid it was too soon, Lexi had chickened out and decided to wait for the perfect moment. Now, that perfect moment would never come.

Hot tears fell from the corners of her eyes, and for the first time since she'd been taken, Lexi gave in to her fears. Sorrow and self-pity overpowered her will to fight. What was the point?

The ropes weren't budging, no matter how much blood flowed from her torn wrists. She had no idea where she was or who the man was who'd taken her. Worst of all, Trevor had no idea where to even begin to look for her.

A loud sob echoed off the room's bare walls as she gave up what was left of her resolve and belief that she would somehow get away. This man, whoever he was, wasn't about to just let her walk away. And no matter how much she wished she could, Lexi simply wasn't strong enough to get herself loose.

At least she'd get to see her mom again. It was the only silver lining in the dark and deadly cloud that overshadowed her.

Lexi's heart rate kicked into high gear when the door to the room creaked open, and the man who'd taken her returned once more. He was carrying a white plastic bucket full of water and what looked like a large hand towel.

Was he going to wash her off? Clean up the blood from

her wounds? That seemed odd, considering the fact that he was the one who'd spilled it in the first place.

She watched as he sat the bucket on the ground next to her and threw the towel over one of his shoulders for safe keeping. Without saying a word, he turned and walked away.

Okay, so that was weird. Lexi glanced down at the water, her dry mouth begging for a taste. Maybe that was his plan. He had to know she'd be thirsty, so he...what? Torturing her by sitting it next to her, but not allowing her to drink any?

Lexi was still trying to figure out the jerk's plan when he came back into the room. This time he was using both hands to carry what looked like a homemade, wooden table. He grunted as he sat it down onto the floor.

The table's legs were grossly uneven, making the top sit at an angle. She almost made a crack about the furniture's clear lack of craftsmanship when she noticed two leather straps, one attached to each side.

Oh, God. Lexi still had no idea what he had planned for her, but she knew it couldn't be good. She watched as the man left the room again, this time returning with a tripod in his hands. After setting it up, he pulled out the same phone he'd used to take her picture earlier and positioned it in a custom cradle on the top of the metal stand.

She decided to try talking to him. Stall him for as long as she could.

"If you're planning to get ransom money for me, you're out of luck." Dang, that hurt. Lexi licked the cut on her lip and kept going. "I have no family left, and there's maybe a few hundred dollars saved in a jar in my closet back home."

The man turned and looked at her with disgust. "You think this is about money?"

Answering honestly, Lexi said, "I don't know. I have no

idea why you're doing this."

Her words seemed to agitate him even more. "I'm doing this because everyone's forgotten. She died, and everyone just went on with their lives like nothing happened."

"She? W-who is she?"

Crazed eyes bore into hers. "My fiancée."

"I'm sorry," Lexi said, surprised that she actually was. No one should suffer that sort of loss. "What…what happened to her?"

"She was murdered."

"I'm sorry," she said again, mainly because she didn't know what else to say.

"You're sorry, they're sorry…everyone's sorry but no one will do anything to the man responsible for killing her!"

And this has to do with me, how exactly? That was the question she wanted to ask. What she actually said was, "H-he got away?"

"Oh, the man who physically ended her life was killed a long time ago. I finally took care of the guy who helped him, but the one…the one who was actually responsible? He's still out there. He's still living his life as if nothing ever happened."

"I don't understand. If this man really is responsible for your fiancée's death and you know who it is, then why isn't he in jail?"

The guy let out an almost hysterical laugh, his voice raising nearly a whole octave. "Jail?" He laughed again. "He's one of the government's golden boys. They're not going to put him in jail. They'd give him a fucking medal before tossing his pretty-boy ass in jail."

The guy was making absolutely no sense whatsoever.

He came over to her, then. Thinking he was going to hit

her again, Lexi shrunk back into the chair as far as she could. However, rather than hit her, he began to untie the ropes from her wrists.

"I'll help you." Lexi was desperate to get through to him. "Tell me his name…the person responsible for your fiancée's death. Tell me who it is, and I'll help you find him. I have a friend who does this sort of thing for a living. He can—"

"Who, Soldier Boy?" He laughed again, moving into a squat to begin working on the ropes at her ankles.

"Soldier Boy?" Lexi parroted, her tone not hiding her confusion.

Still chuckling oddly, he finished his task before resting his elbows on his thighs and saying, "You know, I think you might be onto something. We *should* contact your friend. I'm sure he'll be very interested in what I have to say."

"Okay," she said warily. "I-I don't have his phone number memorized. It's in my phone, and its…crap, it's at the diner." Thoughts of Joe threatened to break her, but she somehow managed to push them back and stay focused. "His name is Trevor Matthews. He works for a private security firm downtown. Risk. It's spelled R-I-S-C. Look it up. I'm sure there's an emergency contact number or something."

The man ignored her rambling and yanked her up from the chair. Lexi would have fallen straight to the floor if he hadn't caught her with an arm around her waist. She'd sat in that position for so long, both of her lower limbs had fallen asleep.

He guided her over to the uneven table. She tried to fight back, to use this as her chance to escape. But with her legs numb and her arms not much better off, Lexi only managed to flail around like one of those inflatable tube guys she'd seen in used car lots.

More than a little annoyed, her abductor forced her to lie down with her head at the end closest to the floor. Again, she tried to move away, but it was no use. He was too strong and had her raw wrists strapped down before she could even lift herself off the table.

"I almost forgot how much you like to fight," he taunted as he walked over to his propped-up phone.

Grimacing from the pain of the leather rubbing against her raw wrists, Lexi called out, "Wait! I thought…I thought you said we could call Trevor. I thought you wanted my help."

"Oh, I do want your help, Alexis. In fact, you're going to help me right now."

He tapped the front of his phone, and its screen lit up. It was too small and too far away for her to make out the details, but she knew exactly what she was looking at…the man had just opened the video app on his phone.

"W-what are you going to do?"

Smiling down at her, he said, "We're going to give Soldier Boy a little show."

Frustration mixed with fear. "You keep saying that," Lexi gritted through her teeth, her voice getting louder and louder. "Who are you talking about? Who is Soldier Boy?"

With a perplexed expression, the man said, "You really don't know, do you?"

She let her frustration fly. "I know you're a sick sonofabitch who gets off on hurting innocent people. I've done nothing to you. *Nothing!*"

"You're right."

His soft words gave her pause. "What?"

"You've done nothing to me. Your boyfriend, however, is a cold-blooded murderer."

Shock reverberated throughout Lexi's entire system. "Y-you know T-Trevor?"

"Trevor Michael Matthews." The man spit out Trevor's name as if it were a curse word.

He then began spouting off facts about the man she loved as if he were reading them from his personal dossier. Facts Lexi only recently learned while staying at his place.

"The only child of Stephen and Judy Matthews. Grew up in a small town just outside San Antonio, then joined the Army after he graduated high school. Became a Delta Force Operator at the young age of twenty-two." The guy's voice lowered as a deadly expression fell over his face. "And Trevor Matthews was twenty-four when my fiancée died as a direct result of his decision."

A picture began to form in Lexi's head. Bits and pieces of the story Trevor had told her the night she was attacked in her home became fresh in her mind. Barely a whisper, she said, "Lisa. Your fiancée was Lisa."

The man rushed toward her then. His hand moving lightning fast toward her face. Grabbing her chin between his strong fingers, his grip was painful as he screamed, "You don't say her name! Your boyfriend sent her straight to her death. He did that!"

His hold on her became even tighter to the point she thought he was going to crush her jawbone. Leaning closely enough for the tips of their noses to touch, he said, "And now he's going to learn exactly what it's like to watch helplessly as the woman he loves suffers and dies."

Chapter 13

"Trev?"

The unexpected voice had him turning. "Liv? What are you doing here?"

Jake's wife stepped out onto the balcony and closed the sliding door behind her.

"Knowing y'all the way I do, I figured you hadn't taken a break to eat. I brought some pizzas. I can go get you a couple slices if you'd like."

"Thanks," he said sincerely. "But, I'm not hungry."

"May I?" she asked, gesturing to the only other patio chair out there.

"Sure." He gave her a nod.

Olivia sighed. "It's nice out here. Peaceful."

Trying really hard not to sound like a complete ass, Trevor turned to his friend and said, "Liv. I know you mean well, but I'm really not in the mood for small talk."

"I know," she whispered with a smile. "I didn't really come out here for small talk."

"Then, why are you here? Really?"

"To make sure you were doing okay."

"Okay?" he said sarcastically. "The woman I love is out there somewhere, hurt and afraid. Some asshole took her and is doing God only knows what to her because of a decision I made nine years ago. And the worst part is, I have no idea how to find her."

"Jake told me the man who took her said she had six hours."

Trevor looked down at his watch for what had to be the hundredth time in the past two hours. "Four, now." He swallowed against the emotions clogging his throat, and on a broken whisper, he turned to her. "He's going to kill her in four hours if I can't figure out a way to stop him."

Reaching across the small table positioned between the two chairs, Olivia took Trevor's hand in hers and squeezed.

"I know it's hard, but you've got the best team in there right now, doing everything they can to find her. Don't give up on her, now."

"I'm not giving up on her," he said shortly. "I'm being realistic." Pulling his hand from hers, Trevor stood and walked over to the balcony. "Other than knowing this is related to an op I went on with Delta nearly a decade ago, we've got nothing."

Standing in the same spot her husband had earlier, Olivia smiled sadly. "You have faith and determination." She put her small hand on his taught forearm. "And you have love. That's not nothing."

"It's not enough!" he nearly shouted, acting exactly like the ass he'd been trying so hard not to be. "Shit, I'm sorry, Liv."

She simply gave him a crooked smile and said, "Don't be. Emotions are high. Trust me, I get it. It wasn't so long ago I was in the same spot Lexi is."

"I know," he said, feeling even worse for yelling at her. "You've been there. What…what do you think she's thinking about right now?"

"I can't say what's going on in Lexi's head for sure, but if I had to guess, it's probably a lot like what went through mine."

"Which was?"

"How I wasn't ready to die. I didn't want to leave the people I loved behind. I kept telling myself not to give up hope. I also remember praying that Jake, and you, and the others wouldn't ever give up on me." Tears fell from Trevor's eyes as she talked, but he did nothing to stop them. "Most of all, I remember praying with everything I had that Jake would know how much I loved him."

Trevor drew in a stuttered breath. "I never got to tell her I love her," he whispered, his bottom lip quivering. "I…I was going to tell her tomorrow at the picnic."

Olivia swiped a hand at her own damp cheek. "I knew it was going to be a special moment for you two."

"I wanted it to be perfect for her. Everything's been such a crazy mess with us as far as dates go…I wanted to create a day she'd never forget. She works so hard, and deserves so much. And now"—a sob broke loose—"Ah, God, Liv. I can't lose her. Not now. We just found each other."

With a hand to his face, Trevor physically tried to keep more tears from falling. A set of small arms reached around him and held him tightly as his shoulders shuddered and his breath hitched again. After a few minutes, he slowly began to regain his control.

Pulling back from Olivia's embrace, he sniffed and ran that same hand down the length of his face. Clearing his throat, his voice came out rough when he muttered, "Sorry."

Olivia shook her head. "You've more than earned a few tears after a day like today. Don't worry. Despite what he thinks, I don't tell my husband everything."

Letting out a weak laugh, Trevor grabbed hold of his friend and gave her a real hug. "Thanks, Liv."

Patting his back, she whispered, "You're going to find her, Trev. I know you are."

"Uh…sorry to interrupt," Derek's regretful voice cut through the sweet moment between friends. Both Trevor and Olivia turned toward the door. "Trev, you got another message."

Steeling himself, Trevor released himself from Olivia's embrace and followed Derek back into his apartment.

He was surprised to see Derek's brother among those gathered in the living room. Homeland Agent Jason Ryker had also arrived and was in the far corner talking to someone on the phone.

Eric immediately came to stand by his side. With a hand to his shoulder, the detective asked, "How you holdin' up?"

"Honestly? Right now, I feel sort of…numb."

"We're doin' all we can to find her, Trevor. You just gotta hang in there."

"I know. I appreciate it, Eric. Thanks."

The two shared a nod before Trevor looked down at Derek. Once again, the boy genius was positioned on the couch in front of his computer. Knowing there was no point in delaying the inevitable, Trevor told him, "Go ahead. Open the message."

"Wait," Olivia said quickly. Eyes filled with regret, she looked at Trevor and then Jake. "I can't. I'm sorry." To Trevor she promised, "I will be here for both you and Lexi after you find her and bring her home safe, but it's just…this is too much. I'm sorry."

"Nothing to be sorry for, Liv."

With a sad nod, she walked over to him and gave him a kiss on the cheek. "Stay strong, Trev."

"I will. For Lexi."

"For Lexi."

"Come on, baby." Jake wrapped an arm around his wife. "I'll walk you to your car." Jake gave him a look as they passed, and he knew his friend needed a moment with his new wife.

Trevor felt like such a dick. He'd been so worried about Lexi, he hadn't stopped to think about how hard this had to be on Jake, too. The memories of that terrifying day when Olivia went missing were still raw for him, too. He could only imagine the emotions all this had stirred up for his friends.

Looking as though he was dreading seeing this newest message as much as Trevor was, Derek waited until Jake and Olivia walked out to right-click his mouse.

There was no text this time. Only a red box with a white arrow in the middle.

"He sent a video," Derek muttered unnecessarily.

With everyone crowded around the back and sides of the couch, Derek looked to Trevor for the go-ahead.

Rubbing his hand across his tense jaw, Trevor gave Derek a nod. With every muscle in his body tightened, he watched as Derek clicked the mouse again.

Lexi was no longer tied to the chair. Instead, she was lying on a slanted, wooden table. There was a man next to her, but his back was to the camera, so they couldn't see his face. He moved to the side, and Trevor had to force himself not to look at Lexi's face.

Olivia was right. Lexi was counting on him and the others to find her, and he couldn't do that if he was too lost in his own emotions to focus on what needed to be done.

"You did well for yourself, Soldier Boy," the man said, still not looking at the camera. "Your girl's a fighter." He ran a finger slowly down one of Lexi's arms. Trevor could see her muscles tense from the bastard's touch, and he'd never wanted to kill a man more.

"*My* girl was a fighter, too," the man said, turning sideways but still not giving them a clear shot of his face.

"He has to be talking about Lisa," Derek said softly from where he sat.

Trevor studied the man in the video with an expert eye. He had no idea who he was.

"They beat my Lisa unconscious that first day," he offered, giving them confirmation that this was, in fact, about what went down in Syria. "Day two, they broke her fingers one by one. Day three, they waterboarded her." The man turned to fully face the camera, giving them a perfect view of his face. "Of course, you already know this, don't you…Trevor?"

Coop whistled quietly between his teeth. "Dude, this guy has a major hard-on for you."

"Shh," Mac chastised him.

"I know you saw the same videos I did." The man from the recording stepped closer to the camera. "Every day for six days I watched while the woman I loved, the woman I was supposed to spend the rest of my life with was tortured in a new, horrific way. You know what I did when I saw that final video?"

Pain filled the guy's crazed eyes. "I begged her to die. I was watching it, part of me knowing she was already gone by the time the video reached me, but still. I sat at my desk, and I screamed at my computer. I yelled at her until my throat was raw, because I wanted her to quit fighting. I wanted her to give up and stop letting them hurt her."

Angry tears fell down the guy's face, but he didn't seem to notice. "And when she finally gave up and took that last, gasping breath…you know what I did?" He paused as if he was actually waiting for someone to answer him, and then he whispered, "I laughed. I laughed with relief because I knew she was no longer in pain."

Trevor watched as the man walked back over to Lexi. His heart felt as though it would pound right out of his chest from the fear of what this man may do to her.

Gently taking Lexi's bound right hand in his, he began caressing her almost as a lover would. "Alexis has such pretty hands, don't you think? So small and delicate."

"Oh, shit."

The two words had barely left Mac's mouth when the man yanked Lexi's pinky finger sideways. Her scream mixed with the enraged voices coming from inside Trevor's living room because the man had just broken Lexi's finger.

"Sonofabitch!" Trevor actually took a step toward the computer. He wanted to crawl through the screen and tear the bastard's heart right out of his chest.

His eyes slid to Lexi's face, his own heart breaking from the pain and fear he found there. She was panting and groaning, but Trevor could tell she was trying to stay strong. Just like Olivia had said.

"Goddammit," Grant bit out from behind him. None of the guys could stomach watching a man hurting a woman. "Tell me you've got something that will lead us to this fucker."

"I'm working on it." Derek's fingers flew over the keyboard. As he typed, a bunch of words and numbers no one else in the room could understand scrolled quickly across the second monitor. "The problem is this wasn't streaming live. If he'd send us one of those, I *know* I could get in."

"Jesus, this is so fucked up," Coop said, walking away toward the kitchen.

"How did that make you feel, Soldier Boy?" The man from the video asked. "Are you sick to your stomach? Feel like you're gonna puke because you had to just sit there and watch the woman you love be tortured?"

He stepped closer to the camera like before. "You do love Alexis, don't you, Trevor? I saw the way you looked at her when the two of you talked at the diner. And the way you ran back up to her house to give her that steamy kiss goodnight."

"This guy was in the fuckin' diner with us?" Derek asked rhetorically, his head swinging up to Trevor's.

But Trevor didn't respond. He couldn't formulate a single word. All he could do was stand there in shock and watch.

"My Lisa had six days, but I'm an impatient bastard. In my last message, I told you sweet, little Alexis had six hours. That was almost two hours ago. Clock's ticking, Soldier Boy. Think your girl can hold on for that long?" The video ended abruptly.

"No!" Trevor started to yell, forgetting this had been previously recorded and then sent to them. He didn't want to even think about what she was going through now.

"I don't get it. If you and Lisa were a thing…" Mac commented right as Jake walked back through the door. "Then, why is this guy acting like she was his?"

"Because she was," Agent Ryker answered her.

Jake stopped when he saw the solemn expressions on everyone's faces. "What happened?" Eric pulled him to the side to fill him in.

"What the hell do you mean, she was *his*?" Trevor turned

to Ryker. "Lisa wasn't involved with anyone while we were together. I never would've been with her otherwise."

"They weren't together while you were with her. It was before. Up until a month prior to joining your Delta Team unit overseas, Lisa Warren was engaged to this guy. Name's Anthony Young. He was her partner, but got reassigned when they made their relationship public. Company policy."

"Engaged?"

"I take it she didn't tell you."

Trevor shook his head. "No. I mean, it was casual. We both knew it wasn't really going to end up going anywhere, but still. We talked about enough personal shit that I would have thought she'd share something like that with me."

"Maybe she didn't tell you because she knew this guy was a total whack job."

Ryker looked at Mac. "You're not far off, actually."

"What do you mean?" Grant asked quietly.

"Long story short, Lisa broke things off because Young became too possessive. He started monitoring her cell records, who she spent time with after work, that sort of thing. According to a close agent friend"—Ryker looked directly at Trevor—"it was what drove her to volunteer for the mission with your team. Prior to that, she'd only been gathering intel from Hadim through a third party asset and satellite conference calls."

Trevor ran a hand through his already disheveled hair. "Jesus."

Mac's voice got a little excited. "That means what happened to Lisa technically was this Tony guy's fault."

"It was Omar Hadim's fault," Ryker stated frankly. "His and the sick sonofabitch he worked for. Thankfully, that guy got what was coming to him years ago."

"Why does Young keep calling Trevor 'Soldier Boy'?"

"According to a coworker of his, that's what Anthony always called Trevor when he spoke about him."

"How the hell did he even know about Trev in the first place?" Coop asked as he returned from the kitchen.

"Apparently, Young went to college with Shane Billows." Agent Ryker's eyes slid to Trevor's. "I guess they were pretty tight back in the day."

His body and mind already on an emotional overload, Trevor didn't even react to that bit of news.

"Who the fuck is Shane Billows?" Coop demanded.

Jake answered for Ryker. "He was one of the two men who died in the set-up the day Lisa was taken."

Even Grant's eyes grew a bit wide at that. "One of your own teammates was giving this Young fucker information about you and this Lisa woman?"

"That's so wrong," Mac shook her head.

"He may not have been purposely reporting to Young," Ryker said, trying to deflate the level of anger in the room. "You have to remember…Anthony Young was CIA. He knew how to get information without it seeming like he was digging for information."

Mac wasn't buying it. "Still seems pretty messed up, if you ask me."

"None of that shit matters, now!" Trevor practically shouted. "I don't care who told Young what. Lexi is the only thing that matters. She's what's important."

"I'm sorry, Trev. I didn't mean to—"

"I don't need your apology, Mac. I need to find Lexi before that bastard hurts her again. Before he ki…kills her."

"That may not be possible," Derek said softly.

"What do you mean?"

Derek shook his head, his expression sorrowful. "I mean, unless he sends us a live feed, we have no way to find him."

"So, we're *hoping* this guy sends us a video of him hurting Lexi even more, only in real time? Is that really what you're saying?" Grant sounded about as pissed at the situation as Trevor felt.

In answer to Grant's question, Derek said, "It's all we *can* do."

****

Lexi had never had a broken bone before, but if she ever made it out of this alive, she'd do whatever she could to never have another one again. Though, he'd only broken her pinky, the fiery pain running through her hand and up the length of her arm hurt like a bitch.

Lying on the table's hard, wooden slats, she had to force herself to take slow, steady breaths so she wouldn't throw up. The man had made that horrible recording for Trevor and then left her alone again.

She was still reeling from the fact that all this was happening because of Trevor. No, not because of Trevor. Because this man blamed Trevor for something that wasn't his fault.

Lexi nearly gave into the sorrow she felt. Not for herself, although she wasn't exactly thrilled about her situation. Heart shattered from the thought of Trevor thinking any of this was his fault.

And how could he not? The man who'd taken her had told him as much.

"Oh, God, Trevor," Lexi whispered brokenly. "I'm so sorry."

She wished he were here so she could tell him. Lexi wanted him to hear her say it was okay. That she didn't blame him, and this man—whoever he was—was wrong. This wasn't Trevor's fault. None of it was.

Most of all, Lexi wanted to be able to tell Trevor at least once before she died that she loved him.

An idea began to form. Maybe…maybe she could talk the madman into sending Trevor a live video, rather than recording it and sending it after the fact. It seemed silly, but she wanted him to hear her say the words as she spoke them. And if he could hear her, there may be a chance she could hear him.

What felt like an eternity later, the man re-entered the room. He walked past her and went over to where the bucket lay next to the chair she'd been tied to. Lexi watched as he picked it up and carried it over, setting it down onto the floor next to her head.

"Time to make another video for Soldier Boy," he said, excitement gleaming in his eyes.

Now's your chance, Lex. The need to have Trevor hear her voice—and her, his—became so intense, she had to physically work to not sound too anxious when she spoke.

"Th-thank you."

Her words made him pause. Looking suspicious, he said, "Now, why on earth would *you* thank *me*?"

Lexi swallowed. "I was just lying here thinking how grateful I was that you sent a recording, and not a live video."

Agitated, he bit out, "Why?"

"I w-was listening to everything you said to Trevor. I can't imagine what you must have gone through when you had to see those pictures of Li…of your fiancée." She almost said Lisa's name again. That hadn't gone over so well last time, so

Lexi was thankful she caught herself.

"And? What's your point?"

"Well, I was just thinking how much worse it would've been had you been forced to watch it all as it was actually happening. She gave him a tiny smile and tried to shrug her shoulder, though it proved difficult with her wrists strapped tightly. "I'm a silver-lining kind of girl."

He actually let his guard down. "You're right. That would have been worse."

For the first time since he'd taken her, Lexi saw a side of him that almost seemed…human. It was gone as quickly as it came. With deadly eyes, he looked back down at her and smiled. "That would have been much, much worse."

Then, without another word, he turned and walked out of the room, leaving Lexi to wonder if her plan had actually worked. She didn't have to wait long for her answer.

He returned with a metal cart holding a computer monitor and keyboard. It looked like a complicated set up…much fancier than the cheap laptop she had at home.

Rolling the wheeled cart into the room, the man stopped at the far wall, angling the monitor so it would fully capture her face. He bent over and clicked at the keyboard for a few seconds, then turned to her and grinned.

"Now, it's my turn to thank you."

Confused, Lexi said, "Me? W-why me?"

His smile grew wider. "Soldier Boy will be with you every terrifying minute. He'll feel your pain as if it were his own. Knowing it's all happening to you in that *exact* moment and there's nothing he can do to stop it will be the ultimate payback for what he did to my Lisa."

Nausea settled in her stomach to the point she almost gagged. Lexi hadn't thought of it like that. She'd only wanted to share one final moment with him. Be with him one last time, the only way she knew how. The last thing she wanted was to cause him more heartbreak than he'd already been given.

Feeling deflated, Lexi let her head fall back against the wood. She didn't even notice the throbbing in her head or hand anymore, her fear and adrenaline apparently enough to dull the pain. "If you're going to kill me"—she whispered—"just do it already."

"Kill you? Oh, we're not to that part yet. Your boyfriend hasn't suffered nearly enough.

Lexi's face crumbled as more tears escaped, falling down across her temples. God, this must be hell for him. He already blamed himself for what happened to Lisa...he'd never forgive himself for this. *What have I done?*

Chapter 14

"Mind if I sit?"

Trevor lifted his head from his hands to see Jake standing next to him. "Sure."

Taking the kitchen bar stool next to his, Jake exhaled a loud breath before saying, "I know you think this is your fault, but it's not."

With his elbows leaning on the granite countertop, Trevor laughed humorlessly as he fisted his hands together in front of him. "I appreciate what you're trying to do, but you can save your breath. That man is hurting her because of me. I know it, and you know it. Hell, even Lexi knows it." *I'm so sorry, baby.*

He stood, but Jake halted his movements with a hand to his forearm. "Hold up a second. Just hear me out."

Trevor didn't sit back down, but he didn't walk away from his friend, either.

"I get where your head's at, Trev. I've been where you are."

Trevor shook his head. "This is different."

"Really? Oh, good." He pretended to be relieved. "So, you weren't just sitting here wondering what you could've done differently to keep this from happening. Or, how one decision you made a lifetime ago could cost you everything. And since this is so different, you definitely weren't just thinking how Lexi would have been better off if she'd never met you."

Shit. Those had been his exact thoughts. Stunned, Trevor stuttered, "H-how did you…"

"I told you. I've been there. And if I remember correctly, it wasn't so long ago that *you* were the one trying to convince *me* that what happened to Olivia wasn't my fault."

Shaking his head, Trevor said, "It's not the same, Jake. The guy who went after Olivia did so because of something he blamed *her* for. Not you. Anthony Young took Lexi because of a decision *I* made." Trevor slapped his own chest.

"Anthony Young is a fucking nut job. Hell, you heard him. He keeps referring to Lisa as his fiancée. The woman broke things off, went clear across the world, and started seeing someone else. Yet, he still believes the two of them were getting married back then."

"Why now?" Trevor ignored the excellent point Jake had just made. "That's what I don't understand. She died nine years ago, so why come after me, now?"

Jake's expression eased. "I wish I knew, brother. But that's one question I can't answer."

"I think I can." Ryker walked up to them. To Jake, he said, "Sorry. Couldn't help but overhear." Both men gave the Homeland agent a nod, so he told him what he knew.

"I was wondering the same thing…why now, after all these years? So, I did some digging. Turns out, Young was actually engaged to someone else recently…another woman who worked for the CIA. They were supposed to be married this spring, but she left him a few weeks ago when she stumbled across a file on his computer. It was filled with classified intel that Young never should have even had access to, let alone had copies of on his personal computer. Apparently, he's been keeping tabs on several people connected to Lisa since her death nine years ago…her family, you"—he tilted his head at Trevor—"and Omar Hadim."

"Jesus," Jake muttered. "He the one who killed Hadim?"

"He put in for three weeks' vacation the same day the chatter about Hadim's resurfacing started to pop up. You tell me."

"You think Hadim's what set him off?" Trevor asked Ryker.

"I think it was a combination of a lot of shit. According to his ex-fiancée, she not only broke things off between them, she also gave him an ultimatum…either he tells their boss what he did, or she was going to. He left for his 'vacation' the next morning, and hasn't been seen or heard from since. Until today."

"Sounds guilty as hell, to me," Jake commented.

Ryker agreed. "From the sounds of it, the guy was already a ticking time bomb. Then, his woman not only leaves him, but says she's going to rat him out. Young had to know he was going to lose his job and probably do jail time for illegally accessing and downloading the intel his fiancée found on his computer."

"Then, word gets out that Hadim's been spotted." Trevor nodded. "It's like he was hit with the perfect shit storm."

"Exactly," Ryker agreed. "And with guys like Young who are already mentally unstable, all it takes is something to throw that switch. Seeing him on that video? Yeah, that guy's hell and gone."

"And he has Lex," Trevor growled. "Even worse, we have no idea how to find her."

"Holy shit!" Derek exclaimed loudly from the living room.

Trevor practically ran over to him, fear shoving his heart into his throat. "What is it? What happened?"

"He did it."

"Ah, God. No." Trevor's fists grabbed the back of the couch to keep himself upright. "He *killed* her?"

"What? No!" Derek looked up at him with widened eyes, he quickly said, "Shit. Sorry, man. I didn't mean to make you think…he's connected to a live feed. As soon as you click, you'll be able to see him in real time."

With slow, controlled breaths, Trevor worked to clear the horrific thought that Lexi had been killed from his brain. He stared back at Derek and waited for more. Thankfully, his friend understood.

"If you can keep him talking long enough, I can worm my way in and figure out where the signal's coming from."

"Then, you'll be able to find her?" Trevor asked, feeling hopeful for the first time since Lexi had been taken.

With absolute confidence, Derek stared him straight in the eye and said, "I'll find her."

Looking down at Derek's unmoving hands, Trevor blurted, "What the hell are you waiting for? Do it!"

"He's set it up as a two-way feed," Derek explained.

Not a tech guy, D's words meant jack shit to Trevor. "So?"

"So, you won't just be able to see him. He'll also see you."

Lexi will be able to see me, too. "Good. Great. Go for it."

"Before I click it open, I need to know how you want to play this."

"For God's sake, D." Trevor ran a frustrated hand through his hair for the millionth time that night. "I want you to hit the damn button so we can connect with the guy, find

Lexi, and get her the hell outta there!"

"And I will, just as soon as I know what the plan is!" Derek yelled back.

"This is getting us nowhere," Mac jumped in. "You both need to calm your asses down for two seconds so we can figure this out before we lose the chance to connect with him altogether." Surprisingly, they did. Mac used the monumentally short timeframe to try to get the plan laid out.

"Derek, say what you need Trevor to know, and fast." To Trevor, she said, "And you listen."

"I have been listening. I just don't understand—"

"She's right, Trevor," Grant joined in on the conversation. "You get one shot to save your girl. You spook this guy, and you lose your only chance to bring her home safely."

For some reason, Grant's words resonated with him. Drawing in a deep breath, Trevor said, "Fine. I'm listening."

"Thank you," Derek said to Mac and Grant. To Trevor he said, "Once we connect, he'll be able to see you. That means, if we're in the camera's view, he'll see us, too. We need to make sure we're nowhere we can be seen. We also need to know what's going to happen when I do find their location."

"What do you mean?"

Derek looked at the others, then back to Trevor. "I mean, the second I get their location, we can head out and go to your girl, but…"

"But?" Trevor prodded impatiently.

"But, if you break communication to come with us, Young's gonna know somethin's up. If you come with us," Derek continued, knowing what Trevor was about to say. "He'll notice the change in background. The movement. He'll be able to hear us talking in the background. All of that."

"And, it'll tip him off," Trevor finally understood.

"Right." Derek sighed. "Which means, you need to let us go after him while you keep him occupied as best you can. I know that sucks, and you want to be there, but finding her is more important, don't you think?"

The reality of what Derek was saying set in. "I need to be there, D. This whole thing is happening because of me. I have to be the one who—"

"I'll take you," Ryker offered unexpectedly. All eyes went to him, but he was looking solely at Trevor. "Get the location. Let these guys go on ahead of us. If and when the connection with this fucker is lost, you and I will head out. I'm in my government vehicle…lights and sirens will get us through traffic in no time. I can also call ahead with the address and get back-up there, as well." Then, with an uncharacteristically softened voice, the Homeland agent added, "I promise I'll get you there as quickly as I can."

From beside him, Ryker put a hand on Trevor's shoulder and said, "I know you want to be the first one Lexi sees, but D's right. The important thing is getting her away from this bastard."

Still feeling torn, Trevor knew Ryker was right. They all were. Shit. "Fine." To Derek, he said, "Do it."

****

A loud dinging sound filled the small room where Lexi was being held, and she instinctively knew what it meant.

The man who'd taken her had been anxiously staring at the computer for the last few minutes. Hearing the sound, he looked at her from over his shoulder and smiled. "Showtime." He turned back to the computer, hit a couple keys, then said, "Nice of you to finally join us."

Lexi's heart physically ached when she heard Trevor's voice for the first time since she'd left for work that morning.

"Let me talk to Lexi."

Fresh tears fell, despite the effort she'd put forth to hold them back.

"You're not the one giving orders here, Soldier Boy. I am."

There was a slight pause and then, "May I talk to Lexi...*please*."

"That's more like it."

The man moved to the side, and there he was. "Trevor," she whispered, trying valiantly to keep it together as she saw his face on the screen.

He was home. She recognized the picture on the wall in the background as the one hanging in his living room. God, she wished she were there with him.

"Hey, angel." he smiled back at her. It was hard to tell, but he looked as though he was on the verge of crying himself. "I'm so sorry, Lex."

She shook her head against the hard wood, the back of her hair pulling when it got caught in the groove. "It's not your fault, Trevor. I know he says it is, but I know the truth about what happened that day. You told me the story, remember? I don't blame you, Trevor. This isn't your fault. It's his." Lexi glared at the man standing to the side, anger sparking in his eyes from her words.

"Mine?" he yelled at her. "This is not my fault, it's *his*." The guy's arm flew out to his side as he pointed to the computer screen. "*He's* the one who gave the order for her to go into that building. *He's* the one who knew Omar Hadim was a traitor. *He—*"

"Told her he didn't trust Hadim, but LISA wouldn't

listen!" Lexi yelled back. Her own words took her by surprise, but damn it…she'd had enough of this shit.

"Baby, no." She heard Trevor's voice warning her, but it was too late. The man was already stomping over toward her, hatred and determination filling his entire being. He grabbed the hand towel from the floor near the bucket of water.

"She doesn't know what she's saying, Young," Trevor yelled through the computer. At least she had a last name, now. "She wasn't there. *I* was. And you're right. This is all on me."

"You're damn right it's on you," the man—whose last name was apparently Young—said. He then started to bring the towel down toward her face.

"*No!*" Trevor's loud voice came through the computer's speakers. "Don't do this, Anthony. Lisa wouldn't have wanted this. She wouldn't have wanted any of this."

The man froze, then. Slowly, he turned from her and looked back at Trevor. "You don't get to talk about what Lisa would have wanted. You didn't know her like I did, so stop pretending you gave a damn about her."

"Lexi, look at me," Trevor's order rushed out quickly. Of course, Lexi looked him right in the eyes. Sad, tortured eyes that conveyed so much pain and anguish it broke her heart in two. "Ah, God, baby. I'm so sorry. I'm so fucking sorry."

"I love you."

Crap. That was not the way she wanted to say it for the first time. But she had no idea what this man was about to do to her, and if this was the last time she got to speak to Trevor, she had to say it now, while she had the chance.

"I know it's early, but I needed you to know in case—"

The towel was placed over her face, stealing her precious view. However, she could still hear his voice.

"Young! Look at me. Don't do this to her, man. She's not a part of this."

"You love her. Just like I loved Lisa. This is the only way you'll truly understand the pain you've caused."

"I…I don't love her. We just started dating. I know what you're trying to do, but hurting her is not going to cause me the pain you think it will."

Lexi lay there, listening as her heart shattered for a completely different reason than before. Almost instantly, her entire body went numb. *How could I have been so wrong?*

Thankfully, the towel hid her tears as a sense of utter mortification began to sink in. She'd just professed her love for a man who, though he seemed genuinely upset by her being held against her will and hurt, apparently had no true feelings for her whatsoever.

But why look so torn up when she first saw him? *Of course. I'm such an idiot.* The man blamed himself for what happened to Lisa. Something similar is now happening to her.

History was repeating itself, and all those memories were coming back to him. His being upset had nothing to do with the fact that he loved her. Trevor was a protector. It was his job, and right now, he was thinking this was the second time he'd failed.

The towel was pulled tighter against her face, and she could hear Trevor shouting for the man to stop. Lexi was so terrified she was shaking. She had no idea what was about to happen, but it didn't take long for her to figure it out.

Cold water splashed against her face. It quickly soaked through the towel and filled her nostrils and mouth. She held her breath and tried to move her head away from the steady downpour, but one of the man's strong hands made it impossible for her to move.

She couldn't breathe. Oh, God, he was trying to drown her. Lexi's legs kicked with the need to move, and her arms felt as though they'd be torn from her body from their strain against the straps.

Her lungs became two burning infernos of hot, molten flames as they begged for air. When she could no longer hold her breath, her body's instinctual need for oxygen took over. She opened her mouth and tried to breathe.

Instead of precious air, Lexi sucked in water. Her own pulse rushed through her ears, and the pressure in her head and chest became more intense than anything she'd ever felt. She was on the verge of losing consciousness when the water stopped and the towel was removed.

The second the man—Anthony Young—let go of her, Lexi turned her head on reflex and vomited. He jumped out of the way as all of the water that had gone down into her stomach and into her lungs came rushing back out.

Between her stomach heaving and the incessant coughing, Lexi couldn't make out what Trevor was shouting at Young. She caught a few curse words and a not-so-veiled threat, but it was hard to hear with her own body wracked with pain and the desperate need to continue breathing again.

"*You sonofabitch!*" Trevor yelled. "I swear to God I am going to kill you."

Now, that, Lexi heard. And she prayed right then that Trevor was able to follow through with that particular threat.

Young walked over to the computer, and with an eerie calm, he said, "You'd have to find me, first. Until then, I'll let you sit there and think about the fact that I'm gonna keep having some fun with your girl." Then, with the click of a button, Trevor's face vanished and the screen went black.

****

"Ah, Jesus." Trevor stood and began pacing his living room. With both hands locked behind his head, he tried hard not to throw up again. "Oh, God. He waterboarded her, Jason. He fucking waterboarded her!"

Consumed with an anger unlike any he'd ever known, Trevor picked up an end-table near one of the recliners. With an animalistic growl, he threw it toward his sliding door. Glass shattered as it smashed through the door before landing with a loud thud on the patio's concrete slab.

"*Goddammit!*" Trevor's nostrils flared, and his chest heaved as he tried to think of what else he could destroy. Thankfully, Ryker was there to stop him.

"We need to go." His words didn't sink in at first, so Ryker tried again. "Matthews!"

Hearing the other man's booming voice, Trevor turned and faced him. "What?" he yelled back.

"They found her, man. Derek got a bead on her location, remember?"

Trevor glanced around his apartment, as if he expected to see the others there, but he and Jason were the only ones there.

"They left while you were still talking to Young. Before he started in on your girl. The guy's less than fifteen minutes away from here…You want to be there when they take this fucker down, we need to go. Now!"

Like a slap to his face, Trevor finally snapped out of it. He ran back to his bedroom closet and, with shaking hands, managed to open the large gun safe there. Pulling out his MP-5 and SIG. Trevor quickly shoved a full mag for each into his jean pockets, and then to Ryker asked, "Need one?"

"Nope," the agent answered quickly. "Got all I need down in the SUV."

With one final look, Trevor gave Ryker a single nod and said, "Let's do this."

Chapter 15

Anthony Young was a monster. A sick, delusional monster. That was the first thought Lexi had when she regained consciousness.

He'd done the thing with the towel and water two more times. The second time, he only stopped because he ran out of water. The last time, he came back with a full bucket and had continued pouring until finally, blessedly, her brain shut down from the lack of oxygen, and she passed out.

Her second thought upon waking back up was that she'd never be able to look Trevor in the eyes again…if she managed to not die today, that is.

She couldn't believe she'd misread things so badly. The moments they shared—albeit not many—had been incredible to her. Magical, even. Hearing him say he didn't love her was a crushing blow to her heart.

She could hardly believe it when he told Young they barely knew each other, after spending the past few days doing nothing *but* getting to know each other better. Well, that and making incredible, sweet love.

God, she felt like such a fool. A hopeless romantic fool. She'd always been a romantic at heart…her whole life she'd dreamed of not just being a successful chef, but also having someone to love and share a life with. Now, she was going to die without having achieved either.

Lost in her own self-pity, she almost didn't notice the man return to the room. She was relieved to see he hadn't brought another bucket of water with him. Thank God for small favors, her mother used to say.

That thought had just passed through her mind when she noticed the large, shiny knife in Young's hand.

"Time to start giving your boyfriend the final act of the show." He came toward her.

"No," her denial was instant and came out much stronger than expected. She fought against her restraints, even though she knew it wouldn't do her any good. "Trevor was right…Lisa wouldn't want this, and you…you don't want to do this."

"You don't know what I want!" He rushed to her and pushed the tip of the knife into her side.

Lexi screamed against the pain. "Yes…I do."

"Oh yeah?" He paused his movements, his voice full of sarcasm as he held the knife in place. "And what would that be, Miss I Know Everything?"

"You want Lisa back," she said quickly. Beads of sweat formed on her forehead. "You want to be able to see her. Touch her. Hold her in your arms and tell her how much you loved her. You want to be able to say everything you ever wanted to tell her but never got the chance to."

Tears from both her physical pain and emotional sorrow fell from the corners of Lexi's eyes and into her damp hair. She fought against the pain, continuing with what she knew to be the absolute truth.

"You want five more minute to just sit and look at her face…her vibrant, *alive* face as she looks back at you and smiles." Then, Lexi whispered, "And you want to hear her say she loves you, too. You'd give *anything* to hear those words, just one more time."

Lexi blinked and was shocked when her vision cleared and she saw tears in Anthony Young's eyes, too.

"I *do* want that," he whispered back. "I want all those things." His eyes hardened, and his voice became stronger. "But I'll never get them. Thanks to your boyfriend."

Young pushed the knife a little deeper, and Lexi screamed louder. He pulled it out of her side and turned away, walking to the keyboard once more.

With her insides feeling as though they were on fire, Lexi hoped to hear Trevor's voice again. Young's fingers hastily clicked the plastic keys, but nothing happened.

"Maybe he's gone," she grunted against the pain.

She tried to ignore how quickly her blood was soaking the side of her t-shirt or the way it was beginning to pool into the grooves in the dry, wooden tabletop below her.

"He's not gone," Young argued, still facing the screen. "He wouldn't leave his only access to you. Not now."

Lexi could tell the man was trying to convince himself more than her, so she played into his insecurities. It was the only move she had left.

With a weak laugh, she said, "You heard him. He doesn't love me. We've never even been on a real date."

"Doesn't matter," he mumbled as he typed in something again. "I saw the way he looked at you. You can't fake that kind of emotion."

"Are you really that stupid? The guy was special ops. He and his team at R.I.S.C. do all sorts of secret, black-ops-type jobs." Lexi grimaced as she coughed a couple times, her body weakening from all it'd been put through. "He could convince you to believe anything he wanted you to. You wouldn't…even know if he…was lying."

Her words were starting to slur, and she'd begun to feel lightheaded. *Because you're losing blood.* Oh, yeah. That.

Lexi blinked quickly against the sudden exhaustion threatening to take over. She had a feeling if she fell asleep now, she'd never wake up again.

"I was CIA, you stupid bitch. I could tell if that man was lying."

"So, was he lying…when he said…he didn't love me?"

She wasn't sure if she was just trying to goad him, or if she truly wanted to know the answer. *Probably both,* she thought sleepily.

"Oh, he was lying," Young said as he bent over the keyboard and continued to try to connect with Trevor. "That man loves you. That's how I know he'd never walk away from his only means of communication with you, now."

When he tried again—and failed—to get a response from Trevor, Lexi said, "T-told you he didn't really…l-love me."

Young faced her, his anger and frustration a living breathing thing. "I wasn't wrong. I couldn't have been wrong. He *has* to love you! Otherwise this was all for nothing!"

The man was losing it, which made Lexi smile. It was odd that she could do so at a time like this…maybe *she* was the one who was losing it.

With her thoughts scattered and the light around her fading, Lexi almost missed it. There was a small sound, like a door creaking. It was there, and then it was gone. Just like that.

At first, she thought she'd imagined it, but then Young's head swung toward the room's closed door. No, she hadn't imagined it. He'd heard it, too.

Lexi smiled again. "They're coming…for you," she said softly.

"Impossible," the man said, even though he didn't take his eyes from the door.

"N-nothing's impo…impossible…with those guys."

Admittedly, Lexi hadn't met the entire team yet. Other than Derek, she hadn't gotten to know the ones she *had* met. That didn't matter. She knew Trevor.

Even if he wasn't in love with her, she knew he'd do whatever he could to save an innocent life. It was just one of the many reasons she'd fallen so hard and fast for him.

"Shut up!" Young ordered, his crazed eyes on hers. He pointed the bloody knife toward her. "You make one more sound, and I'll slit your throat ear to ear."

Laughing silently, Lexi moaned against the pain the movement had caused. "You're going to kill me…anyway. M-might as well d-do it…n-now."

"I said shut up!" he yelled even louder.

Good. Lexi had wanted him to be loud. She was too weak to yell for help and had been hoping to rile him up enough for Trevor and the others to hear.

Because she had no doubt they were here. They'd finally found her. She glanced down at her side and the growing pool of blood on the floor. Trevor and his team had found her…she just prayed they weren't too late.

****

"Damn it, D, watch the doors," Trevor whispered angrily from behind him as the team made their way into another part of the building.

"Sorry," he whispered back, still moving forward. "My ass

bumped the damn thing."

"Shh," Mac ordered them both to get quiet as she stepped into the open area and stood next to Trevor.

As promised, Ryker had hauled ass and gotten them to the location where Lexi was being held in record time. The team was just about to breach a door on the side of the abandoned factory when they'd pulled up.

With their plan already in place, Trevor hadn't wasted time Lexi didn't have arguing about not getting to go in first. After Grant checked the door for any explosives Young may have put into place and declared the entry safe, Jake led the team into the large, open space. Trevor only just stepped inside the building himself when they heard Lexi's blood-curdling scream.

Trevor nearly lost it, then. He tried barreling his way to her, but thankfully Coop grabbed his arm from behind, and Derek turned and pushed against his chest to keep him in place.

Once they got him to calm down and look at the situation objectively, he realized they were right to stop him. If he went charging in, Young would most likely kill Lexi before he had a chance to prevent it.

As hard as it was, Trevor forced himself to move slowly, just as he would if this were any other op. He had to put the fact that it was his Lexi on the other side of that wall. Had to forget about the fact that she'd told him she loved him…right before she was tortured in one of the worst ways possible.

I'm here, angel. Hang on just a little longer.

The team continued on through another wide, open space. Sets of steel beams ran across the high ceiling above them as others stood upright along both sides of the building. It was like walking through a steel giant's ribcage.

Light from the broken, multi-paned windows running along the length of the room shone in on them as their boots made their way silently across the floor. Glass, dirt, and other debris littered the floor, and they had to step carefully so they wouldn't give their presence away.

"I said shut up!"

The loud, angry voice made them freeze.

"He sounds pissed," Mac said on a low whisper.

Part of Trevor wanted to smile, knowing Lexi was giving him hell. *That's my girl.*

"We need to go, now," Trevor whispered back. "She pushes him too far, he'll kill her for sure."

"Agreed." Jake kept his voice low. He looked toward the closed door in front of them, then back to Trevor. With one look, he silently asked, Trevor, "Can you handle it?"

Without hesitation, Trevor gave his boss and best friend one, sharp nod and mouthed back. "I'm good."

The team made their way closer to the door. With an assessing eye, Jake tilted his head in response and then used hand gestures to give orders to the rest of the team.

He raised a hand and started counting down from three. Just as he got to one, Trevor grabbed his arm and shook his head.

Their team leader's face twisted with confusion. Not wanting to talk for fear they'd be heard, Trevor pulled his phone from his pocket and quickly opened his notes app. His thumbs flew over the screen as he typed what he wanted to say.

Can't all go in. He'll panic…can't risk Lex.

He held his phone up for Jake to see. Jake's eyes scanned the message. He then took the phone from Trevor and typed his own.

Not going by yourself

Trevor saw the message and shook his head. Grabbing the phone, he wrote his response with

No visual. Unknown position.

The swapping of messages continued.

Jake: I'll text Ryker. See what he knows. His group may be outside and ready.

Trevor: No time.

Jake: Can't let u go in alone.

Trevor: Won't make a move on me until he kills her. He won't get that chance.

Jake looked pissed as he considered what Trevor was saying. Trevor took the phone back.

Have to do this. Has to end now.

After reading Trevor's words, Jake looked at him, then back to the phone. Typing one, final message, Jake handed Trevor his phone back for the last time.

You get killed, I'm gonna kick your ass.

As serious as the situation was, Trevor's mouth turned up in a slight grin. He slapped Jake's arm and stepped around him, leaving his friend to explain it all to the others.

Standing just outside the door, Trevor paused a moment. He sent up a silent prayer that, no matter what happened to him, Lexi would be safe. Then, he reached for the doorknob.

With his trusted MP-5 aimed and ready to shoot, Trevor looked back at his team. They were standing a few feet from him, ready to have his back, if needed. Giving them one final nod, Trevor turned the knob and walked straight into Hell.

Lexi was still strapped to that godforsaken table. Her hair was wet, and a dark, wet stain took up most of the right side of her gray t-shirt. *Blood.*

Unable to think about that now without risking them

both, Trevor quickly assessed the scene with an operator's eye. A cart with a computer set-up was to his left, and there was a small window on the wall opposite the door. Trevor stood at Lexi's feet while Young stood behind her head. Trevor would never forget the image of that bastard holding his knife at Lexi's throat the way he was now.

"Take one more step, and she's dead."

Ignoring the other man, Trevor allowed himself one second to glance at Lexi's face. She stared back at him, her eyes filled with pain and something else. Love. She was looking at him with more hope and love than he deserved.

Incredibly, she gave him a shaky smile and whispered, "H-hi."

Trevor's throat physically hurt from the pressure as he worked to swallow against the emotions there. Not reacting was the hardest thing he'd ever had to do.

Sliding his eyes back up to Young's, Trevor said, "You have two seconds to step away from her, or I will end you."

"Go ahead!" Young shouted. "That's what you're good at, right? Ending people's lives?"

"I didn't kill Lisa." Trevor forced his voice to remain calm.

"Maybe you didn't take that knife to her, but you may as well have! You sent her in there. You made that decision!"

"No, *she* made that decision!" Trevor raised his voice. "I told Lisa Hadim couldn't be trusted. I tried to talk her out of it, but *she* kept insisting we go in."

"But you didn't go in! You weren't the one who was taken and…and tortured."

"No," Trevor said matter-of-factly. "I wasn't. And I'll never forgive myself for not putting up more of a fight. But hurting her"—he tilted his head toward Lexi—"isn't going to bring Lisa back."

"No, but it hurts *you*." Young started to press the knife against Lexi's skin.

"Stop!" Trevor begged. "Please. I'm the one you want, right? Let her go, and you can have me."

"T-Trevor…no," Lexi said softly, her voice sounding too damn weak.

Ignoring her, he pulled his aim away from Young. Holding his weapon out to the side and putting his left hand up in surrender, Trevor said, "See? I'm putting down my gun." Going completely against protocol, he slowly bent down and sat his rifle on the ground. Standing back up, he said, "Now, I'm unarmed. You have all the control here."

"I know I do. I don't need your arrogant ass to tell me that."

"Fair enough." Trevor took a slow, easy step forward as he spoke. "So, what do you say, we let her go?" Another step. "You know who I am, and what I do." Another step. "I'll get you a hell of a lot more leverage to work with than a civilian." One more step. *Just a couple more and I'll be close enough to take the asshole down.*

"Stop!" Young pressed the tip of the blade against Lexi's throat again. She winced, and a small drop of blood formed, then slid slowly across her delicate skin. "Don't come any closer, or I swear to God I'll kill her."

"Okay, okay." Trevor raised both hands palm up. "I'm stopping. Just ease up on the knife, there, all right?"

"Fuck you. You think I'm gonna do anything you say? Because of you, I lost my fiancée!"

Knowing it was a risk, Trevor decided to try to piss the guy off enough, he'd come after him instead of hurting Lexi.

He shot up another quick prayer and said, "Which one? Because you seem to have bad luck with those."

Young yelled again. "You don't know shit about me!"

"Oh, really? Your most recent fiancée found out about your little obsession problem with me and Hadim, as well as the fact that you illegally accessed classified CIA files. You're looking at some serious prison time for that, Tony."

"Fuck you!" Spittle flew from his mouth as he shouted.

The guy was definitely getting pissed. More importantly, in his rage, he'd taken the blade a few centimeters away from Lexi's throat. Just a little more, and Trevor would have the opportunity he needed.

"And let's talk about Lisa. All this…" Trevor gestured to Lexi, hating the fear and panic in her eyes. "All this is to avenge a woman who'd left you."

"That…doesn't matter." Young stumbled over his own words. "She…I…we were meant to be together."

"Really?" Trevor forced his body to relax and his voice to sound casual. "Funny. Lisa told me she wanted nothing to do with you."

Rage began to build in Young's eyes. "Shut up! She never said that. Lisa loved me! We were going to get married."

Keeping a close eye on the blade near Lexi's throat, Trevor pushed on. Chuckling, he said, "She flew half way across the globe to get away from you. She left you, then she was killed, and you somehow managed to convince yourself that she still loved you."

"Shut up," Young warned.

Another quick glance at the trembling knife told Trevor he was on the right track. Taking a step closer, he said, "She didn't love you, Tony. She didn't love you, and this newest fiancée of yours didn't love you anymore, either."

"Shut. Up." Young clenched his teeth together.

"Is that why you went after Hadim? You couldn't handle

another woman leaving your crazy ass? Or was it the thought of going to prison and becoming someone's bitch that drove you to find Hadim and torture him to death?"

"I killed Hadim because that bastard lied to Lisa*!* He *tricked* her. She liked him. Told me about him even before she left for Syria. Said he was kind and wanted to help Americans. He was lying to her the entire time, so yeah, I fucking tortured him. You know what he told me just before he died?"

Trevor shook his head, his eyes bouncing back and forth between Young's and that knife.

"I asked why he did it. You know what his answer was? Money." Young laughed almost hysterically. "Money! He helped kidnap and torture Lisa for *fucking money*! The whole thing was this long, elaborate con. Get an American agent to trust him. Help that agent gain some wins and then bring her in. They used her as a fucking example, and he got paid for it!"

Using his free-hand, Young wiped some sweat from his brow. "Hadim told me everything. He confessed to it all…and then I slit his throat." He took a deep breath and then said, "You and Hadim…the others. You all took the woman I loved away from me. My life was never the same after that. Now, I have nothing. Nothing to look forward to…nothing left to lose. You do, though. Don't you, Soldier Boy? It's time you finally learned what it feels like to lose everything that matters to you."

Trevor saw it in his eyes, then. His heart pounded against his ribs with the force of a kick drum because he knew what was coming next. A loud roar filled the room as he leapt forward, unaware that he was the one yelling.

"No!"

His entire body shot forward just as the blade began to

slice into Lexi's skin. In one fluid motion, Trevor pushed his left hand against Young's chest and used his right to grab the hand that held the knife. He pulled it away from Lexi's throat, careful not to let the sharp edge cut her any more than it already had.

With a loud growl, Young twisted the blade toward Trevor. The tip sliced Trevor's forearm, but there was too much adrenaline running through his veins to feel it.

He let go of Young's wrist just long enough to wrap his arm under and around Young's forearm. As hard as he could, Trevor then slammed the heel of his hand against the outside of Young's bicep, pushing the upper portion of the man's arm forward. At the same time, Trevor pulled the lower half of Young's arm back towards him, in the opposite direction. The man's ulna and radius bones snapped instantly.

Young howled, his cry of pain echoing off the concrete walls. On reflex, his hand opened and the knife started to fall. Trevor caught it before it could hit the ground.

Moving with unexpected speed, Young swung his left hand up and around in an attempt to take the knife from Trevor's hand. The two men struggled, Trevor using his entire body to push Young back against the wall—away from Lexi.

Young pushed against Trevor's wrist with surprising strength. The man had clearly been trained in hand-to-hand, but thankfully, Trevor was better.

The door to the room burst open, and the rest of the team entered the room at the same time he drove the blade of the knife straight into Anthony Young's heart. Trevor looked into the set of wide eyes looking back at him.

"Lisa…was…m-mine," the dying man sputtered out. Blood spewed from his lips. Some began to trickle down over his chin.

"No, she wasn't," Trevor groused. "She wasn't mine, either. But Alexis?" He had to swallow because even though she was lying right behind him, he had no idea if she was even still alive. "She is mine. And you never should have touched what's mine."

"G-go to…h-hell," Young barely managed to say.

Staring back into the eyes of a madman, Trevor snarled, "You first."

He twisted the knife before yanking it free from Young's chest. He didn't wait for the bastard's dead body to hit the floor before spinning around and taking in the scene before him.

Mac had already freed her wrists from the restraints, and Coop had taken off his shirt and was using it to put pressure on the wound at her side. Derek and Grant stood on the other side of the table between it and the wall and Jake had his hand on Lexi's throat.

Ah, God. "Lexi?" he said her name hesitantly as he walked stiffly to Jake's side.

Assuming Jake was checking for a pulse, Trevor wasn't sure what he'd do if his friend gave him that ominous shake of his head like he'd seen on countless ops. But as he got closer, he saw the most beautiful, half-lidded eyes staring back up at him. She was alive.

"Alexis!" Trevor exhaled, his relief so profound he nearly collapsed. He laid a gentle hand on her forehead, careful not to touch where she was bruised.

"T-Trevor." She smiled up at him as best she could, but then her eyes caught the blood on his other arm, and she scowled. "Your b-bleeding."

Having forgotten all about the cut, Trevor quickly glanced

at his arm and back at her. "It's nothing, Lex. Barely a scratch."

"Yeah," she whispered. "I got…s-scratched…t-too."

After everything she'd been through, she still had her sense of humor. Jesus, she was amazing.

With a half-laugh, half-cry, Trevor paid no attention to the tear falling down over his cheek as he spoke.

"You sure did." He swallowed against that painful knot again and told her, "You did good, Lex. *So* good. I'm so proud of you, baby."

"H-how did…find m-me?"

"Shh. Don't talk, angel. There'll be plenty of time for all that later. Right now, I need you to save your strength. Can you do that for me?"

Trevor looked to Jake who had removed his hand from the cut on her neck. Thank God, it wasn't very deep. "She's fading fast, Jake."

"Ryker's medics just got here. He's bringing them in now."

Knowing she would be taken to Homeland's private medical facility made him feel slightly better. They had the best doctors and nurses on staff, including Olivia.

Wanting to check her stab wound for himself before the medics came in and took over, Trevor smiled down at Lexi. "I'm just going to take a quick look at your side, okay?"

"'kay," she whispered back, her voice so soft he could barely hear her now.

Giving Coop a nod, the younger man removed the bunched shirt he'd been holding against Lexi's side and stepped out of the way. Carefully, Trevor lifted the hem of Lexi's own blood-soaked shirt and got his first view of where Young had used his knife on her.

As gently as he could, Trevor inspected the wound. Lexi

moaned when he pressed around it, trying to assess how deeply she'd been cut. Thankfully, he didn't think the bastard had damaged anything major, although she'd need some tests run to be sure.

"Sorry, angel." He kissed her forehead. "I'm done. You're going to be just fine."

"P-promise?"

He smiled. "I promise."

Her eyes started to close.

"Lex?" She didn't respond, so he ordered her sternly, "Alexis, I need you to open your eyes and look at me."

Her eyes finally fluttered back open, and he blew out a breath. "That's good. You've got to stay awake for me, angel."

"So…tired."

"I know, baby. I know you're tired, but you have to stay awake."

Ryker entered the room, followed by two medics.

Despite the fact that her pinky had been broken, Lexi reached her hand toward his. "S-stay?"

Not wanting to cause her more pain, he gently grabbed hold of her thumb and used his to caress the skin on the back of her hand.

"I'm not going anywhere."

The corners of her mouth curved slightly, and his aching heart swelled. Though, it was about as far from ideal a place as it could be for this sort of thing, Trevor kissed her temple and whispered into her ear, "I love you, angel."

They were the last words she heard before she lost consciousness.

Chapter 16

The next few days were like a blur. Nurses and doctors invaded Lexi's space nearly every waking second. Even with heavy pain meds, sleep was nearly impossible with all the blood-pressure checks, wound checks and re-dressing, and chart updating. By day three, Lexi was ready to pull her hair out.

"I want to see Joe."

Dressed in a pair of yoga pants and an oversized t-shirt, Lexi looked up from her hospital bed and waited for Trevor's response. She had a feeling she already knew what he was going to say.

As expected, Trevor gave her the same, perfectly pleasant smile he'd been wearing since she woke up in the hospital three days ago. "I know you do, angel. But his room is on the floor above this one. I'm not sure you're ready to be up and moving that much, yet."

I already had one mother. I don't need another one. Guilt instantly assaulted her as she finished that thought. Trevor had literally risked his life to save hers and hadn't left her side ever since. He'd bent over backward making sure she had everything she needed.

She should be ashamed of herself.

It was just so frustrating. Lexi was fully aware of the fact that she wasn't one hundred percent yet and wouldn't be for at least a couple more weeks. She also knew she was perfectly capable of riding in a wheelchair up an elevator and down the hall to see one of her dear friends. One who'd nearly died because of her.

No, not because of her. She wasn't to blame for Anthony Young's actions, and neither was Trevor. However, Lexi suspected he didn't share those same beliefs.

That would explain why he'd been her shadow every second of every day since he'd found her in that awful warehouse. Trevor had been doting and kind the entire time.

But he hadn't kissed her like he had before all this happened. He definitely hadn't said the three little words he'd whispered to her before she'd passed out from blood loss that day. *Because he hadn't meant them.*

Accepting that reality, Lexi woke up this morning and decided she was going to do what *she* wanted for a change. And right now, she wanted to see Joe. If Trevor wouldn't take her—

Lexi slowly swung her legs over the side of the bed.

"What are you doing?" He was at her side in a heartbeat. "Here, let me help you."

"I don't need your help, Trevor," Lexi said more shortly than she'd intended. His surprised expression made her feel even worse than before. "I'm sorry. I didn't mean to sound so snippy. It's just…I know I can get myself into that chair." She looked at the wheelchair parked in the corner of her room. "And I was hoping you'd push me to see Joe. If you don't want to, I can see if Olivia can help me."

"No," Trevor protested quickly. "There's no need to call Olivia. I'll help you."

She could tell he wasn't happy about it, but at the moment, she didn't care. She was tired of being in that damn bed. Plus, if he didn't feel the same for her as she did for him, there really was no need to keep hovering over her as if he did.

"Thanks," Lexi mumbled as he helped her into the wheelchair. She hid her grimace as the stitches in her side pulled. Resting her partially-casted hand in her lap, she sat quietly while Trevor pushed her out of the room.

Once they got to Joe's, Trevor knocked on the door and waited. Hearing Joe's voice telling them to come in was like music to Lexi's ears. She'd promised herself she wouldn't cry, but when she saw him sitting up in bed and laughing with Caleb and Gina, the tears began to pour.

"Alexis," Joe said, his voice still raspy from all the smoke he'd inhaled. "What are you doing out of bed, girl? You should be resting."

"That's what I tried to tell her, but you know Lex," Trevor teased.

"Yes, I sure do. Stubborn to the core, just like her mama. Those nurses and doctors tell you things for a good reason, young lady."

Lexi didn't even mind the razzing she was getting, because it meant Joe was alive.

"Don't let him fool you, Lex," Gina said. "Just this morning, I came in and found him out of bed and half-way down the hall before any of the nurses even realized he'd left his room."

"What?" Joe said innocently. "I wanted my coffee, and no one was around to bring it to me."

Caleb said, "Guess neither one of you are good at following directions." Under his breath, he added, "Not that I'm surprised."

"Hey," both Lexi and Joe said at the same time. The room erupted in laughter.

God, it feels good to laugh again. Holding her casted hand to her side to help with the pain the movement caused, Lexi looked up to find Trevor staring down at her. The emotion behind his eyes something she couldn't place.

"Well, I'm glad you're here," Joe said to Lexi. "There's something I've been wanting to tell you." He looked at Gina and Caleb. "All of you, actually."

"Okay." Lexi looked at him as they all waited.

"It's about the diner."

"Oh, Joe. I'm so sorry," Lexi apologized, but Joe didn't want to hear it.

"Now, look here. Neither one of you"—he pointed first to Lexi, then to Trevor—"is responsible for what that sonofabitch did. He was his own man who made his own decisions, and I don't want to hear another word about it."

Blinking at the stern tone of his voice, Lexi said, "Okay." Because really…what else could she say?

"Yes, sir," Trevor respectfully agreed at the same time.

"Good. Now that *that's* been settled, what I wanted to tell you was, I've decided not to rebuild the diner."

"What?" Gina asked, clearly shocked by Joe's revelation.

"But, Joe…that diner's you're whole life," Lexi said softly.

"That's precisely why I'm not rebuilding."

"I don't understand," Caleb said from the chair he'd pulled up closer to Joe's bed.

"Don't get me wrong." Joe shook his bald head. "That diner's been a wonderful business to own. And you all"—he looked around the room—"you've become my family. But, I'm not getting any younger. I still have most of my wife's life insurance, and it's been collecting interest since she died. I've also managed to put some money away here and there over the years, so I'll get along just fine."

"Are you sure?" Lexi asked softly.

"I haven't been this sure about something since the day I hired you."

Lexi's eyes welled up, even as Caleb said, "Wait a minute…you hired me a long time after you hired Lex."

Joe just looked at him and grinned. "I know."

Gina, Lexi, and Trevor all laughed while Caleb pretended to be offended.

Once the laughter died down, the room went silent for a bit. After a short stretch of time, Lexi gave Trevor a look and somehow he knew what she needed without her even saying it.

Pushing her over to the bed, he helped her stand. Carefully, Lexi leaned down and gave Joe the best hug she could without tearing her stitches. She kissed him on the cheek and said, "I'm so glad you're okay."

"Don't you worry about me, Alexis. It'll take more than some punk like Anthony Young to take me down for good. I do wish I'd been the one to kill the sonofabitch, though." Joe looked at Trevor. "Thanks for bringing her back safe, son."

"You don't ever have to thank me for that."

Trevor's eyes slid to hers, and Lexi could have sworn there was love there. That couldn't be right, though. She'd heard what he'd told Young. *I don't love her. We barely know each other.* Those crushing words hadn't stopped running through her mind since she'd woken up to find him waiting by her bedside.

"As far as work goes for you three," Joe gave Trevor an odd glimpse before bringing his attention back to her, Gina, and Caleb. "I have a feeling everything's going to work out just fine."

Lexi wasn't sure what that was all about, but by the time they said their goodbyes, she was too exhausted to ask. Trevor pushed her back to her room and helped her into bed. When he leaned down and kissed her forehead in that annoyingly sweet way he'd been doing lately, Lexi's heart sank a little more.

****

"Come in."

Joe's raspy voice came from the other side of the door. Trevor pushed it open and peeked his head inside. "Olivia said you wanted to see me?"

"I did. Come on in and shut the door behind you."

Trevor did as he was told and stood at the foot of Joe's hospital bed, waiting to hear what the man had to say.

"Alexis asleep?" he asked.

"She is. And I really don't want to be gone long, just in case she wakes up. So, if you don't mind…"

Joe smiled, his gold cap gleaming off the harsh florescent lights. "Straight and to the point. I like that." He gestured toward the plastic chair near his bed. "Have a seat, son."

Again, Trevor obeyed the former Marine's order and sat down. "So…what was it you wanted to talk to me about?"

"Alexis."

"What about her?"

"She loves you," Joe said bluntly.

"Yes, sir. At least I hope she does."

"Oh, I know she does. What I don't know for sure is how you feel about her."

Joe waited for a response. Trevor gave him the truth. "I'm in love with her, sir."

The older man's straight face began to curve. "You plan on marrying her?"

"Yes, sir. That is, if she'll have me. It's still early, but…"

"Nah," Joe shook his head. "It's never too early when you know it's right. Too late, now that can definitely happen. You wait too long or don't make your intentions clear…women don't like to wait around forever for a man to make up his mind."

"Sir?"

Joe reached into the neck of his white t-shirt and pulled out the chain he was wearing. At the end was a set of dog tags…and a small, silver ring.

Trevor watched as Joe slipped the chain up over his head and then proceeded to undo the clasp. Holding one end up, he placed his other hand below it, catching the tags and ring as they fell off the chain and into his palm.

Holding the tiny diamond ring up, Joe said, "This belonged to my wife. I kept it after she died. For some reason, I just couldn't bear to part with it." He looked up at Trevor and held out the ring. "Now, I know why."

"Joe, I can't accept that."

"It's not for you. It's for Alexis," Joe teased.

Trevor chuckled. "I know. Still, I can afford to get her a ring."

"I know you can. This isn't about that." Joe inhaled deeply. "Helen and I…we couldn't have children of our own. Alexis is the closest thing to a daughter I've ever had, and I know my wife would be tickled pink if she knew that girl was wearing her ring."

Trevor leaned forward and reached his hand up over the railing. Taking the ring in between his thumb and forefinger, he studied it.

It wasn't overly huge or flashy. It had a square diamond in the middle that he guessed was half a carat. Several smaller, round diamonds outlined it, as well as the top portion of the band. It was exactly the style of ring he would have picked out for Lexi had he had a million to choose from.

"It's perfect."

"Just like my Helen."

Trevor looked up at the man and smiled. "And Lexi."

Joe tipped his head. "And Lexi."

Clearing his throat, Trevor slid the ring into his jean's pocket and held out his hand for Joe. "Thank you, sir. I know this will mean a lot to her."

Joe took his hand. "Enough of this 'sir' shit. We're practically family now. You can call me Joe."

"All right." Trevor smiled. "Thank you, Joe."

Trevor started to stand, but Joe stopped him. "There's one more thing I wanted to discuss with you before you go."

Nodding, Trevor sat back down and listened.

****

The next morning, her room was a bustle of traffic. She'd really wanted to talk with Trevor, but they hadn't had a minute alone.

Nurses kept coming in and out to check on her. Then, two guys from R.I.S.C she hadn't met yet—Coop and Grant—and the woman they called Mac came by to see Trevor and check on her.

They all seemed really nice. Well, Coop and Mac, anyway. Lexi had gotten a few laughs watching those two banter back and forth with each other. Grant had been so quiet she wasn't quite sure what to think of him, yet.

They all left, but around lunchtime Derek and Jake came by. Trevor had already filled her in on Rob's accident a few days prior, but Derek informed them both that Rob had succumbed to his injuries and had died the night before.

Olivia came in right as they were leaving. Lexi watched as she and Jake shared a few passing words, then kissed each other goodbye.

Smiling at Lexi, Olivia said, "So…you ready to blow this joint, or what?"

"I get to go home?"

"Got your walking papers right here," Olivia held Lexi's release papers.

"Thank God." Lexi exhaled, quickly adding, "Not that you haven't been great."

Chuckling, Olivia came over and pulled a pair of medical gloves from her scrub pocket. "Trust me. I completely understand how you feel." The two women shared a look, before Olivia looked over and said, "Hey, Trev. This isn't going to take long. Why don't you go get your truck and bring it around front?"

He looked at Lexi like he didn't want to leave her side for one second. Olivia picked up on it, too. With a teasing tone, she said, "Oh, my gosh…would you stop being such a worry wart and go?

With an almost embarrassed look, Trevor gave Lexi a half smile. "I'll be right back."

"I'll still be here," she teased back.

The minute the door closed behind him, Lexi let out a

loud, exaggerated sigh.

"That bad, huh?"

Her head snapped up to Olivia's. "Oh, no. Trevor's been great. He's been here every day and has helped me with everything..."

"And he's stuck by you like a mama bear afraid to leave her cub. It's okay, Lexi. What you say in here stays with me."

Looking up at Olivia while she put a small bandage where her IV had just been removed, Lexi whispered, "It's exhausting. He's been hovering over me ever since I woke up. He won't let me do anything for myself, and he hasn't..."

"Hasn't what?" Olivia asked as she took Lexi's vitals one last time and entered the information into her tablet. "Kissed you?"

Lexi felt her eyes grow bigger. "H-how did you..."

Olivia chuckled. "I told you I'd share the story of what happened to me someday. Well, the short of it is, the man who took me the first time found me again a few months later. Thankfully, Jake and the others rescued me, but...here. I'll just show you."

The other woman turned around and lifted the back of her scrub top. Lexi could only see the bottom portion of Olivia's back, but it was enough to understand what she was trying to show her.

Gasping at the crisscrossed scars, Lexi said, "Oh, Olivia. I'm so sorry."

"It's okay." She shrugged it off casually as she pulled her shirt back down and turned to face her. "I'm good now, but after it happened...when I was healed enough and ready to do...certain things "—her neatly trimmed eyebrows waggled up and down—" Jake wasn't having any of it.

"Really?"

"That man was so afraid he'd hurt me it took *weeks* for me to convince him I was healed enough to have sex again. I thought I'd lose my mind trying to find new ways to seduce him."

Lexi held her side as she chuckled. "That does make me feel a little better. I don't know. I'm not sure Trevor feels the same about me as I do him."

"And how do you feel about him?" Olivia asked bluntly.

Unable to lie, Lexi whispered, "I love him."

Smiling wide, Olivia said, "Then, I'd say you two are right on track with each other."

"But he hasn't even really kissed me. Or said that he loves me. Not since before I was brought here."

"He's worried you blame him for what happened."

Lexi frowned. "He told you that?"

"Didn't have to. Like I said before, those guys are all the same." Olivia carefully sat down on the bed next to Lexi's legs. "Think about it. Anthony Young's sole purpose for doing what he did was to get back at Trevor. How do you think Trev feels knowing—in his mind—he's the reason you're in here?"

"I never thought of it that way. I mean, he's seemed…different since I've been in here. Still sweet and caring, but distant." Lexi thought for a moment then looked back up at Olivia. "I don't blame him for what happened. I know none of this is his fault."

"Does he know that?"

"Well, I never said that to him…but he should know that I'd never blame him for what Young did."

"Maybe he's thinking you should know that he's keeping his distance because he's worried about how you'll react if he doesn't."

Hope began to blossom as Olivia's words sank in. "We need to talk."

Olivia laughed. "In my experience, that tends to do wonders in situations like these." Standing, she gave Lexi her papers. Then, she gave her a gentle hug. "I know the name of a wonderful therapist. When you're ready, give me a call. I'll introduce you."

"Therapist? Thanks, but I don't know that I'll need one. I feel fine."

"Right now, you do. But once the craziness settles, you may find yourself needing to talk to someone. When that time comes, let me know, and I'll do everything I can to help."

"Thanks, Olivia. For everything."

Olivia gave her another hug before leaving. While Lexi waited for Trevor to come back, she thought about the conversation they needed to have and what she was going to say.

****

Trevor was almost to Lexi's room when Olivia stepped out into the hallway. When she saw him walking her way, she smiled and came toward him.

"Hey. You got a second?"

Concerned, he looked at the door to Lexi's room and asked, "What's wrong. Is she…"

"She's fine, Trevor. Actually, that's what I wanted to tell you."

"That she's fine?"

Olivia grabbed Trevor's hand. "That woman in there is a lot stronger than you think. And, despite what's probably going around in that head of yours, Lexi doesn't blame you for what happened."

"She…she said that?"

"Yes." Olivia smiled up at him. "Trevor, she knows it wasn't your fault. We all do. You're the only one still hanging on to that guilt. I know what that did to you after Lisa. You have a second chance at happiness, and she's waiting for you right there, behind that door. You can either waste another nine years blaming yourself for what happened to Lexi, or you can spend the rest of your life being happy with the woman you love."

Standing on her tip-toes, Olivia leaned up and gave him a kiss on his cheek. "Be happy, Trevor. You deserve it." Then, she stepped around him and began to walk away.

She'd made it half way down the hall when Trevor turned and hollered for her to stop. Thanks to his long legs, it didn't take long for him to make his way over to her.

"Do you still have the stuff at the ranch I asked you to get the other night?"

"For your date?"

"Yeah."

Olivia smiled knowingly. "Yes. Would you like for me to call Jake and have him get everything set up?"

Trevor nodded. "I'd appreciate it."

Pulling out her phone, Olivia said, "I'll call him right now."

"Thank you." Trevor leaned down and gave his friend a peck on the top of the head before turning back and walking to Lexi's room.

Almost an hour later, they were pulling into Jake's driveway.

"It's beautiful." Lexi sounded wistful as she stared out at

the expansive green hills and trees. "This is all Jake's?"

"Yep. And Olivia's, of course." Trevor put the truck in park and turned off the ignition. "Wait here. I'll come around to help."

Before she could argue, he got out and walked around to the passenger door. Opening it up, he held his hand out for her.

"Thank you."

He looked down at her and smiled. "Of course."

Lexi drew in a deep breath of the clean, country air. "Olivia's so lucky to live here." She glanced down toward Jake's barn, and her eyes lit up. "They have horses?"

Trevor smiled. "You ride?"

"No, but I've always wanted to."

"Okay."

"Okay?"

"Sure. You get yourself healed, and I'll take you riding."

Lexi smiled, but the spark in her eyes dulled slightly. "Trevor, what…what are we doing here? I thought when we left the hospital, you were just going to take me home. To my house. Or"—she hesitated slightly—"I thought we might go to your place so we could talk. So, why are we here?"

"I still owe you a date," he said matter-of-factly.

"A date? *Now?*" She looked at him like he was crazy.

Trevor simply shrugged. "Why not?"

"But, I'm…" Lexi looked down at herself. "I just got out of the hospital. I'm in yoga pants and an old t-shirt."

"Which is perfect for what I have planned. As long as you're feeling up to it."

"I…um…yeah. I guess so."

"I was hoping you'd say that." Trevor reached down and swooped her gently into his arms.

Lexi let out a tiny squeal. "Trevor!" She grabbed the back of his neck for support. "What are you doing?"

"It's a long walk down to the barn, angel. Don't want you tiring out before the date even starts."

Though she looked like she wanted to say something, Trevor was relieved when Lexi gave in and laid her head against his shoulder. *God, I've missed having her in my arms.*

After carefully making their way to the barn, Trevor sat Lexi down into the side-by-side Jake had sitting out, waiting for them. Not wanting to waste any time, he drove it out past the horses and into the wide, open land behind the structure.

He went slowly and did everything he could to miss any bumps or divots that might make the ride uncomfortable for Lexi. He couldn't help but smile at her reaction when they crested one of the hills and she saw what was waiting for them.

Her face lit up like a little kid's when she turned to him. "A picnic?"

"You like picnics?"

"I *love* them! My mom and I used to go on picnics all the time when I was little."

The nervous tension he'd had since leaving the hospital eased knowing he'd planned something she'd enjoy. He brought the side-by-side to a stop, and though it wasn't a tall step like his truck, he still came around and took her good hand as she stepped down.

Standing in front of her, he kept hold of her hand as he spoke low. "I was hoping you'd like this."

"I love it. Thank you."

Taking a chance, Trevor leaned down and kissed her on the lips. Her bruises and cuts were already healing nicely, but he still kept the kiss gentle for fear of hurting her.

After the kiss ended, he guided them to the area Jake had set up for them. There was a large blanket resting on the grass. In the center was a bucket of ice with a bottle of champagne, two champagne flutes, a vase with some freshly cut wildflowers, and a covered platter. Next to the bucket was a cork screw.

Jake had remembered everything.

He helped her sit before lowering himself beside her. "You doing okay? I brought your pain meds with us, just in case you needed them."

"I'm good." She shook her head. "I took some ibuprofen before we left the hospital. And I don't want anything stronger." She eyed the bottle of champagne. "Especially if I get to have a glass of that."

Trevor smiled as he reached for the bottle. After popping the cork and pouring them each a glass, he lifted the cover off the platter. It was filled with an assortment of fruit and chocolates.

"Wow. I can't believe you did all this."

"Well, like I said, I had some help. I'd actually planned an entire day, but—" Trevor cut himself off abruptly when he realized what he'd been about to say.

"It's okay to talk about it, Trevor." Lexi rested her casted hand on his jean-covered thigh. "Actually, I think we need to."

She was right. Swallowing hard, he set his glass down. "I'm so sorry, Lex," he whispered. He glanced up at her big, beautiful eyes. "I never meant for my world to come crashing into yours. Knowing he hurt you because of me…" His damn voice cracked, and he lowered his gaze, the guilt making it impossible to keep looking her in the eye.

Setting her own glass down, Lexi eased herself to her

knees and scooted in front of him. Taking his hands into hers as best she could, she said, "Look at me, Trevor."

Knowing he could never deny her anything, Trevor did as she asked. He was stunned when he saw no anger or resentment there. Only love.

"I know you blame yourself for what happened, but you need to know that I *don't.* This wasn't your fault. It was horrible, and I'm sure I'll have nightmares for months, but not because of you. When I dream about you, I'll be dreaming about how relieved I was when I saw you come through that door. I'll dream about the way you were willing to give yourself over to that monster, just to save me. And…" She licked her lips nervously. "I'll dream about the way it felt to hear you say you love me. Even if"—she paused, before taking a deep breath and lifting her chin—"even if you didn't really mean it."

Didn't really… "Of course I meant it, angel."

"You do?"

Trevor hated that she'd doubted that for even a second. "I wouldn't have said it if I didn't mean it, Lex. I've only held back because I wasn't sure how *you* felt." He used a finger to swipe some hair from her forehead and tuck it behind her ear. "After everything you went through, I was afraid you'd hate me forever. Not that I'd blame you."

With her good hand, Lexi grabbed hold of his raised wrist. "I could never hate you, Trevor. I love you." She leaned up and kissed him this time.

Trevor allowed himself a moment to give in to his need for this woman. The tip of his tongue hit the seam of her lips, and she opened for him for the first time since their nightmare had ended.

He poured all the love he felt for this woman into that

one, slow kiss. After a few glorious moments, he pulled away and whispered, "I love you, too, angel." Surprisingly, Lexi's shoulders shook with a light chuckle.

"Not exactly the reaction I was expecting."

"I'm sorry." She gave him another short, sweet kiss. "I was just thinking about how right Olivia was."

"About what?"

"She said you and I really needed to talk to each other. That it would probably help us a lot. Guess she was right."

Trevor smiled. "The woman usually is. And speaking of talking…" He sat up a little straighter. "There's something else I wanted to discuss."

"Okay." Lexi sat back and grabbed a blueberry from the plate. Popping it into her mouth, she said, "What is it?"

"The diner."

Confused, Lexi said, "There is no diner."

"No, but there's still the land the diner used to sit on."

"I don't understand."

"Here." He leaned up and pulled an envelope from his back pocket. "Maybe this will help."

Lexi took the envelope from his hand and opened it awkwardly. Once she got the papers out, she unfolded it and began to read.

"I don't understand," she repeated. "This looks like a property deed."

"That's because it is. It's the deed to the piece of land Joe's Diner was on."

She looked up at him, her cute as hell brows wrinkling together just above her nose. "Why do you have the deed to Joe's land?"

"Because it's not Joe's land anymore." He looked her and smiled. "It's yours."

Stunned and still clearly confused, Lexi opened her mouth—probably to tell him for the third time that she didn't understand—but Trevor cut her off at the pass.

"I went to visit Joe in his room last night while you were sleeping. He gave me that"—Trevor tilted his head toward the papers in her hand—"and said he wanted you to have the land."

"Why in the world would Joe give me the diner's land?"

"So you can have a place to build your own restaurant."

Her adorable eyes grew as big as saucers. "My own…Trevor, I can't build a restaurant. Even with this land, I'd still have to find the money for the construction, plus all the licensing fees that would go with it. This was sweet of Joe"—Lexi folded the papers back up and started to put them into the envelope—"but there's no way I can afford to do all that."

"Yes, you can."

"How?"

"With my help."

"I can't ask you to—"

"You're not asking. Truth is, I've been thinking for a while about finding something to do with the money I have saved up."

Trevor raised himself to his knees and took her hands into his. "Thought I'd find a good business to invest in. Maybe a nice restaurant. Nothing too fancy. Someplace elegant, but simple. A place people can go for a nice meal."

He lifted her good hand and kissed the back of it. "What do you say, angel?"

****

Lexi's eyes welled with tears when she heard Trevor recite how she'd described her idea of the perfect restaurant. The fact that he remembered almost word-for-word the way she'd described her dream made her hope for things she'd thought would never be.

"Trevor?"

"I want you to have the restaurant you've always wanted. And before you try to argue, this isn't a hand out, and I don't see you as some charity case. We can set it up as a small business loan, if you want. I've already talked to my attorney, and he's going to draw up the papers as soon as I give him the green light."

"So, we'd be…business partners?"

"As far as the restaurant is concerned, it will be yours to build and run how you want. I'll be a partner in name only."

Lexi's mind whirled with a little fear and a whole lot of excitement. *My own restaurant.*

"As for the rest, well…that's up to you."

"The rest?"

"I love you, Alexis. I don't want to just be your partner in business. I want to be your partner in life. I know it's fast, but I don't care. My heart knows what it wants, and it wants you, angel."

He cupped her face with both hands. "I want you by my side and in my bed. I want to share your joy and sweat and tears while you make your dream come true. I want to come home from a job and know that you'll be the one waiting for me when I get home."

Lexi knew he was trying to act calm and collected, but his eyes gave away too much. She watched as Trevor pulled something from his pocket and drew in a nervous breath.

Lexi lost hers as he held out the most beautiful ring she'd ever seen.

"This belonged to Joe's wife."

Gasping, she wiped the tears from her eyes. "J-Joe gave that to you?"

Trevor nodded. "I don't want to wait, angel. I want to tie myself to you in every way possible. I know in my heart we belong together. The only other thing I need to know is…will you marry me, Alexis?"

Oh, my God! The warmth from his touch and the love reflected in his eyes filled her to the point she thought her heart would burst.

"T-Trevor, I…I don't know what to say."

He kissed her, his lips brushing against hers as he whispered, "Say, yes, angel." He kissed her again. "All you have to do is say, yes."

With tears of joy streaming down onto her cheeks, Lexi smiled back at the man of her dreams and whispered softly, "Yes."

Want to read more about R.I.S.C.'s Alpha Team?

Turn the page to see how it all began:

TAKING A RISK, PART ONE

(Available on all major platforms)

Keep reading for a peek at Book 1
in the R.I.S.C. Series…

"One of the best books I've read in a long time. If you like Susan Stoker, you'll love Ms. Blakely's R.I.S.C. Series." – USA Today Best Selling Author Elle Boon.

"2019's breakout author. Blakely's debut novel has all the makings of a sexy, thrill ride." – Best Selling Author, Riley Edwards

Excerpt from

Taking A Risk

Part One in the R.I.S.C. Series

Available at Amazon Books
and all major platforms!

Chapter 1

Something was wrong. Very, *very* wrong. The metallic scent of copper filled the air as a red stain appeared on Cody's chest. Olivia's eyes locked with the young male nurse as his grey shirt quickly became saturated with his blood. Yet, she remained frozen. Her own body and mind battling against her efforts to understand.

Moments before, a series of thundering pops had filled the warm, humid air. Time stood still while men continued to yell. Screams echoed all around her, and still, she felt no fear. Olivia felt…nothing.

Her gaze slid back up to Cody's face. His always hilarious—and often inappropriate—jokes had kept their spirits raised in the midst of such devastation. Looking at him now, though, Olivia didn't see his contagious smile. Instead, she found a face twisted with pain. Eyes that were filled with confusion and fear. Then, like a puppet losing its strings, Cody's body went slack, his muscles rendered useless.

She watched numbly as his head slumped forward, and he slid from the log upon which he'd been sitting. Cody landed with a sickening thud in the dry dirt. Olivia was still trying to comprehend what was happening when another terrified scream pierced the air.

Turning slowly, she saw that, much like Cody, the rest of her new friends had begun to fall. Movement to her left caught her attention, and she looked back just in time to see Malani, the young woman who'd lost so much in the storm, drop to the ground by her feet.

Wide eyes stared into Olivia's, their rapidly expanding pupils conveying the fallen woman's desperate plea for help. Seconds later, Malani's head tilted to one side; her beseeching gaze no longer there. Olivia realized that *nothing* was there anymore.

No light. No laughter. No life. If Olivia didn't know any better, she'd almost think that Malani was—

Dead.

The word slammed into her with brute force, bringing Olivia back from wherever her shocked mind had escaped. The scene sped into focus, and she finally, *finally* understood. Her group was under attack, and with an indescribable horror, Olivia realized she was the only one still alive.

Dear God.

Adrenaline surged through her body as her belated fight or flight response kicked into gear. She shot up from her log and spun around in a dizzying attempt to assess her situation.

Several men—at least ten—were quickly approaching. They appeared local and, with one exception, were all dressed in head-to-toe in camouflage, each carrying an automatic rifle at their side.

Olivia's initial thought was to fight, but going up against these men would be suicide. She was far too outnumbered, not to mention unarmed.

The well-dressed man headed straight for her. He wore all black, from his dress shirt down to his shiny, black shoes. He would have reminded her of a Wall Street businessman if not for the long, jagged scar running down the right side of his face. The puckered mark, paired with the set of deadly eyes now focused solely on her, sent waves of terror pulsing through her veins.

Instinct told her this was the man in charge, and given the way he was looking at her now, Olivia knew she was as good as dead. Despite her odds, she refused to just stand there, waiting to be slaughtered. She had a snowball's chance in hell of escaping, but she still had to try.

With one final look at Malani and her other fallen comrades, Olivia bolted toward the road leading away from their camp. She thought she heard laughter coming from behind her, but the sound of her own blood rushing through her ears made it impossible to tell.

Leg muscles burned as she forced them to work harder than ever before. Tears fell from her eyes as she thought of her dad and brother. Of the mother she never really knew.

Her entire family was already gone—taken from her far too soon—and Olivia found herself praying that when the bullets hit, she wouldn't have to wait long before seeing them again.

Another image flashed before her eyes. One that nearly brought her to her knees.

Jake.

More tears came as Olivia realized she'd never see her best friend again. Never be on the receiving end of his sexy-as-sin smile or hear his deep-chested laugh.

Even more heartbreaking was the knowledge that she'd never get the chance to say everything she'd always wanted, but, even at thirty-one, she'd been too afraid to. *Why didn't I tell him?*

She should have shared her feelings with him years ago,

rejection be damned. At least he would've understood how deeply she cared for him. That just thinking about him could make her smile, even at the worst of times.

A person should know that, right? Everyone needed to know they were loved. *Especially,* someone as good and kind as Jake. And now, it was too late.

Oh, God! A loud sob escaped her throat as she forced her tiring legs to keep moving. She was going to die without ever having the courage to tell Jake she was in love with him. That single thought was more painful than anything these men could ever do to her.

Though she'd never been shot, Olivia knew to the depths of her soul that a bullet piercing her flesh would be nothing compared to the pain searing through her heart at this very moment.

With more thoughts of Jake and a lifetime of regret, she glanced back over her shoulder. The scarred man was right behind her, now. He raised his gun, and Olivia screamed.

She tried to run faster, but it was too late. He was too close, and her body had nothing more to give. She squeezed her eyes shut and pictured the last thing she wanted to take from this world.

Jake's handsome face appeared in her mind's eye. He smiled, the movement deepening the shallow lines bracketing each side of his mouth. His piercing blue eyes sparkled back at her.

I love you.

The words whispered through her mind just before a sudden, sharp pain exploded in the back of her head. And then…nothing.

****

Jake McQueen couldn't think. God Almighty, he couldn't *breathe.* The dizziness and nausea hit him like a freight train as he reached for the remote, desperate to block out the nightmare playing before him. He willed his thumb to press the power button, but his fingers refused to follow the simple order.

"The brief clip you just saw was from the memorial service held yesterday in honor of the eight men and women who were violently murdered in what authorities are still reporting as a drug-related raid. Five weeks ago, the group of American doctors and nurses arrived in Toamasina, Madagascar to offer volunteer medical aid to those in need. As I'm sure most of our viewers already know, Toamasina was one of the many areas devastated by the massive hurricane that hit Madagascar early last month."

Jake shook his head, his denial instant and final because no way, no *fucking* way was this really happening. The media, the so-called authorities…they had to be wrong.

Ah, God, not her. Anyone *but her!*

He continued listening to the TV, searching for something, *anything* that said this was all just some horrible mistake. But the longer he sat there, the more Jake's unwavering wall of denial began to crumble. Everything he'd just seen and heard pointed to only one truth—Olivia was dead.

Last week, while he and his team had been completing their most recent mission, her entire group had been gunned down. Their bodies burned beyond recognition. A week ago.

Jesus.

Finally regaining some bodily control, Jake raised the shaking remote. He refused to sit and listen to another goddamn word about how she'd been brutally gunned down and then fucking *burned.*

Just then, Olivia's face filled the oversized screen. His thumb froze in place. He couldn't tear his gaze away now if his life depended on it.

Jake knew the picture well. He should, he'd taken it the day Olivia received her nursing degree. She smiled back at him from his TV, her laugh from that long-ago moment forever captured.

A pair of gorgeous, hazel eyes with their mesmerizing swirls of greens and browns bore deeply into his own. They were eyes he'd always sworn he could get lost in. Jake blinked, and her name appeared on the screen in bold letters beneath the picture.

Olivia Bradshaw.

His best friend's little sister. The girl he and her brother, Mike, had spent countless hours of their childhood tormenting…all the while, protecting her with everything they had. She was also the same girl who'd grown before his eyes into the most beautiful, compassionate woman he'd ever known. And the most stubborn.

Olivia had given him so much shit throughout the years, challenging him at every turn. Despite all her sass—or maybe because of it—Jake had never wanted a woman more.

For years, she'd been the star of more fantasies than he could count. The cause of more wet dreams than he'd ever admit. She was also the only woman who'd managed to steal his heart, and last week she'd died without knowing the truth about how he really felt.

A rush of bile hit the base of his throat and Jake barely made it to his kitchen sink before losing the fast-food lunch he'd scarfed down on his way home. A few minutes later, his hands shook so violently that it took three tries to get the damned faucet turned on so he could rinse the rancid taste from his mouth.

After running the garbage disposal, Jake splashed his face with cold water before reaching for the nearest dish towel. In a daze, he wiped the moisture from his skin before tossing the towel aside. His hands became two vice grips, grabbing hold of the sink's edge, his knuckles white from the strain.

Hanging his head between his shoulders, Jake summoning every ounce of his training to force some much-needed air into his lungs. After several controlled breaths, he attempted to calm himself. To accept the unacceptable…Liv was dead.

He thought about the last time he saw her. Regret quickly filled his gut when he realized it'd been nearly two full months. *Too fucking long.*

When his team wasn't away on a job, Jake and Olivia would talk on the phone or hang out whenever they could. Just as friends. No matter how busy they both were, he always made sure he saw her before leaving town again. Except this last time.

His team's most recent job had been the very definition of last-minute. Jake had been home a whopping forty-five minutes, and hadn't even had time to unpack his bags from the previous job when he got the call from his handler at Homeland, requesting a hostage location and extraction.

He'd barely had time to shower, let alone see Olivia, before heading out again. So, he left her a voicemail, promising to make it up to her as soon as he got back. Now he'd never get that chance.

Filled with sorrow, Jake squeezed his watering eyes shut. Rather than blocking out the pain as intended, his mind instantly conjured up images from their last day together.

The two had eaten and talked. They'd laughed. More than

anything, they'd laughed. *I can still hear her laugh.*

It was always like that with her. They could joke around effortlessly, or just sit in comfortable silence. When it came to Olivia, everything was easy. Especially loving her. So, why the hell hadn't he ever told her?

You know why, asshole.

Jake had vowed a long time ago never to reveal his true feelings. For several reasons. To start, she was his best friend's little sister. As cliché as it may be, the unwritten rule between guys was very real. You didn't date your buddy's sister…or do anything else with her. Ever.

Sure, her brother had been gone for the better part of ten years now, but when Jake's feelings for Olivia had first begun to change, Mike had still been around. Jake had no doubt that Mike would have kicked his ass from here to Timbuktu if he'd ever known even a *fraction* of the thoughts Jake had entertained about the other guy's sister. Especially the ones involving Olivia naked and in his bed.

By the time she'd lost her brother, there were other, more serious, reasons preventing Jake from taking things further. *Come on, dickhead. Own up to it. It was the fucking lies that kept you from making your move.*

And Jake *had* lied to her. About his job. The way he felt. Then there was *the* lie. The one that had the power to destroy her.

Sometimes, Jake would be with her, and he'd forget. They'd be hanging out, and she'd tell him a funny story about something that had happened in her E.R. He'd be listening to her talk, and the guilt of his betrayal, the secret that years ago he'd sworn to *never* reveal, would momentarily vanish.

Unfortunately, it never lasted. The damn thing was always there, hovering over him like a cloud of poisonous gas, just waiting for the perfect moment to swoop in and destroy the most precious thing in his world.

It didn't matter that every lie he'd ever told Olivia stemmed solely from his need to protect her. Good intentions or not, Jake knew holding on to those secrets meant he'd never get the chance to be with the woman he loved.

It had to be that way. Not only to keep her safe, but also because Olivia deserved the world on a fucking silver platter, and Jake knew he could never give her that.

He did, however, give her as much time as he could between jobs. Since starting R.I.S.C.—the elite private security firm he owned—Jake had actually managed to never leave for an extended op without seeing Olivia first. This last time was the one and only exception.

Not once, though…not one time in all his years had Jake ever considered that he'd get back and *she* would be the one gone.

Ah, Christ. Liv is gone.

His empty stomach convulsed again, and no amount of training could stop it. Minutes later, when the dry-heaves finally subsided, Jake's quivering legs managed to take him back to the couch.

He sank down and rewound the broadcast. As much as he dreaded it, Jake needed all the information he could get before determining his next move.

****

TAKING A RISK, PART ONE
is available on all major platforms!

Amazon
Apple
Barnes & Noble
Kobo

Want to connect with Anna?

Sign up for her newsletter! You'll receive exclusive excerpts from her latest books, up-to-date news on upcoming releases, cover reveals, contests, giveaways, and more!

www.annablakely.com

Stalk Anna Here:

FB Author Page: facebook.com/annablakely.author.7
Instagram: instagram.com/annablakely
BookBub: bookbub.com/authors/anna-blakely
Amazon: amazon.com/author/annablakely
Twitter: @ablakelyauthor
Goodreads:
goodreads.com/author/show/18650841.Anna_Blakely

Made in the USA
Columbia, SC
28 July 2019